The
Importance
of Now

Paul Schumacher

Black Rose Writing | Texas

ISBN: 978-1-68433-717-0
PUBLISHED BY BLACK ROSE WRITING
www.blackrosewriting.com

Printed in the United States of America
Suggested Retail Price (SRP) $18.95

The Importance of Now is printed in Garamond

*As a planet-friendly publisher, Black Rose Writing does its best to eliminate unnecessary waste to reduce paper usage and energy costs, while never compromising the reading experience. As a result, the final word count vs. page count may not meet common expectations.

Author photo by Colin Sibert and Max Stevens.

Praise for Paul Schumacher's first novel,

The Tattered Box

"Schumacher tells his story in clear prose, and John's first-person narrative is buoyed by an infectious enthusiasm for the world around him. Overall the book is a pleasant exploration of familial bonds across generations and the timelessness of youth."

−*Kirkus Reviews*

"I rate this book 4 out of 4 stars. The premise of the plot is original and very well written. I would recommend this book to anyone who needs a life lesson on cherishing the people in your life and the stories that they tell you."

−*Online Book Club*

"A beautifully written story that is multi-layered with rich symbolism. I highly recommend this book for the rich message it offers that moments of the past, present, and future co-exist between generations."

−Linnea Tanner, author of the *Curse of Clansmen and Kings series*

"*The Tattered Box* is a wonderful read that prompts us to consider what mementos in our lives we would gather to tell our stories."

−Dr. C. Thomas Reiter

"As a first-time novelist, Paul Schumacher has written a treasure. This book could be a movie like *Field of Dreams* with some of the magic of *The Notebook* or *The Letter*. Great read...poignant, humorous and touching stories that may cause your eyes to moisten."

−Dr. Patrick Williams, Ed. D., Master Certified Coach

"A well-written and enthralling novel told through parallel stories of two generations, both searching for answers and closure in an emotion-filled past."

−*Sublime Book Review*

For Gail:
I love you.

Author's Note

This story is told in both the past and the present using multiple points of view. First person is used throughout, with the person listed in the chapter title along with a date in the beginning to help orient the reader. All of Aidan's chapters happen on the same day, so it's only listed once. There are also letters and police reports written by many different characters. Immerse yourself and enjoy!

The Importance of Now

"Be happy in the moment, that's enough.
Each moment is all we need, not more."
–Saint Teresa of Calcutta

"To forgive is to set a prisoner free and
discover that the prisoner was you."
–Lewis B. Smedes

I slammed the accelerator but only inched forward on the icy road, my tires spinning with a high-pitched whir. A Suburban hydroplaned across the intersection and smashed directly into my door. Glass, steel, and rubber splashed the sky. The other driver flew into his airbag. Blood poured from his nose.

My head punched the steering wheel. A gash sliced across my forehead. Blood smeared my eyes, blurring the devastation. My legs propelled under the dashboard, snapping my left ankle. My cell phone flew out of the cup holder and soared through the windshield.

It was the worst possible way to end such an epic day — all my actions, all the words spoken, both mine and hers. Never to be repeated.

But it only had a lifetime of meaning because of what came before.

And I never spoke about it with anyone.

Until now.

Chapter 1 – Aidan

November 5, 2017

I hated going up, but I had to. The staircase was steep and narrow, with a loose railing on one side and a sorry wall of chipped paint on the other. The old, decaying steps squeaked and moaned with every nudge of my feet, loud enough that my mom must have heard me.

The attic felt eerie, almost haunted. A single lightbulb hung in the center, creating an army of shadows, and the scattering of junk provided way too many places to hide. My friends would have said it was the perfect place for hide-and-seek, but I'd disagree.

I had to find the letters. How else could I finally meet my father? My feet slid across the floorboards as I searched in every direction but the right one. I knew I'd recognize them because they were addressed to me.

I had no idea where to start: stacks of boxes, huge piles of clothes, and mounds of games and toys. I dashed over to the blue and green Fisher Price boat, my favorite toy only a few years earlier. I kneeled down, blew away the thin layer of dust, then pulled out the diving board in back. My favorite character, Eddie, leaped off the board, flipping in my hands before diving into a stormy sea.

I dropped Eddie. He'd survive on his own.

"Whatcha doing up there?" yelled a voice from the bottom of the stairs.

I knew it. "Just lookin'…"

The creaking steps frustrated me even more. I rounded up Eddie and the boat and threw them back in the box. My mom wasn't about to see me playing with them. I was 13 after all.

"What are you looking for, Aidan?" Her question bounded up the stairwell, way faster than she was.

I stepped away from the box as her head peeked out from the stairs. She balanced against the railing, brushed back her reddish-brown hair, then adjusted her shirt to make sure it covered her belly.

"Nothin'." My hand instinctively rubbed my face, checking for newly cropped pimples that further spiraled my life into chaos.

"You must be here for something." She paused for her breath to catch up. "Ah… so much stuff. I haven't been up here in a long time. So many memories in one place."

I stood up but forgot about the wooden beams extending down from the ceiling. Boom! The sound of my smacked head startled my mom.

"Oh! Are you alright?" She instinctively reached out to help, but I leaned aside.

"I'm fine…" I massaged the top of my head and inspected my hand for blood. There was none.

I liked being taller, but the six inches I'd gained in the last year drove me crazy. I became awkward and clumsy, trapped in this bizarre costume that only changed the way I looked.

"Let's get some ice. That'd make it feel better."

Gee, Mom. Offer me milk and cookies while you're at it.

"I'm fine."

"Let's at least head down. It's too dark up here for my liking, and… it's scary. I'll make lunch. What would you like to eat?"

"Not hungry." I crossed my arms, acting like the little kid I knew I wasn't. The dry wood echoed my feelings.

"Then what do you want?" She spoke so firmly, but her voice was filled with desperation. I could always tell. "If you don't tell me, then I can't help you." She always thought of herself as this grand problem solver, as if her life's purpose was to fix other people's brokenness, especially mine. If only she knew what I wanted.

I shoved my hands in my pockets, pushing down my jeans that hung loosely around my hips. What did I want, besides someone who listened? Where to begin when my own life had turned against me. But whatever it was, it sure wasn't something she could give.

"I'm looking for a stack of papers. Some letters."

She froze, stuck in a gasp. "I'm not sure I know what you mean." She kicked her feet and stared at nothing. A lie. She clearly knew.

"Yeah you do! Letters written by all kinds of people. About my dad. I know they're up here. I wanna read 'em." I flailed my hands and pointed my fingers, thrashing about like someone reluctantly learning to swim.

"I wasn't going to give you those for a while. They contain way too much for you to handle right now." Her rushed tone reeked of guilt.

"Well, ever since Zach mentioned them, I've gotta know. You can't hold them back from me. I've gotta see 'em."

My mom took two steps toward me and put her hand on my shoulder. I shrugged it away. "Honey, please. They were going to be a special gift on your sixteenth birthday."

"That's forever! You have to show 'em to me! Or I'll... I'll run away!" Every muscle from my neck down to my hands tightened. An annoying reflex. My body felt achy and beaten as if all my wrestling had been physical. It wasn't. "Why are you laughing? I mean it."

She thought I was kidding, that I'd never do such a thing. Last year, I wouldn't have. Maybe not even last month. But things were different now. I wanted to run — chasing something just as much as escaping something else. It had to be better than what I had now. I didn't see how it couldn't.

"Oh, Aidan. It's just..."

"Just what? Why don't you ever take me seriously?" My hands trembled. I could barely control them. They fell behind my back and latched onto each other as if grasping for an ally. I considered them lucky. The only way I could make my life bearable would be to take control, and that meant doing it on my own.

She finally spoke. "The determined look on your face, the way you twitched your nose as you spoke, that gritty sound in your voice."

"What does that mean?" My head shook. Her words never made much sense to me; her convoluted, confusing riddles drained my brain of all things comprehensible.

My feet dusted the floor. She watched, then looked directly into my eyes, this time more determined. "You're so much like your father."

Holy cow, she mentioned him. The world abruptly stopped. Planets aligned. Stars exploded. I got a girlfriend. Why she didn't faint from exposure or sprint away like a raging lunatic was beyond me. She was obviously out of her mind.

It was my chance to pounce. "Then tell me about him! I wanna get to know him. Either you tell me... or let others do it through the letters. I've got a right to know."

She chuckled. "We should head downstairs. You have homework to do."

My hand swept away her question. "You never want to talk about him. What was he like? I mean, he mentored other boys besides Zach, right? How did that end? Why didn't you two get married? How did he die? See… I have so many questions!"

She sat on a large cardboard box, probably filled with a year's worth of clothes. She leaned back and glanced up at me, her only child, making me either special or the disappointment of something more.

"I think about your father every day." Her voice suddenly soft and airy. A whisper. "I'm sorry I've kept him from you. He's difficult to talk about. Not because I don't love him, but because I still do." Her cheeks reddened as she rubbed them.

My hands slid back in my pockets, and my shoulders shrugged. "Have you ever wanted something so badly you'd do anything to get it?"

She wiped her forehead, sweat forming in beads. "You're definitely your father's son." She shot me yet another dissecting stare. "I love everything about you, from who you are to who I think you're going to be."

The far corners of the attic were so dark, I couldn't even see where they ended. The light only went so far. It was an infinite space that either contained nothing or everything.

"Yeah… someone who never knew his father." I scratched up and down my neck, mimicking a chokehold but with less pressure.

"Of course not! I was going to show you them. And do you think I'm ready?" Her hands flipped in her lap. "There's a time and a place for everything."

She could have said every baseball game has a bat and ball for all I cared. It meant nothing. "You told me a few days ago there's no better time than the present." I swayed back and forth, stranded on the rear deck of a lost ship.

She rubbed under her eye. "And that was in regard to doing your chores."

"And how is this any different? You should be proud of me for listening."

"I am proud of you. You just…"

"Deserve to read the letters?" I splashed a grin. She was always a sucker for that.

She took a deep breath of the dense, dry air and partially returned the smile. "I've loved watching you grow up. My dream is for you to figure out what you want out of life."

4

"That's what I want, too." I tried to look outside, but the lone octagonal window was smudgy from dirt and grime. "And it's to meet my father."

"You know that's not possible."

"That's not what I meant." My eyes weaved back and forth along the floorboards, looking at the gaps, the grain, and the knots. It was old wood that had seen better days. Neglected yet sturdy.

She inhaled again. "While I loved your father, he made some awful mistakes. There's a past you're definitely not ready to hear about."

"That's so bogus. Maybe I am ready!" If only she knew my plans to ditch, she'd let me read them. She'd have to.

She massaged the back of her neck. "You're only 13. It's too much, too soon." Another judgment. I raised my hand in mock defeat. She continued, "Let's eat lunch." She stood up and headed towards the stairwell, her footsteps landing hard against the floor.

I was losing her. Fast. So I went in for the kill. "Don't you want me to grow up to be just like him?"

Her hand banged against the railing. I jumped. "Aidan, please stop! It's not just you to think about here. I'm not ready, okay. I don't want to read them, and we need to stop talking about them." She turned and descended the first two steps.

There was no way I was giving up now. I stood up, this time ducking beneath the cruel beams. It was my turn to be determined. I marched toward the boxes.

"Where are you going?" She yelled. "Listen to me! Come back here. Now!"

I stood next to the elephant-sized pile of boxes, squatted down low, and stretched behind it, daring to find cobwebs and dust bunnies and anything else that wanted to hide.

I held the yellow envelope in front of my chest and untwisted the string to open it. "They're in here, aren't they?"

"This is a terrible idea. I don't think we should." She came back up and walked behind me but stopped just short of arm's reach. Her face was crimson — a blotchy but deep red. "How'd you know they were here?"

"You were glancing over there this whole time."

"Let's do this later. I need to give you a background first…" She reached out for the envelope, but I twisted away and kneeled. This was so typical of us: my determination was a continued source of frustration for her. She sighed.

Why didn't she accept me for who I was?

I placed it on the floor and stooped down next to it. A thin layer of dust covered its side. I sneezed.

"You're not ready to read these, Aidan." She stood there, shifting side to side just below the light, her immense shadow covering everything, including me. She reached again over my shoulder, but I held the envelope against my chest.

She hadn't a clue what I was ready for.

I wiped my hand on my jeans then stared at the envelope, suddenly in sheer darkness. I dreamed of what the letters contained, words etched in gold. Could they really be mine? I reached inside and grabbed the entire stack, then flipped through them. Each one was written by someone different. I recognized all the names, some only vaguely.

But the more I looked, the more I was confused. "I see a bunch of letters from a lot of different people." The papers shuffled in my hand. "Why'd they write 'em? And when?"

"That's part of the background I need to explain."

"Then what's the other stuff?"

She crossed her arms, her hip flexed to one side. "Police reports." Her words slurred as if she spoke a dirty word. She extended her palms. "Don't say I didn't warn you."

"Was he that bad?" My look was not returned.

She glanced out the window, focusing on either the smudge or the limited view. From her angle, I knew there was nothing she could see outside. She never answered.

I stepped out of her shadow and sat down on a white covered box made of sturdy cardboard. The light was harsh yet helpful. The papers flashed in my hand. "I'm reading these."

Similar to me, this was now beyond her control.

I scanned the letters again. Most were in cursive, barely legible to a kid my age. Who uses that anymore? I had no clue where to start, so I placed the letters aside. Curiosity got the best of me. "This report's from a long time ago…"

She glanced at me and scoffed, annoyed as always by my directness. I almost felt sorry for her.

I cleared my throat then dove in headfirst, having no clue what I was getting into. Far from it. But that was also the reason why I did it, to learn what I didn't know.

Turns out, I didn't know much at all.

Chapter 2 – Shawn

September 6, 2003

Nothing was there to greet me, not a doorman, not a gargoyle or a lion, not even a security camera. But I didn't need an introduction. The place was just as I remembered: gigantic lobby with glossy linoleum flooring, wood-paneled walls splashed with promises to change the world, and a large crucifix hovering over it all.

"Shawn Stevens! My how you've grown," boomed a voice from the dark corridor. "You must be a foot taller since I last saw you." He stepped out of the darkness with a hand extended.

I shook it. My fingers brushed against my sweatshirt, then fell back into my pockets. "Four years is a long time, Pastor Mike."

This was my old church. I grew up here, or at least got older. So many memories, from a disastrous Christmas pageant when I was a bearded wiseman who tripped over sheep, to a youth lock-in where I scored my first kiss, to an over-indulgent potluck where I threw up on the same girl two years later.

"If that's the case, then I'm ancient. How old are you by now?" His hands fell on his belt, the sleeves of his white shirt rolled up around his elbows, his navy tie loosened around the collar. He still appeared in reasonable shape but was rounding above the waist.

"Turned 18 a while ago."

It was only two weeks, but who's counting?

"Time flies." Mike chuckled while brushing his fingers through his graying hair. "How's your mom doing? Haven't seen her in a while."

I had no idea how to answer that. Yes, it had been a while. "Doing well. She's happy to have me home." I smiled. Putting my mom and happy in the same sentence was an awful oxymoron.

The last time my mom attended church, she felt defenseless to the gossip and piercing looks, clearly directed at her. At least, that's what she told me. I wasn't there. She became this miserable widow who couldn't control her son. Compassion was like water: life-giving in doses but drowning in torrents. After that, she told me she had to leave. She didn't have a choice.

"Nice to see you come back. I wasn't sure if I'd ever see you again." His words hung in the air like the mission poster behind him: blatant and to the point.

But he was right. I didn't think I'd come back either.

Then why did I? Nostalgia? Revenge? In some ways, I hoped the place had completely changed — a total makeover where many things were discarded, including some of the people. But part of me didn't want it to change at all, like it was this life-size diorama of my childhood, suspended in time, back when everything was perfectly normal.

He continued. "We should catch up. Do you have time?"

Either way, I had to visit. This was my previous life all wrapped up in a neat, little package. Was it salvageable? I hadn't a clue. But I did know my current life desperately needed a replacement.

"Ah, sure. I'd like to look around first if that's ok."

"Be my guest. Stop by my office when you're done."

Mike took a quick step back, bent forward, then extended his arm as if granting me permission. I headed toward the large hall, my feet pounding up the wide stairway.

The door was unlocked, so I let myself in. It was smaller than I remembered, yet large enough to store a childhood of memories. Every weekend, there was a youth event to keep me out of trouble, from Fongo Bingo to Monopoly marathons to Three on a Couch. Great memories, even though they didn't succeed.

A small stage sat on one end, opposite the kitchen. Racks of chairs were in the corner next to a stack of long, foldable tables. The place felt hollow. The shiny floor reflected the row of windows, blurred and undefined like a distorted version of reality.

I left the hall, hopped down the steps, then walked across the lobby to the auditorium. The door swept open, letting out a rush of air. Stained glass rainbows painted the pews. I easily picked out where we sat every Sunday. How could I forget?

The place was full of contrasts: bright lights to dark mahogany pews, a chilly air mixed with the scent of burnt candles, spacious yet confining. My jumbled emotions were no different.

I had no clue how they could all co-exist.

The unmistakable kingpin of the place was the white marble pulpit towering high above the congregation. It protruded off a raised platform — shiny, smooth, and about as subtle as a stairway to heaven. Even the altar behind it looked puny in comparison.

I had to see what it was like to stand up there. I walked up the steps to the lectern and glanced out across the sea of pews, a figurehead suspended off the bow of a ship.

It wasn't the most sacrilegious thing I'd ever done — far from it. But it felt like breaking an eleventh commandment. It was high and lofty with a landscaped view of the entire sanctuary. Everything below seemed so small and insignificant, like pawns in a giant game of chess.

I stepped off. I had seen enough.

●　　●　　●

"Hey Mike." I peeked my head into his office. It was easy to find, the only glimmer of light in an otherwise eerie hallway.

"Come on in. Have a seat." Mike stood up behind his huge, sprawling desk. Stacks of papers covered the front, some more stable than others.

Two chairs with rounded, wooden backs faced the desk, angled toward each other as if staged for counseling. I chose the one on the left.

He sat down, then boomed a question across the room. "How've you been, Shawn?" It startled me, partly because I didn't want to answer it. But it was inevitable.

I scratched my stubbled chin and glared at the largest pile on the desk, a Jenga-like heap that would be the first to fall when the rapture hit. "Pretty good, all things considered."

"You know…" Mike's eyes darted side to side as if a gazillion topics swirled in his head. Knowing him, it was probably true. "I miss your father. You do know he and I were best friends back in college?"

"Yeah, he'd mentioned that." I paused. "He was… a fun-loving guy." I fidgeted in the chair, then leaned back and crossed my legs.

Why did I come here again?

My eyes drifted to the crowded bookshelves behind him: ancient manuscripts, study guides to explain them, and self-help books to recap how little they're followed. From leather-bound Bibles to thin paperbacks, all spread across the shelves and standing at attention like soldiers.

"Sorry for bringing him up. I just think of him... and you and your mom so often." Mike raised his eyebrows, his mouth creased into a weak smile. "I wish life hadn't dealt you such a bad hand."

I placed my arms on the armrests and shrugged my shoulders. I barely understood his analogy. The only card games I knew were Poker and Sheepshead, my motives too obvious for me to be any good.

"Well, it's great to be home again, away from the ranch. I couldn't stand the place."

I mostly understood why they put me away. I deserved the punishment. Sheep should be separated from goats like children from convicts. But what if they're one and the same? I was more a threat to myself than I was to society.

Mike rocked in his chair. "So, what was the boys' home like? What'd they make you do?"

I pivoted toward the small window, the only natural light entering the place. But it never left, sucked away forever like a black hole. "Honestly, I'd rather not talk about it."

Or maybe I was ready. I didn't know. My mind was too cluttered for my life to make any sense, not to say it did. Love and hate. Give and take. Alone yet surrounded by people. More contrasts.

That so-called home messed me up more than it cured me of anything, that's for sure.

Mike flashed the paleness of his palms. "Sorry, I... I shouldn't have asked so much."

I wanted to tell him what I really thought: how the years of isolation forced me to miss what I had, how my life dwindled to nothing, and how the only emotion I owned was a loathing for where I was, a prison by every definition.

I wanted to tell Mike everything. But I also knew there would be no going back, and I wasn't ready for the consequences. At least not then.

"I've been thinking about something." Mike pointed his finger at me, popping the air. "I've got a proposal I think you'll like."

Chapter 3 – Aidan

Case Number: 55397221

Date: 14 February 2000

Reporting Officer: Deputy Gonzales

Prepared By: CPL Currie

Incident Type: Aggravated Robbery

Address of Occurrence:

857 Elm Street, Clearfall, CO 80543

Witnesses:

Michaela White: Store owner. Female, 56, African American

Evidence:

Closed circuit surveillance footage

Fingerprints (taken from soda can)

Weapon/Objects Used:

Smith & Wesson Model 29

On February 11, 2000, at approximately 19:20, an armed male entered Log Cabin Liquor and stole $235 and a pack of cigarettes from behind the register. The security camera at the store recorded the incident as the suspect threatened the store owner, Michaela White, and demanded Mrs. White give him money from the register.

"This kid came in and immediately ran to the counter," White said in her witness statement. "Then he flashed a gun in my face and yelled obscenities, forcing me to hand over cigarettes and money."

White described the suspect as a white teenager, about 5'9", dark hair, and wearing a Clearfall High School letter jacket and blue jeans. There were no other customers at the time.

After grabbing the money from the register, the suspect ran out of the store. It had rained that afternoon, and White identified the suspect's footprints in the mud outside the door.

Deputy Gonzales arrived on the scene at around 19:42, responding to White's 911 call. After reviewing the security footage, Deputy Gonzales noticed the suspect had grabbed a soda can but later dropped it. Forensics performed fingerprint analysis on the can, leading to a suspect.

While the security footage never showed a clear view of the name on the letter jacket, the single soccer pin on the front also helped identify the suspect.

On the evening of February 13th, Deputy Gonzales stopped by the home of Shawn Stevens who fit the description and was in the area at the time of the incident. Mr. Stevens, a juvenile, was brought in for questioning along with his mother, Ms. Ellen Stevens. He admitted to the crime and was arrested on charges of aggravated robbery, petty theft, and unlawful possession of a deadly weapon.

• • •

"This is crap!"

"Aidan! Watch your language." My mom's only obsession was catching my sorry attempts at swearing. Life was unfair.

My long-lost father was a gun-flashing thief. Great. I didn't know if I should rip up the report into a million pieces or store it away as further proof of my insanity.

"Why would he do this?" My arms flailed. "This is so bogus. I… I just don't get it."

"This was why I told you we should wait." Her hand waved in front of her rising chest. She glanced over at the pile of boxes. "He was about your age, if that matters."

"Yeah, that matters." I laughed at the absurdity. "It's not something I would do, but there's a lot of dumb kids in my class."

"Then you'd understand."

"So, you're saying my father was dumb?"

"Of course not!" She rubbed her chin. "I'm just saying he did something he wasn't supposed to do and was too young to figure out why." She shifted her hips to the right, her shadow moving to a deep corner that was already dark.

"I'll have to use that excuse sometime."

She barely acknowledged me. "You have to understand. This was the day after his father's funeral. He was sad and mad and every other emotion you can think of."

I stood up, rubbed my shoulder then placed my hands in my jean pockets. They slid even further, reminding me how hungry I was. My stomach grumbled. "How'd grandpa die?"

She shook her head, obviously surprised by my question. She wrapped her arms around her upper body, looking as uncomfortable as I felt. "A drunk driver."

I scratched my chest through my thin, raggedy T-shirt. This was all news to me. My mom never talked much about the past, but I guess I never asked much, either. "That must have been awful." I paused, then mumbled. "But at least Dad knew his father."

She stared into my eyes. I turned away. There was nothing to see. "Yes, he knew his father. But your grandpa still died when your father was young, right at the age when your father needed him the most."

Why was she explaining that to me? I should have been lecturing her, telling her who I was, what I thought and felt, and most importantly, what I never had. I was a ghost who no one noticed, including her. Especially her. "Yeah, but… he grew up with his dad! I'm sure it was terrible and all, but at least he had that."

On the other hand, I had nothing. No father. No memories. A whole lot of nothing. Life was very unfair. I always felt like I was doing life blind, as if I needed a guide but never got one. I feared running into things, where stubbing my toes was the least of my worries. But it also had to do with what I missed seeing.

"Now, Aidan…" Her low, springy voice sounded like a teacher scolding me for throwing a pencil. "You had it tough, I get that. But consider the circumstances of others. What if I died and you had to live with Grandma?"

Now there was something I didn't want. She spoke in more riddles than my mother. "I guess so."

I didn't know what else to say. The Colorado weather, the figures of girls in my class, my voice, my height, my privates. Things changed. I got it. But everything else was supposed to stay the same.

"It was difficult for your father. He took it pretty hard, and his life spiraled out of control. Took him four years to get back on track with three of them stuck in a boys' home. And then… Well, then he met me."

"Mom, really? It's not like you saved him or anything."

"No, I didn't." She rubbed her hands together. "But we all helped in some way. This isn't just his story, Aidan." She watched me closely for my reaction, but I didn't give one. "This is one part his story, one part God's, and one part everyone else's." She paused for a moment, then finally continued. "Most stories are like that."

My stomach growled. "So… what else does this mean? My grandpa died when my dad was young, then he stole from a store."

She leaned against the wall near the small window, balancing against her shoulder. "There's coincidences you should know about. Some that changed your life, too."

There she goes again. Somehow, she thought I was old enough to have a changed life. "What do you mean?"

"Well…" She stared straight ahead, her eyes hazy and flat. "Your father also died in…" She brushed her cheek, folded her arms, then swallowed hard.

"In what? How did he die?"

"Sorry, I can't. Not yet. It was so similar, yet so different."

I waited for her to elaborate, but she wasn't going to. The stillness of the attic felt even more haunting, like right before the black cat jumps out in a horror movie. I shivered. "Didn't Grandma stop him? I mean, the robbery. Didn't they have relatives in town?"

She sighed as if settling for reality. "They weren't close to anyone else in the family. Not sure if any relatives even showed up for the funeral. And Grandma… she's a whole other story."

I kind of knew what she meant but wanted to hear her explain it. "Whadya mean?"

"Well, a part of her died when Grandpa did." My mom looked down, staring at the rustic boards. "It's tough to lose a spouse. It really is."

I placed a hand under my shirt, pushing upward against my rib cage. My skin was soft and warm. "For Grandma and Grandpa, yeah. But you weren't married to Dad, right?"

Her right arm reached around and rubbed the fingers on her opposite hand. "We never got the chance."

"Wait, wait, wait. I'm confused." There was a deeper issue that annoyed me. "Dad spent three years in a home… for robbery?"

She brushed back her hair just above her ear. "No, not just robbery. It was what happened afterwards. That's what really got him in trouble." Her hand swayed in front of her. Turns out, the black cat was just the decoy. "Let's switch to the letters. Those will help explain things, and, believe me, there's a lot to explain. Plus, they're a lot more enjoyable." She grabbed one and handed it to me. "Here, read this one. You remember Harry, right?"

I shook my head. I wasn't about to argue with ditching the police report — way too depressing and super confusing. Anyway, the letters were what I came for.

"'Of course I remember Harry." I chuckled, my mind flooded with odd, peculiar memories, the only kind to have with Harry. "How could I not?"

Chapter 4 – Shawn

September 6, 2003

"I'm interested to hear your proposal." I scratched the bridge of my nose, distracted by an itch.

Deep down, I still wondered why I came. This church was where I used to spend much of my time — most of my childhood, actually. But that didn't mean I had to go back. The problem was, while I knew God was still there, I also knew my dad wasn't.

Mike balanced his arms on top of his desk, snapping his swivel chair. I angled back, leaving enough space for words and emotions.

"I know the last few years have been difficult for you," Mike started. My eyes shut, and my arms wrapped across my chest. "Now hear me out. You'll like this. I know firsthand the power of God's forgiveness. He embraces us for who we are, no matter what we've done."

"Um, I thought you were proposing something." My foot tapped, shaking my entire leg. I must have come for something, but it sure wasn't a lecture.

Mike's return gaze was steady, with a tilted head and toothy grin as if staring at an innocent child. Ironically, I was neither.

I swallowed hard, my mouth tasting like car exhaust. I searched around the piles on his desk, looking desperately for a bowl of mints or candies or something. Anything.

"I do tend to run off." He laughed, his arm extended to balance his awkwardness. "Anyway… we have a mentorship program this year to love and support kids as they mature. Parents are great, but I'd like to see others involved. Young people such as yourself."

The room was shrinking rapidly. Luckily, the black hole couldn't implode as it already contained too much.

"What does this have to do with me?" I was the poster child for those who slipped through the cracks, the one who got away. Maybe I could stand by the door wearing a 'Don't be like me' sign around my neck. That'd work great!

"Well… I was wondering if you'd like to mentor a few boys." He stared at me, but I didn't return it, unable to focus on anything in front of me. Everything was fuzzy and stunningly misplaced, including his sanity.

"You're kidding, right? They didn't throw me into Agape for three years for nothing." My neck pulsed to the beat of my heart. "There's laws against people like me hanging out with kids. I'm too young. No way I'm qualified."

I looked behind him, my eyes grasping for something to focus on. Rows and rows of massive volumes lined the bookshelves. At the end stood a small, yellow paperback with frayed ends, slanting sharply against the others. It was a lone man supporting a wall.

Mike looked unfazed. "I know your past. Believe me, I thought and prayed for you every day. But, I'd like to think beyond that. I'd like to give you a chance at a fresh start."

"Thanks for visiting, by the way."

"I couldn't!" He wiped his mouth then rubbed his cheek. "I wasn't on the list."

"What the… What does that mean?" My legs crossed, the chair hard and uncomfortable. A dull ache traversed my spine. No wonder counseling sessions were so painful.

"Never mind. Long story." His nonchalance told me it really wasn't.

"Anyway…" I tried to wave everything aside, my hands eventually landing onto my thighs. "I'm not sure if I want a fresh start, let alone deserve one." The paperback suddenly resembled a man toppling a wall, or about to die trying.

Mike reached across the desk and grabbed a ballpoint pen, clicking it multiple times before leaning back again. "I can't tell you to want one, but I can tell you you deserve one. We all do."

I knew the Bible stories, heard all the sermons and parables and lessons. Seventy times seven. Got it. But they didn't apply to me. "Haven't I crossed a line where I'm not forgiven?"

I didn't even know what *forgiven* meant, as if this gray-bearded guy sat on a cloud and handed out 'Get out of Jail Free' cards to anyone who asked. Seriously. How do I even ask, let alone know where to go to get one?

"No, you haven't. And you can't. Ever." Mike propped his forearms on his desk. "You'd make an excellent mentor. These kids want someone to look up to and teach them right from wrong. We all have experiences to share, and you'd get a lot out of it as well."

Mike paused, but I didn't flinch. There was so much implied in what he said, so much between the lines, and none of it made any sense. My experiences were about as share-worthy as a toothbrush.

"I'm not sure it's a good idea. I have a record, you know."

He knew what I'd done and sharing it with impressionable kids would be a crime in itself. I was a thief in every sense of the word. The last thing I wanted to do was teach some kids to be just like me.

He rubbed his forehead, his thoughts as deep as my past. "I've considered that, but your records were sealed. There's no way for anyone to know. This is your chance to move on."

I scratched my head, confused as ever. Something was terribly wrong about this, even I could see that. And what if I didn't want to move on? In some ways, I still wanted to stay a kid. Making up for lost time, I guess.

"Tell you what..." Mike sighed. "Let me know if you're interested by tomorrow afternoon. Your timing is impeccable as it starts next Wednesday. I have one opening left, and I'm having a hard time filling it. It's been waiting for you this whole time, just like God planned."

This time, the bookshelves stared at me, telling me my life was not a story worth telling. Where was God when my dad died? Why didn't He prevent me from doing what I did afterwards? What was God's plan when I was locked up in that rotten home? I swore God was a director who either had no control over his actors or was staging a tragedy with me reluctantly cast as the lead.

"I'll think about it." I reached back and rubbed my neck, not knowing what else to do or say.

"That'd be great. It'd be a fun, fulfilling experience for you. And for them."

I leaned forward, no words or emotions left. "I've gotta run. I'll let you know, ok?"

"Sounds good. And say 'hi' to your mom for me."

I shoved hard against the desk and stood up in one brisk motion. Mike extended his hand. I lazily shook it. There was so much left unsaid, so much I didn't explain. But I couldn't, at least not yet.

The floor of the lobby was spotless, still damp and smelling of cleanser. It would only stay that way for so long before getting trampled on again. A vicious cycle. Why someone even bothered to clean it was beyond me.

Chapter 5 – Shawn

September 6, 2003

I waved my hand to acknowledge my buddy in the back of the restaurant. The place was dimly lit and more crowded than ever, but I knew where he'd be sitting.

McGrady's was nothing special. Padded booths slotted the walls, while the interior was a haphazard maze of tables and chairs and people. I maneuvered my way to the back while avoiding the reeking hazes of cigarette smoke.

"Hey Shawn! Nice to see you, bud." Phil's arms draped over the backrest like a Mafia Don. His jet-black hair contrasted his pale complexion, an artsy look even though he'd never picked up a paintbrush in his life.

"Hey there, Phil." I slipped into the opposite side of the booth just as the waitress stopped by.

"Welcome! What can I getcha to drink?" She tilted her head with a half-smile. Her complexion was so defined by makeup, I couldn't even tell what she looked like. "Water, please. Thanks." I returned the smile.

"Going for the hard stuff off the bat, eh?" joked Phil.

"Always do, man." I pushed against the side of the backrest. "I have to put up with you."

I pointed at him as if he was guilty of something. Truth be told, he always was. His smirk further proved my point.

An eruption of cheers pierced the smoky air. Colorado just scored their second touchdown, stealing the lead back from UCLA. The bulky TV sat on a black metal plate, suspended from chains directly above the booth next to us. I had a great view, even though I didn't care in the least.

"Bruins stink," moaned Phil. "Almost as bad as you. Definitely not as good as the Buffs."

I ignored his rip on my football skills, or lack thereof. "Going to any games this year?"

"The old man's gettin' cheap. Maybe later." Phil was more than willing to accept tickets from his father, just like everything else he was handed. But I liked him. Mostly.

He angled his head upward then toward me. "Whatcha been up to, Shawny? Making the most of your newfound freedom now that you've left the ranch?"

His jaw jutted outward with his skin stretched tight. I always wondered if he had any body fat at all.

"Yeah, no kidding. I can finally do what I want." Far from the truth. I had no money and no concept of what I wanted. But at least I had control, however useless it was at the moment.

The waitress dropped off my water. I grabbed a quick sip, providing a nice interruption. Everyone wanted to talk about the home that wasn't. Everyone except me. I guess when I fell off the planet for four years, people wanted to know what happened. But if I didn't know, how do I explain it to someone else?

"Hey, didn't you say you were going somewhere yesterday?" asked Phil.

"Yeah…" I brushed back my hair, feeling matted and oily. "Not a big deal. Stopped by church and talked with my old pastor. That's all."

I expected to catch Phil's thoughtless reaction, but the game was captivating him. He perked up. "Sounds like fun… unless of course he reminded you of everything you've ever done wrong in your life." He scratched his neck. "Which is a lot."

"Shut up, Phil." In some ways, he was still that irritating fourth grader with a faucet of humor that he never learned to turn off. Unfortunately, breaking old habits was hard, for both of us.

"So, what did you and the priest talk about?"

"He's a pastor."

"Ok, let's call him Reverend. What's new with the guy?"

I shook my head. "You're impossible."

"Funny, that's what the waitress said right before you came. Apparently, she doesn't have any grandchildren."

"You're kidding, right? Man, you've never been known for your eyesight… or your brains."

We both laughed then took quick swigs of our drinks. My mom never understood the two of us, why we were even friends. Honestly, sometimes I didn't either.

But my selection of friends had dwindled to one. Everyone else ditched when they heard what I did. Can't say I blamed them.

"So… what'd you and the sheik discuss?"

Water washed away only part of the disgust. Phil's snide comments were like orange traffic cones — ugly and annoying, yet swerving to avoid them made them even worse.

I kept my eyes on my water glass, sparkling under the bright overhead lights. "I walked around. Wanted to see the place because I could." My arms landed flat on the table. "Then I stopped by Mike's office."

Phil snorted, making me cringe. Church meant nothing to him, as if it only existed to be the butt of his jokes. It would be the last place he'd ever set foot in.

"We talked." I watched Phil, his thoughtlessness splattered on his face. He despised not just the building but everything that came with it, including the rules and the people. "Although, it went in a totally different direction than I thought it would."

"Did he ask you to start a homeless ministry?"

"What? No!" I swallowed hard, my Adam's apple feeling like a pebble stuck in my throat. "But the place felt different."

"All the busybodies left to start a cult?"

"What does that even mean? Sometimes, I don't know about you." My ice water was again a diversion, a sorry attempt at cooling me off. "You're awful tonight."

He ignored me. "So, what'd you talk about?" He looked at me with a casual glance. "You could be a security guard and beat up all the patrons who avoided the offering basket."

"No, I…" I breathed deeply, wondering what to even share with him. Was it worth it? I said it anyway. "He asked me to mentor some boys." I hoped for a change of topics, from the odd and insulting to the normal and civilized.

"You? Yeah right." Phil's blurt trailed into laughter. He was almost drowned out as the Buffs got another first down. Almost.

"You know…" I clenched my teeth then placed my hands firmly on the table like a lion eyeballing his prey.

I knew what he was thinking. Not only was I a worthless kid, but I had become a worthless adult with no foreseeable skills to speak of, let alone to teach or imitate. In a lineup of potential mentors, I'd bring up the rear. And it annoyed me that everyone knew, especially him.

"I'm probably not going to do it." I tried to loosen my shoulders, releasing a heat that surged up my neck. But it only made me warmer. "I have no idea what to tell some punky middle-schoolers. I mean, what do I talk about for goodness' sake?"

I looked up at the television then over at Phil, still entranced by the game.

He suddenly spoke. "You could teach them a lot, like how to provide aid and comfort to those less fortunate." He stared at my hands. "Oh wait… as long as the defenseless guy isn't drunk out of his gourd. Then you pound the crap out of him."

I leaped onto the table and punched Phil squarely on his jaw. His head snapped back against the wall, barely missing the padded booth. Our water glasses knocked over and spilled.

I jerked my hand up and down. The sudden pain was intense. I reached out and grabbed the front of Phil's shirt. He was still in a daze.

My eyes blazed into him. Shaking hands. Instant sweat on my brow. A flaring intensity scorched my throat. But the real fire was deep inside, down to my core. The embers had smoldered far too long.

Phil grabbed his mouth with his hand, attempting to sustain the swift flow of blood. It had already dripped down his neck and soaked his collar.

A hand tugged on my shirt, a feeble attempt at reeling me back. I pivoted on my knee and shrugged off the helpless waitress. I glared back at her then slowly removed my hand from Phil's shirt, both full of sweat and blood and guilt.

The force of the counter punch propelled me backwards, my leg slamming against the table. My head hit the back padding. My cheek felt swollen and damp.

"Enjoy the parting gift, Shawny boy…"

I reached up and patted the blood dripping from my nostrils. I grabbed a napkin, already damp from the spilled water, and attempted to stop the bleeding. Shards of broken glass splashed the floor.

"You ok?" asked the waitress. "Let me get a rag."

I stood up and pushed her aside. The piercing glares of judgment and confusion were everywhere. Too many people, not nearly enough space. I had to do something.

I tried to speak, but no words came out. I pointed with my left hand, the blood-soaked napkin held tightly in my right. The server station and front counter were a blur as I ran past. The front door banged open and thwacked the rubber stopper protecting the flower bed.

I took one more wipe with the napkin then tossed it into the row of flowers. I gently touched my nose with my index finger, catching drops of blood that I wiped on my jeans. They were a mess, just like me.

I reached into my pocket, pulled out my Motorola flip phone, and found the contact I was looking for. "Count me in" was my quick message.

I threw the phone into my pocket then bolted to my car.

Chapter 6 – Shawn

September 6, 2003

I flew out of the parking lot with bloodstains streaked down my shirt. At the first stoplight, I yanked it over my head and threw it out the window, a ghastly reminder of what I had become. My hand slammed on the steering wheel with such unrestraint it hurt.

It was way too early to head home. My mom would ask a ton of questions, and I wouldn't have the heart to lie. Too late to head back. The past could never change. I had to go somewhere. So I drove.

My life had fallen into a deep abyss dug by everyone around me, and it started with my father. I was furious he was taken from me, and even angrier he had become that important.

My mother, on the other hand, was no help. She was an animal lost in the forest, hunting for her herd, never seeing anything besides the pack of wolves behind her.

My friends. Non-existent. I just smashed the one remaining in the face. Everyone else? Gone.

But they didn't know what really happened. No one did. The newspaper even got it wrong. The rumor mill churned out the small-town definition of truth which was good enough for most, yet bad enough to ruin my life.

Did I have a choice in my actions? Of course. But that assumes there was something else I should have done, or something others would have done in my place. Wouldn't anyone act the same way I did?

I was miserable, confused, and furious — at God for taking my father and at myself for taking it so personally. God messed up my life just as much as I did. Worse yet, I didn't even value what I took. Sadly, no one else did either.

And now, Mike wanted me to be a mentor. One of us was certifiably crazy. What did I get myself into? Maybe I looked the part, perhaps even acted like one sometimes. Or maybe he thought I was just like my father. That was a mistake. Mike didn't know the real me. No one did, not even me.

I wiped my blurry eyes, enough to make out a sliver of road. Blood streaked down my cheeks, diluted by tears.

Beyond the thin shoulder was a deep ravine, overgrown with tall grass, thick weeds, and enough garbage to fill a dump truck. Was I the first to notice?

A slight turn of the wheel and I'd be gone, slamming into the ravine with such a potent force, my car and I would become a twisted pile of nothingness.

And not a single soul would notice.

Only my hands had any semblance of control. They gripped the steering wheel, white knuckles encircled by blotchy red. I tried to tell them what to do, but they didn't listen. My head overruled, and this time, my heart agreed. One clouded and empty, one heavy and full.

But I focused on my hands. My senseless hands.

They failed again.

Chapter 7 – Shawn

September 7, 2003

I trudged into the kitchen, focusing on all the things I didn't want to think about. Nothing was immune to my path of destruction: my face, hands, pride, and friendships. The bathroom mirror already told me how I looked. I was just beginning to grasp how I felt.

"Nice to see you rise from the dead. How late were you out boozing?" My mother, always the kidder.

The sink was stacked high with dirty dishes, a normal state I still couldn't get used to. Spaghetti sauce stuck to plates like glue, lumpy milk sat in glasses, and ketchup-stained tableware resembling the shirt I threw out roadside.

I wondered what she did all day. She probably felt the same about me. "I wasn't boozin', and it wasn't late. What time is it?" I had no idea. Time had no meaning.

I sat down on a chair and angled my body so my unharmed side faced my mother. I folded my fist under my chin and slanted my head toward the window, resembling *The Thinker*, although looks were deceiving.

"After noon, I know that." She glanced up at the clock hanging above the sink. She was right. "Want breakfast or dinner?"

"Very funny. Breakfast is good. Thanks." I wasn't hungry, but at least it bought me some time.

"Cereal's in the cupboard." She barely motioned.

"Ah, Breakfast of Champions."

"You can eat it, too."

"Gee, thanks."

I grabbed everything I needed. The spoon clanked on the bowl and the milk jiggled against the box of Wheaties. I encircled my mom like the moon with my dark side hidden by my own shadow.

She sat down across the table from me, her mug still steaming. She held the side of it with one hand and gripped the handle with the other. Her forearms were tense. "What happened?"

"Whadya mean?" I tossed some cereal and milk into the bowl then spooned a mouthful.

"I'm not blind, Son. Where'd you get that?" She extended her finger toward my guilt-ridden face.

I stopped mid-chew. "Where'd I get what?" My mouth full of food. Milk dripped down my chin.

She almost laughed. "Oh, c'mon. I wasn't born yesterday. Who punched you?"

My chin snapped upward while my spoon clanged on the table. "How'd you know?"

She motioned outside. I turned to look but didn't get it. "Your reflection in the window." She tilted her head to the side then sipped her coffee.

I reached up and dabbed the underside of my eye, feeling tender and spongy. "A parting gift from Phil."

She scrunched her nose, forcing a scowl. "You've gotta be kidding me. You two've been friends forever, although I've never understood why."

I bent to my right and tucked one leg under the other. At least they didn't ache like everything else. "Well, I did punch him first." I tossed in another bite.

She cleared her throat, dislodging a clog of cynicism. "That explains it." The steam veiled her face but not her anger. "Want some?" She raised her mug.

"Sure. That'd be great." I shoveled more cereal into my mouth, leaning over the bowl like a lapping dog. Milk spilled onto the table in odd, random shapes.

Her eyebrows raised, lips pursed. "Get it yourself."

I grabbed a mug from the cupboard, poured from the pot, then sat down again. Too lazy for creamer. She strained to inspect my eye. There were so many shades of black and blue and purple, each with a matching rawness and sensitivity.

"Should heal in a week... unless you start another brawl."

"I'm not starting another brawl." I mumbled into my bowl, leaning further forward so I didn't have to look at her. Contrary to popular belief, getting into fights was not a habit of mine, although dealing with her was.

In normal families, I assumed this would kick-start a productive life lesson about how to treat others. Turn the other cheek type stuff. Not mine. "Well, I don't know. You might." She crossed her legs and let out a deep sigh. Her breath smelled like charred firewood.

I took another bite, ignoring her as much as I could. "I stopped by church yesterday. Mike says 'hi.'"

She took a sip, then stared out the window as if our conversation hadn't even started. A stone-like presence. Her emotions either deserted in a drought or raged back in a flood, with a mind that ran circles around her motionless figure. I could always see her thoughts, just never understand them.

"Mom... did you hear me? I stopped by and talked to Mike." I downed the leftover milk from my bowl even though it tasted sour and was barely drinkable. The spoon chimed when it hit bottom.

Spots, creases, and lines appeared on her complexion like rings on a tree trunk. The poorer the conditions, the more pronounced the markings. Her psyche could only handle one life-altering storm. Unfortunately, hers was still ongoing.

She slanted her head, focusing on a not-so-distant memory that danced in the yard, just begging to be watched. It had visited before, too many times to count. I let it be hers, never looking to see what it was.

I swallowed hard, mimicking the gurgling coffee pot.

"That's nice, dear," she finally answered, sounding convinced of nothing. Sadly, it was the reaction I expected.

"Mike's doing well... in case you wonder," I almost spat, the coffee tasting as bitter as the burnt timber it smelled like.

She sprang to life. "What does this have to do with you and Phil? I'm lost."

My hands were cracked and irritated, victims of the high desert air of Colorado. My nonstop scratching didn't help. "Mike asked me to be a mentor."

"You?"

"Yes, me!" My shoulders jumped. "And I'm gonna do it, too."

She attempted to suppress her giggle with her mug, but it didn't help. Not at all.

"Thanks for the support." I leaned back. "Appreciate it."

"What am I supposed to say? That you should waltz out of prison and teach some kids what not to do?"

"It wasn't prison."

"Close enough."

I walked over and jabbed a chunk out of a coffee cake that sat in a 9x13 glass pan on the counter. At quick glance, I didn't see any mold. "I'll tell 'em my story. That should align them with God's plan."

"Shawn!" Her glare was hotter and ten times more intense than the coffee. "Don't be such a pessimist."

I sat back down at the table and laughed. "Ah, you've taught me well." I munched on the stiff, powdery cake. Crumbles scattered on the table, right next to the milk splotches.

There was so much wrapped into what we said. My mom and I had been separated for years, besides her occasional visit. We were a family of two, but I used the term loosely. Nature vs. nurture didn't matter. I learned enough from her about pessimism, not that my life hadn't taught me my share.

When did it start? I was never sure if my dad was the equalizer who kept her at bay or the igniter who started it all when he died. Sadly enough, he was at fault either way. But I still blamed her.

"Anyway… I'm doing it. Like it or not."

I had so many memories of my father, and they always came back at awkward times. Back when I was five, we went boating on Carter Lake up west of Berthoud. It was a beautiful day until it wasn't. A howling wind came out of nowhere, stirring up a choppiness to the otherwise calm water. All three of us were there, my dad steered our small motorboat up and down the waves, while my mom and I hung on for dear life.

We both got drenched as the frigid water crashed over the front of the boat, each wave seemingly larger and colder than the last. I laughed it off. What a blast! My mom? Not so much. She was so mad at my father for that, and I never understood why. First, it was a shoreline tongue lashing. Then came the silent treatment. They didn't fight much, but that one was a doozy.

"Those kids will teach you a thing or two about respect. Lord knows you need it."

I wished she didn't waste her words, on me or anyone else. There were so few of them. "Should be easy. They're just middle schoolers." There was nothing I hadn't seen, nothing I hadn't heard. It wasn't that long ago. "What could go wrong?" I plucked off a large chunk of helpless cake and threw it in my mouth.

She reached across the table, trying to touch my arm but coming up short. I recognized the attempt, and the failure. It had been years since we last hugged, let alone an intentional touch of a hand. That closeness left our family at the same time all the bad stuff crept in, as if there was only enough room for one of them.

"I wouldn't count on that." She glanced at my mess of hair then narrowed her eyes. "I'm still lost. How'd this lead to a fight with Phil?"

"Ah, yes." I finished chewing, then wiped my mouth with my index finger. "I told Phil about mentoring. Let's just say he wasn't that supportive, especially for me."

"Can't say I blame him." She downed the rest of her mug with ease only because it tasted so familiar. "We all make mistakes. Some more than others… like you."

I devoured the last bite, then scooped crumbs from the table and threw them in my mouth. "At some point we have to move on."

My comment was so loaded, so full of raw emotion. It was an entire chapter neither of us wanted to write, let alone discuss. For starters, she didn't even know what *moving on* meant, let alone how to do it. If anything, her four-year rut only showed me the opposite.

The topic ended before it even started. If there was anything I learned since my father died, timing was everything.

"Would you believe it starts Wednesday?"

"Do you get any kind of training?" She stared at my unshaved chin, the harsh stubble in desperate need of attention.

I scratched my chin and laughed. "For what?"

"Oh nothing. Nothing at all."

Chapter 8 – Shawn

September 10, 2003

I was blown away when I stepped through the church doors. Parents and kids were everywhere. Some stood in confined circles, some walked about, all resembling a giant pinball game. The kids looked so young — scrawny, pimpled, and wearing clothes that fit better yesterday. The five years between us was an eternity. A lifetime for me.

I propped myself against the corner wall, crossed my arms, and watched. I had no desire to stand out, but it was obvious I did. Teenagers hoping to be older, parents wishing they were younger, and me feeling like the average.

The kids were hilarious to watch. They twisted and fidgeted their gangly bodies as if out of place in who others thought they were. They talked, yelled, ran around until their shirt collars got yanked, and generally tried their best to be as annoying as possible. I remembered the angst well enough to recall I was trying to forget it.

The parents, on the other hand, scratched behind their ears, glared at their kids as if assuming the worst of them, while casually glancing at their watches, wishing time was different, less cruel.

As for me? Everyone stared like I was an unwelcomed outsider just waiting to do something unlawful. If that included running away, then maybe I was. The outer courtyard appeared to be a great escape route — bushes and shrubs to hide behind, a clear path to my car. This whole mentoring shindig wasn't going to work, a disaster from day one. Two wrongs did not make a right.

Instantly, as if on cue, the auditorium doors popped opened. Pastor Mike descended into the crowd, shaking hands and talking to everyone he came across. He gestured in my direction as I wasn't hard to miss. I acknowledged with a slight wave. As he walked toward me, my hands fell to my side.

"Great to see you, Shawn!" Mike briskly shook my hand, vibrating his tie. "I've been looking forward to tonight. The kids are going to love this."

"Is this new?" Whatever *this* was. "Or did you have this last year?" My eyes darted side to side, with random kids glaring in my direction. Adults, too. They obviously had no idea who I was, which I counted as a good thing.

"Nope, just started this year. Tonight's opening night!" His hands gestured outward like a showman, appropriate since the place resembled a circus.

"I'm excited, too." My smile only mirrored his. I couldn't help but fiddle with my watch, twisting it back and forth around my wrist.

He pointed to my shiner, standing out as much as I felt. "I bet that's an interesting story."

"It sure is."

Mike was too preoccupied — glancing around the room, waving at people — to ask any more. His focus shifted back to me, head nodding upward and smile deserting his face as if second-guessing his invitation. At least I wasn't alone. As far as I could tell, we were both in way over our heads.

He placed his hand on my shoulder. "We'll chat later." He walked away with his promise and threat both suspended midair. His hand raised in an awkward salute, then dropped to greet the next guy over. They exchanged a few words, then Mike announced to everyone it was time to start.

The cattle call began. Every parent and his or her mini-me entered the auditorium and found seats near the front. The first ten pews filled, so I sat in the eleventh. I hoped to go unnoticed, but that was highly unlikely.

Some kids sat with their parents, some as far away as possible. Either way, their choices were based on their parents, and the game of it looked downright silly. But the kids hadn't a clue they were even playing.

"Welcome! Nice to see everyone here." Mike placed his hands together as he glanced across the audience. "I'm expecting this to be a great year for our youth program. And judging by tonight's turnout, we're off to a wonderful start."

The kids were all listening, facing forward and keeping their hands to themselves. I figured it was more out of curiosity than any kind of eagerness to start something new.

Mike continued. "Psalm 145:4 states that 'one generation shall commend your works to another.' In this simple statement, God commanded us to be mentors for the next generation. The mentors here tonight have taken time out of their busy schedules to spend it with you guys. And they want to teach you how to navigate life."

I shook my head. Was this my mistake or Mike's? My worst fears came to life. If I were a parent, would I want someone like me as my kid's mentor? This was wrong in more ways than I could count. The stained glass felt like plates under a microscope, and all of us were subjects in a yet-to-be-determined experiment.

"As far as schedule every week, we'll continue to blah blah blah. But then in the second half, we'll split up and blah blah blah." At least that was what I heard.

The kids looked even more blindsided than I was, sitting towards the front, mouths open, eyes blurry, heads slightly downward. Excitement, anxiety, and fear, all mixed into one.

"You kids wanna meet your new mentors?" asked Mike with a big smile. It wasn't returned. The kids were dumbfounded, as excited about meeting their mentors as my mom was in finding out I'd be one.

"It's not my dad, is it?" came a timid voice from the front row, a ponytailed girl sitting beside her embarrassed father. The thought of my mother ever mentoring was hysterical.

Mike laughed. "Since you asked, I'll make sure it is, Liz."

He called off the names of every group. Each mentor stood up after his name was called, the kids suddenly reacting like it was a popularity contest: claps, cheers, and howls. To me, it was glaringly obvious why. Every mentor was a parent they already knew.

Had Mike forgotten? Changed his mind? Gotten around to doing a background check?

I drowned in uncertainty, caught between an island of naïve kids and a distant land of unforgiving adults.

Proving Phil wrong was one thing, but teaching kids how to navigate life? You've got to be kidding me. Had they forgotten who I was? I rubbed my forehead with the palm of my hand, unsure which one was wiping the other.

I gripped the armrest. This was my chance to leave.

"And our last mentor, but certainly not least…" Mike paused for an eternity. "Shawn Stevens."

He motioned to me in the back, and a wave of people turned their heads. My black eye glowed like a lighthouse. Everyone sized me up for all I was worth: my age, height, and reputation. Luckily, nobody seemed to recognize me.

This was no longer the place where I grew up, and I couldn't decide if that was a good thing or a bad thing.

I sat down and instantly thought of my mom. Her last visit to church was a train wreck — the death of her husband, her no-good prodigal son. Her family was gone: one temporarily, one forever. But why did everyone stare? Was it the shock of knowing someone so stricken by grief?

Mike called off the boys' names for my group, but I barely listened. He told each group where they'd meet and handed every mentor a sheet of icebreaker questions.

My eyes and thoughts glazed over it all.

•   •   •

We sat down in a circle, the rock-hard floor jolting my spine. They moved nonstop, one of them clicked his teeth, and at least one of them desperately needed deodorant. They all glanced around the room, but it was obvious they were stealing glimpses of me.

"So, why don't you tell me your names and what grade you're in?" The sheet I was handed was worthless, with questions I couldn't answer let alone ask eighth grade boys to. It landed on the floor quicker than I could ask my first question.

One boy sprang into action. "Hi! I'm Harry." One hand extended while the other tucked his wrinkled shirt into his jeans, twisting around his small frame. "And that's Peter, Sebastian, and Zach. We're the fearsome foursome, ready to attack the world!"

"And he's Moron." Zach was a striking kid with intense blue eyes who smacked of confidence. He wore a tight spandex shirt with black nylon sweats. His muscles yelled insults.

"You can call him Jockhead if you want," snapped Harry.

"Nice one. Come up with that on your own?"

"C'mon, guys. Settle down." My pitiful attempt at restoring order. I felt like a substitute teacher, expecting classroom mutiny at any moment.

But they were just as out of place as me. Young. Incomplete. Their bodies were disproportioned, their social cues non-existent. Oversized kids disguised as miniature adults. Uncomfortable and awkward yet confident enough to push limits. More than enough to be dangerous.

"What happened to your eye?" Peter would have hidden behind his glasses if he could — soft-spoken, wandering eyes, and a persistent downward slope to his head. Apparently, though, he was willing to ask pointed questions.

I shifted my legs and placed my hands behind me on the floor. They all watched with blank stares as if seeking greatness but settling for mediocrity.

"I had me a scuffle the other night. Someone said the Broncos stink, so I smacked 'em. As I walked away, I slipped on some shotgun shells and hit my eye on the 12-gauge leaning against the table."

The boys stopped moving, their eyes squinted. I smiled, trying hard not to laugh. At that point, they would have believed I went to grade school with Keira Knightley.

"No way, the Broncos are awesome!" Zach responded, seemingly oblivious to sarcasm. "They're drafting me after college." Oh my. I was surprised this kid even noticed others were in the same room.

"Are not!" shouted Sebastian, a tall, skinny kid with reddish, brown hair and cowboy boots to match. "Football's a stupid sport, anyway. Try a real sport like soccer."

"You gotta be kidding me! Soccer's for sissies. Football's where the action is."

"Yeah, if you mean concussions and broken necks." Harry reached around his side, making another awkward attempt at adjusting his shirt.

"Listen here, Mr. Potter," This Zach kid was a real winner. "What do you know about sports, anyway?"

"Hey, hey boys! I was kidding." I laughed at their creative insults and lackluster idiocy. "My shiner has nothing to do with football, or guns, or anything else. But I did have a fight with a friend."

Awkward silence.

Peter finally spoke up. "How does he look?" He squirmed like the others but appeared older with neatly cropped blond hair I was certain his mother meticulously combed every morning.

"Hopefully worse," I mumbled. "Can we get back to you guys telling me about yourselves? What grade are you in? What's your favorite subject in school? If you were an ice cream flavor, what would you be?" I rubbed my neck. "You know, the important stuff."

Older did not make me wiser. A leader I was not.

"Well, all he cares about is gym class, while I'm much more mature and well-rounded." Harry stood up, threw his arms to his side, and waddled around like a penguin.

Zach pounced on Harry and wrestled him to the ground. He twisted Harry around, his legs wrapping him into a nylon vice. Sebastian tackled them both, followed by a reluctant Peter. An all-out riot erupted as each one jumped on the next, creating an infinite pile.

"Boys... Stop!" I yelled, but it was as if I wasn't there. The other groups strained their necks to watch. Lucky for me, they were far away, but their agitation was obvious.

I started to sweat as I toyed with my collar. My back muscles ached so I leaned forward, ready to explode and scream at the top of my lungs. Anything to get them to stop. But I couldn't. These were kids.

It only escalated. Zach was the strongest as he wrestled the others to the ground in one swift motion. They soon ganged up on him, with each grabbing an arm or leg. But they were no match for Zach. He grappled his way to the top only to be swarmed again.

The world's first perpetual motion machine.

Yelling. Laughing. Best of friends becoming the worst of enemies. Or the other way around. No clue.

I sat there, helpless and confused. They clearly weren't going to listen, especially to me. It was complete chaos at its finest.

Why did I do this?

Chapter 9 – Aidan

Dear Aidan,

I hope all is flying, man! I haven't seen you in years, and by the time you read this it might even be a few more. I'm hard to track down ever since I cleared my pilot's license. I'm a traveling fool.

According to what your mother told me, you must be a strapping young man by the time you read this. I decided to write it early just because I couldn't stop thinking about it.

I remember when you entered this world. I was so young, I had no idea how to process any of it. I was ecstatic to welcome you, don't get me wrong, yet my thoughts and emotions ran elsewhere. Ever since the day that stork dropped you on your mom's doorstep, you have always been a spitting image of your father (that's a compliment, by the way). It's why I always enjoyed being around you. I hope your mom didn't get sick of me dropping by.

I remember the day I met your father. He had short, dark hair and a shiner on his right eye to match. I didn't know what to think of him and honestly, I was intimidated. We were five years apart in age, but it was light years to me. What do 13-year-old boys do when they're uncomfortable? We were noisy and fidgety and gave your dad a splitting headache!

But it was perfect timing. The week before we met, my father had moved out of our house. I was still trying to figure out my new normal, but I didn't make a big deal about it. In fact, I covered it up and pretended all was well. But it really wasn't. I hated my life.

That was precisely when your father waltzed into the picture. I didn't know much about what I wanted, but I did know I wanted to be just like him. Even when I found out about things later, I still admired him. He listened, even when we talked endlessly.

Ultimately, he was there for me when I needed someone the most. And for that, I will always be grateful. Of course, I needed to figure out who I was before he knew who he was rescuing, but that's okay. He forced me to do just that.

Hold your head above water, kid. Be there for others. Listen and learn whenever you can. Honestly, it would be the ultimate compliment.

May God watch over you, and may you find peace and happiness in everything you do.

Take care bro',

Harry

•   •   •

As weird as it was reading a letter from Harry, it didn't compare to Harry himself. I only remembered meeting him a few times, but the last time I saw him, he wore red leather pants with his hair dyed to match. He taught me Algonquin and then demonstrated their traditional, native dance which totally freaked me out.

"Was Harry always screaming for attention?" I asked.

"Always." My mom rubbed her cheek. "Partly because he didn't get any at home."

I totally understood what it was like to live in a place where no one cared, where I'd leave, and no one would notice. One momentous day, in the not-so-distant future, I'd get home from school, use the same stupid key that hung around my neck like a dog collar, then with my mom at work, I'd slip out of the house and make it all the way across town before she'd ever figure it out. It would work, I knew it.

"He's funny. Weird but funny." I tugged on my ear, almost forgetting my mom was listening.

"He certainly is." She tilted to the right, her hand resting above her belt.

I held the letter tightly in one hand and skimmed parts of it again. Timing. That's what I thought of. Not a stopwatch, but more like an engine. His dad leaving, my dad arriving, and the combustion of it all.

But I still had questions. Lots of them. "Why did Dad have a black eye? Did he just have a fight?"

My mom sat down on a box across from me and swept back the hair above her eyes. "He did. A disagreement with a friend."

"Like the time I punched Brian on the playground?" That wasn't a good memory for me or my mother. But he deserved it, pushing kids down and stealing my friend Sarah's swing. Someone had to stand up to the buffoon.

She shook her head. "Kind of like that. Oddly enough, it's what convinced him to mentor his boys."

She finally appeared as interested in the letters as I was.

"Why would that be?" My head snapped upward, and the corner of my mouth sneered. *His boys.* The possessiveness of it. The authenticity. I hated it. "Makes no sense."

The more I thought about Harry's letter, the more I realized I had more questions than when I started.

"Well... his friend didn't think he could do it."

"What friend?"

"The one who punched him."

"Doesn't sound like a friend to me." I scratched the side of my stomach then sat up and adjusted my T-shirt, wishing the box I sat on didn't feel like such a rock. "What would mentoring prove anyway?"

She kicked her feet and stared at the floor. Her fingers shot up a peace sign, although she meant it differently. "Two things: your father didn't think he could, and because he needed to learn something." She knew more than she said. Way more. And for some reason, she wasn't sharing it.

But she did get my attention, and it was at least something to hold onto. "I thought he was the mentor. How can he learn anything?"

She tucked in her legs, shifting her body side to side. "You need to learn a few things about mentoring."

"I probably do." I scratched my cheek, my skin flush yet dry. "So, how'd you and Dad meet?"

She rustled through the papers, grabbed the one she was looking for, then handed it to me. "That's this one."

Chapter 10 – Shawn

September 14, 2003

The rain picked up its pace, and my dirty windshield quickly became layered in mud. The wipers on my filthy, old Mustang were pathetic, and worse yet, I was desperately low on wiper fluid. My vision was awful.

I pulled over into the first gas station I saw. The lot was filled with cars, all newer and nicer than my jalopy. I pulled into the only open space, right between a nondescript minivan and a souped-up Charger.

Blam! My front bumper pounded against the curb. I trembled in frustration, then uttered obscenities I'd rather not repeat. I pulled back the sleeve of my flannel shirt and glanced at my watch. Late for work. Again.

I ran inside the building but abruptly stopped past the entrance. People were everywhere. As the door closed behind me, I maneuvered around an old lady, my arm brushing against her raincoat and drenching the side of my shirt. It was a tight aisle, so I twisted my body and took a long stride with my front leg, never noticing that the tiled floor had become a giant, slippery puddle.

My foot slid. My leg flailed. I reached out to brace my fall, catching the corner of a display rack. I slammed against the floor and was pelted with raining corn chips. Some crunched underneath me like the crackle of a loudspeaker.

When the chip shower ended, I reached over and grabbed my hand, still aching from its encounter with Phil's face. It braced my fall, but my instincts continued to inflict wounds. Now my wrist and elbow were sore.

I was furious and embarrassed. The bright florescent lights were not the only things glaring down on me, as the store clerk's Coke bottle glasses magnified his eyes. Laughter I expected, help I didn't want.

I sat there for a moment while the world stopped around me. At least I knew how far my life could plummet, an abyss far worse than the weed-infested, roadside ravine I passed days ago.

A soft hand touched my shoulder. I almost swatted it away thinking it was a buzzing fly.

"You ok? That sure was a hard fall," she said.

I rubbed and shook my arm then looked up to greet the lady with the sopping wet jacket, the one who forced me to make a fool of myself, the one with the soft, comforting hands and reassuring voice.

But it wasn't her. She had long, chestnut hair tied tightly into a ponytail that bobbed side to side as she bent down to help. Her red raincoat shone under the lights, and her smile speckled with laughter. She had spotted dimples on her cheeks, noticeable on her soft, smooth complexion.

Any hopes of her not noticing a clumsy goofball stumble onto the floor were dashed. But I noticed her as well, and she was difficult to ignore.

Her hand reached out to help me off the floor. I stood up next to her — about a head taller than she was — then brushed myself off. We both laughed as some chips fell off my shirt. I hastily put the display back to together, but the cross bar was bent in the middle making it about as worthless as I felt. I placed it on the shelf, right next to my ego.

"Thanks." I blurted. "I should have watched where I was going." The sad part was I actually did watch; it was the thinking angle that I missed.

"Lots of people fall for Fritos, you know," she pointed out. "They're tasty, especially with soup and a sandwich."

I laughed, glancing at the pathetic display that was entirely my fault. "I just wish that lady wasn't so desperate to grab all the bags. I had to beat her to it. I had to."

"And that you did. No one in the store doubts that."

"Gee, thanks."

I shook my shirt, and the last remaining chip fell into my hand. I threw it in my mouth. She grinned, her face so gentle, almost enchanting. Freckles dotted her cheeks.

I was staring. I turned away. I was lost. *What do I say?*

"Hi, I'm Grace." She stretched out her hand, breaking the silence between us.

"I'm Shawn, fearless leader of the Frito patrol." I tried shaking my head, but it didn't move. I had just made a complete fool of myself to the most beautiful woman I'd ever met. First action now words. I was officially a moron.

She burst with laughter then reached back and stroked her ponytail. Her indigo eyes were so deep and vast, I couldn't believe I just noticed them. Her gorgeous, seascape eyes.

She helped me put the damaged goods back together, at least what could stand on its own. We both reached for the last bag, our hands briefly touched, but I let her grab it. She placed it on the lowest shelf then stood up next to me.

"Thanks for your help." I couldn't help but watch her every move. "I appreciate it."

"No problem." She pointed up past her cheek. "Looks like you caught a hefty punch. Must have a habit of fighting ladies for chips."

I completely forgot about my shiner, which was now more spotted red and green. Christmassy minus the joy part. I reached up and dabbed it, unsure how sensitive it would be. Still raw and tender, covering a whole range of textures and emotions.

"Yeah, happens to me all the time." The heavy rain was letting up outside. "Well, maybe only once. A gift from a friend. A parting gift."

"I'm so sorry, I bet that hurt."

"Gave him a matching one." I shrugged my shoulders. "What are friends for besides sharing?"

I raised my hands in mock confusion. But I remembered what friends were for. Absence made the heart grow fonder, I guess. Provoked by the past, Phil mocked the present, and I defended my future. All three were horrible choices, but I had to live in one.

I realized work was barking for my presence. And squawking, and purring, and every other noise caged animals make. But what could I do? The pet store was a job, and my past didn't exactly lend itself to great employment.

"I've gotta run…" I reached out, grasping for a little more time with her. "Say, speaking of soup and a sandwich, would you wanna catch a bite to eat sometime?"

My voice raised as I spoke, desperation dribbling off my lips. I hoped my newfound bravery wasn't wasted. She stared at my eyes. I wondered if she heard me.

I was new at this game. Girls only inhabited my dreams at the boys' home. Did I say something wrong? Come on too strong? I read everything so poorly.

"Only if you bring the Fritos." She reached into her purse, her hand shaking ever so slightly. She jotted down a number then handed it to me.

I couldn't help but wonder what she thought. She had just met a bruised and clumsy also-ran, in a gas station no less. She was humoring me, laughing on the inside, waiting to tell her friends the joke that I was.

I nodded in acceptance, but my mouth didn't cooperate. "Sure, I'd be glad to."

"I'll see you later, then." Grace gently raised her hand as she turned to leave. "Bye."

"Bye." I waved as she turned to walk away, wondering if there was more I should have said.

The rain finally stopped so we both headed to our cars. Her rust-covered Jeep was almost as old as mine, making me less embarrassed about my junker. At least I wasn't alone.

I slid into my front seat, brushed back my damp hair, then unfolded the paper she had given me. Her name and phone number were written large and loopy with consecutive zeros drawn into a smiley face.

I looked up right as she drove away.

Chapter 11 – Aidan

Dear Aidan,

I remember the day I met your father. He got tangled in a store display and landed hard on the floor. I had stopped to grab a quick breakfast when I watched him slip and fall. Some might call it an accident (us meeting, not the display falling over :-), but I would beg to differ.

First thing, I never eat at McDonald's. Why I stopped there, I have no idea. Second, I was taking a different route due to construction on Pace. Third, I severely overslept and was running an hour late for my classes. And lastly, I would have completely missed seeing him if I had entered through the restaurant. But they were mopping the floors, so I took the other entrance.

He was the most charming man I'd ever met. He was courteous, kind, and funny. It scared me how physically ill I felt that day. I had no idea what my future held, but I suspected it involved him.

Of course, in some ways I was wrong. We wouldn't be together forever. But who is, really? He left my life just as quickly as he entered. But because of you, he will always be with me. You are his legacy, and his pride and joy.

Your father was far from perfect. He was stubborn, unaccepting of people he didn't like, severely lacking self-confidence, and he blamed others for his own predicaments. But I loved him anyway.

I like to think I saved him in a way, from re-entering his destructive past to providing a glimpse of a future. But I didn't entirely. That's giving me way too much credit, and him not enough. To me, saving is a group effort, never just an individual.

Deep down, he cared so much about others. He always wanted the best for your grandma and me, and he was willing to fight for it, no matter what. He convinced us to do earth-shattering things, and I am the better for it.

You're so much like him. You have the same childlike humor, identical brown eyes where I can read your thoughts, and a similar empathetic yet 'know what you want' personality where the future is crystal clear. He would be proud of the kind and driven young man you've become. Funny how I did all the work carrying you (for nine whole months!), yet you turned out just like him.

But I wouldn't have it any other way. You are a lasting memory for me and everyone else honored to have met you both.

You are our son, and I will always love you.

Love,

Mom

•   •   •

Did my mom know the lady who forged this letter? Because it sure wasn't her. It was open and honest, as opposite of reality as nice, middle-school girls.

"Why didn't you tell me this in person?" The air in the attic was as coarse as sandpaper. My throat was scratchy and moving made me itch.

There was no way I was waiting until I was 16 to find out who my father was. Crazy. Abusive. Holding this back was both an insult and a punishment.

She watched me fidget with my legs, stretching my jeans down toward the floor. "I don't have an answer, Aidan. I... I guess I'm just not good at talking about difficult topics. Never have been."

"But why? Zach tells us to open up about stuff. It's cool to share." It was odd to say as I'd never told her anything like that before. "Maybe you need a mentor, Mom."

She burst into an awkward laugh. "You might be right."

Whether she admitted it or not, she did need a close friend. Her life revolved around me and work, and she opened up even less than I did. She was the one ready to detonate.

"Trust me." I winked poorly, my eyes shutting with a long, heavy blink. "You should listen to me more."

She brushed back her hair, revealing a face outwardly more insecure and wrinkled than yesterday. "Yup."

The edges of the paper felt dry and sharp. "Why did you request these letters?" I held it loosely between my thumb and index finger. "Did something trigger you to ask?"

"Well… you're almost the age your father was when Grandpa died. I didn't…" She scratched the inner part of her eye. "I wanted your life to be different. I wanted you to know who he was. I just didn't think you'd be ready so soon."

I glanced at the letter still held lightly in my hand. I felt ready for anything, although my mom would have said otherwise. "So, what did he convince you to do that was so earth-shattering? Bungee jump? Sky diving?"

She snapped her head back in this seemingly natural way. Totally odd. "I wish it were that easy."

"Then what?" My lips puckered then split. "What in the world could you possibly do that's earth-shattering?" The thought was mind-blowing. Moms don't do earth-shattering things. They just don't.

"Aidan, really? I used to be young once, you know."

"Yeah… I guess so." *Like fifteen years ago.*

She paused and sighed before finally answering. "You'd better keep reading. I'm not ready to tell you everything about your father."

"What did he do? Was it another fight?"

"Yes and no. A fight for his life, perhaps."

"What does *that* mean?"

Why didn't she tell me what she knew? Adults were way more confusing than kids. No doubt, kids can be cruel, but at least we're not protective of things we don't even own. Spit it out for goodness' sake. I can take it.

"He made a huge mistake, Aidan, one that cost him a lot. But he reconciled, if you know what that means."

"Like when the teacher forced me to say I was sorry to Brian even though I wasn't, and he deserved it?"

"Kind of like that." Her slow, word-by-word response wasn't very convincing. "But more complex."

"You mean, like my math homework?" I was grasping for some kind of meaning or explanation. Something to keep me afloat.

"Similar." She nodded. "Difficult but solvable."

There was so much up in that attic, most of it I didn't recognize. But even the familiar stuff had changed. My box of toys was crammed full of stuff —

LeapFrogs, Fisher-Price boats, and all kinds of books and games — still trying desperately to be noisy and colorful and significant.

But they all lost their importance years ago.

Maybe they were trying to tell me something.

Chapter 12 – Shawn

September 26, 2003

I found my favorite collared shirt and threw on the stone-washed jeans I had just bought at Sportsman's Warehouse. Took me a while to find them behind the camouflage gaiters, duck decoys, and smoothbore shotguns. The place was literally a nightmare factory for birds.

I headed back to the bathroom and stared at the mirror, still steamed over after my shower. I admired my soft, stubble-less face, massaging my smooth chin and neck. It had been a while, entirely by choice.

I despised shaving — the dryness, the itchiness, and irritation in so many forms. I was conditioned as much as a Pavlovian dog. The boys' home was where it started — a ranch beyond a dusty butte, nestled into a small, pine-studded valley. Looks were deceiving.

Rain or shine, they'd work our tails off every day. Every stupid day. I tended to horses, cows, sheep, and every beast on the planet, beating the sun out of bed as if it were a contest. Hours of work before breakfast — bundles of hay for the horses who showed their appreciation by crapping shovelfuls, and mounds of slop for the thankless pigs filled with cucumber shavings and melon rinds from last night's dinner. Man, I hated the mornings. I learned how to be a rancher, whether I wanted to or not.

Everything was forgettable, yet I knew I'd remember it forever. The schedule and rules were fun-sucking vacuums, and the constant yelling made me wonder the purpose of my existence. I made friends with no one. Didn't even try.

Sure, there were many other boys there, and we shared everything from meals to chores to showers and bathrooms. But they were the rough ones, the criminals, the discarded castaways of life. I was the guiltless one who only slipped after someone else messed everything up. Mixing breeds at the dog pound was not advised.

Of course, one jerk named Nick always wanted to pick a fight with me. Don't ask me why. He was well over six feet and packed over 200 pounds of ripped muscle, but he didn't scare me in the least. His constant provoking, from smashing my food to throwing half my clothes in the pigpen, was never enough to set me off. Sure, he tried. But I always restrained myself. I guess I was smart enough to seek out the easy targets and avoid the ones that required taking a chance.

Then there was Roger. He was one of the adults — I refused to call him a leader — who bore a remarkable resemblance to Tony Soprano. Another kid who'd been there longer than me said Roger was a former cop who worked the beat on Colfax in Denver. Not surprising. His daily goal was to pick up where Nick left off. Nothing I ever did was good enough, from making my bed to cleaning up after dinner to shoveling the horse crap. He called his approach tough love, but I sure didn't take it that way.

So if the goal of the place was to change me, it sure did its job. The concept of replacing negative behavior made total sense. They just didn't give me anything positive to replace it with. What I needed was not what I got, and because of that, ended up more damaged than how I went in.

And that's why I despised shaving. Nobody else saw me, and nobody cared. So why did I have to shave? Why subject myself to something I hated when I already endured enough? I never got an answer, partly because, I admit, I never expected one.

I ran down the stairs as fast as I could, landing hard on the bottom step. I swung around the bannister, feeling like I was being watched.

"What?" I slipped into my dress shoes and sat down to tie them. "I'm looking forward to the great food."

My mom rolled her entire head. "Like it's the food."

But I swore I saw a glimmer of excitement in her face, like she wanted me to get out of the house in more ways than one. My pathetic social life was hanging out with Phil, but that ended as abruptly as a 1-2 punch.

"Bye." I dashed toward the front door.

"Don't do anything I wouldn't do," she bellowed from the living room.

I peeked around the open door. "That's a long list."

"Yup." She had this unfinished look on her face, staring blankly yet tranced into thinking of what else to say. This was my first date in years! Wasn't that worth a 'Have a great time, Son. I love you?' Apparently not.

I didn't even look in the backyard. Some dancing memory had made its bold return. I knew it.

Stepping outside felt like this ceremonious crossing, as if moving on had an entryway. But I shook it off. I knew I hadn't changed, and it was obvious the world hadn't either.

I hopped into my Mustang and left to pick up Grace. At the first stoplight, I glanced again at her address. She was past the railroad tracks in Mary's Farm. I'd been through that area so many times to see Phil, flying by her house without realizing the significance.

The neighborhood had such a nostalgic feel to it: large porches, narrow streets, and back alleys leading to detached garages. Time travel without a machine.

I parked my car in front of the cream-colored brick house then grabbed the slip of paper in the cup holder to triple-check the address.

I stepped out of the car and started up the sidewalk. Bordered by azaleas, the wide steps led to a front porch with a white, wooden swing hanging in the corner. As I reached the top step, the door swung open. Grace hurried out and shut it behind her.

My entire body shuddered. Her gray sweater and dark brown leggings were so chic and stylish, I swear she had just jumped out of a fashion magazine. And her tiger print flats made my insides melt. Yeah, she looked hot.

"Hi, Shawn."

My hand swept upward to distract her. "Hey Grace. Doing well this wonderful evening?" The sky was dark and endless, stars sparkled. It was a beautiful night.

"Doing great, actually." Her face beamed, further dissolving me from the inside out. "I was thrilled you called yesterday. I've been thinking about this ever since."

Somehow, I discovered the courage to call. Days passed before I finally did. When I asked, her slight pause made me wonder if she covered the receiver to disguise her laughter. But then she said yes.

"The anticipation of hanging out with a wonderful guy like me drove you nuts, huh?"

"I'm sure that's it…" She nudged me, knocking me off balance. I needed that.

I dashed in front of her and opened the passenger door, which sounded like silverware in a garbage disposal. I cringed. Apparently, a full bottle of WD-40 wasn't enough.

"Why thank you." She slanted back ever so slightly. "I appreciate a gentleman."

"Since he's not available, I'll gladly fill in." My cheeky grin was silly but intentional. I closed her door then jogged to the other side, my Oxfords tapping on the concrete.

"Where are we headed?" Such a loaded question. I guess the answer depended on where she assumed we started from.

"You'll see." I revved the engine then reached over to buckle my seatbelt. She crossed her legs and re-adjusted her sweater, flashing those shoes. I sat up straight, rubbed my hand down the side of my leg, then drove off looking for an adventure that most likely already found me.

• • •

We pulled into the parking lot at Cinzzetti's, just adjacent to I-25 in Northglenn. Rows and rows of cars were lined between islands of grass and shrubs, the freeway noise only noticeable if you focused on it.

"I love this place!" She yelled as soon as we pulled around the corner of the nearby Lowe's. Her entire body stretched upward.

We parked way in the back, the luxury sports cars kind enough to leave me room. I walked around and opened her door. The light post directed my way, stealing the spotlight off the Viper for just long enough.

"It's been a while since I've been here. You?" I closed the door behind her, flinching again at the horrid sound.

"Maybe a couple of years. My brother can spend days here. Literally."

We made our way across the lot and through the front lobby. A family of kids sat on a bench, each younger and messier than the next. The youngest boy had spaghetti stains all over his shirt; his jade eyes staring at me as I walked past. I smiled. The water fountain had calcified, nostalgia at its best.

The restaurant resembled an Italian marketplace with scattered food carts and tree-lined walkways leading to rooms filled with tables. Renaissance paintings, mahogany doorways, wrought-iron railings. It was a museum disguised as a restaurant.

We were ushered past the dessert cart to an intimate table deep in a corner. The lady had read my mind. We rounded up some food and sat back down. A large tree loomed above, secluding us from the overeating patrons around us.

I compiled the first bite on my fork then glanced at Grace. "I have to admit, I was worried the guy who answered was your boyfriend." I stuffed a pile of food into my mouth.

"No, silly... that was my brother, Todd. He's always messing with boys who call. Just ignore him."

"Happens often, I take it?" My eyebrows popped.

"Wouldn't you like to know?" She took her first bite, a dainty sliver of salad.

In the depths of my mind, she was already taken. Her boyfriend was captain of lacrosse or tennis or wherever you turn up your collar and surround yourself with nameless clones. He didn't even exist, and I already hated him.

"It was perfect timing." she pointed out. "I was about to head to school for my afternoon classes."

"Oh, where do you attend?" A large family of five scooted around the tree to get to their table, each with heaping piles of food on their plates. I was disgusted and jealous as I feasted on my own sloppy bite of lasagna.

"Front Range. Taking some nursing classes and hoping to finish soon." She turned around and glanced at the family.

"Why'd you choose nursing?"

She smiled. "Well, my dad's a doctor, and I was always intrigued by healthcare. I didn't know if I could hack it as a doctor, so I pursued nursing."

"You'll make a great nurse." I swiped the long string of cheese hanging from my chin and smeared it on my napkin.

"I'll learn to treat wounds after brutal attacks at gas stations."

"She was rude, wasn't she?" I pushed the rest of my lasagna against a breadstick, then ate it.

"I was talking about the corn chip display."

I covered my mouth and laughed. "Ha, Ha. Very funny. No, I could just tell."

"Really? How?"

"Well, you seem to be... compassionate. And driven."

My eyes finally adjusted, the dark corners of the restaurant visible. I glanced at Grace then across the room where Mona Lisa stared at me. Such contrasts.

"I do care a lot about others, almost to a fault. I sometimes don't care enough about myself."

I twirled my fork in the spaghetti, pushing it against a large spoon. "You can say that again. I know what you're talking about." I stuffed a clump of food into my mouth.

"What do you mean?" She cut into a golf ball-sized chunk of meat and ate half.

I purposely took another bite of spaghetti, a perfect and delicious way to delay my response.

"You can tell me." She angled her head to the side like a needy dog wanting a treat.

I finished chewing then wiped my mouth with my napkin. "All right, already. Jeez…" It was her look that got me, that condescending stare where someone pretends to care.

She glanced down at her plate and ate the other half of the meatball. Random noises abounded, but the silence was excruciating. Loneliness in a crowded room was all too familiar, but that didn't mean I liked it.

"Sorry, I just… I'm not as open about things as I need to be." I spoke softly, the distinct voice of guilt. My real problem wasn't being open. It was being vulnerable.

"Well, you'd better be. Lord knows I need to work on it, too." She smiled, but with a closed mouth and clenched jaw. She meant what she said.

"Yeah, I know. It's been a long road." I played with my food, pushing it around my plate but not taking any bites. An entire reel of memories flashed in my mind, from camping trips deep in the Roosevelt Forest to playing catch with a baseball in our backyard, my glove barely fitting over my small hand.

It was haunting yet vivid, somehow both a gift and a curse. I couldn't wrap my head around why or when, lost in a clutter of recollections. I shook my head. It was too much.

I didn't even know how long we sat there. Maybe I was still, maybe I moved. She finally broke the silence. "What started you down that road?"

I breathed deeply. I had to. Too much to say if only a few words to say it in. "My dad died four years ago."

The past whirred by, and there was nothing I could do to stop it. My dad and I were skiing in Winter Park. I was nine going on fourteen, thinking that rushing life was a brilliant plan. The sun was warm, but light snow fell all day. I had just tumbled for the umpteenth time on the easiest bunny slope. But he didn't care. He wanted me to succeed no matter what, even though I let him down, over and over again.

He raced over, skating with ease on the packed powder, tucked his massive hands under my bulky jacket and lifted me up, brushed the snow off my coat, then nudged me on. I wanted to cry, but he wouldn't let me — not because it wasn't manly but because perseverance was. We skied until the slopes closed. No one else was out there, at least no one who mattered. I didn't think I could ever learn to ski, but I also learned being wrong was a good thing.

She continued staring at me, her forkful of salad stopped midair. My answer was evidently not what she was expecting. "I'm so sorry. I… I didn't know. That must have been tough."

Tough. Yes, as a matter of fact, it was. And terrible and miserable and life-altering awful. Ever since then, my God-given life had been defined by that one horrendous week.

"It wasn't something I ever thought would happen, not that anyone ever does." I rubbed my temple then brushed back my hair. "Never occurred to me to say goodbye. I was blind-sided, like a sucker punch. And like it or not, it has become my lens to view the world."

"I guess you just have to live every day to its fullest."

"Whatever that means…" I had heard it all before, clichés bought off the shelf for so much more than they're worth.

"Ok, then…"

It was the one trait I liked least about myself. I assumed the worst intentions in people, and I had no idea why. It defined me. I was not made with mistakes, but I've sure committed my share since.

My left hand extended, my right cradled my fork. "Sorry, but you'd be surprised what people say afterwards." My eyes rolled just thinking about it. But she seemed different. At least I hoped she was. I gave her a pass.

"I bet."

The background felt distant. "Ok… so how does improving your present affect your past? Isn't it already said and done? I mean, living life to its fullest is great, but…" I rambled on, not even sure if what I said made any sense. But I took the risk.

She positioned her fork on the rim of her plate, right next to the scraps of lettuce and lone remaining crouton. "You're right… in some ways. You definitely can't change your past, but you can control your reaction to it. Bad things happen and moving on is part of life, which isn't to say it's easy."

We had just met, and she could already read right through me. She spotted it a mile away. Or in this case, across a table.

"I don't know… I just wish there was a rewind button." I didn't want sympathy but apparently needed it. "You ever feel like that? Like, if only you knew then what you know now, you'd change the way you did something? That's confusing…" My forearms rested on the table, straddling my plate. I had gotten closer without realizing it.

"No, no. Makes perfect sense. I get that feeling, too. My grandma died a few years ago, and now I suddenly think of all these questions I wished I'd asked her. Life can sure stink sometimes." Her nose scrunched, acting out her words.

I reached up and dabbed the underside of my eye, still tender even though it looked fine on the surface. "I'd give anything to have one more conversation with my father — to ask all the questions I never asked, hear all the stories I never heard, and soak up every word like I'd never hear it again."

She gifted me this beautiful smile, but I couldn't return it. This was too raw, too close to home. To me, this was life.

"How's everything been since then? Difficult for you and your mom?"

It was a question I didn't want to hear let alone answer. But it was inevitable. She wanted to know where I'd been, what I'd done. Even I asked that. Everyone did. But to tell her everything that happened would be like throwing mud on her salad — disastrous for the meal, even worse for everyone around it.

I wanted to tell her my entire story from start to finish, I really did. But I couldn't. She'd judge me even more than I already judged myself. "It's been difficult, but we've managed." I tilted back against my chair.

She looked at me as if my sentence ended with dot-dot-dot. There had to be more. And she was right. There was more. Much more.

"And how have you managed?"

How do I answer when I hadn't managed at all? How do I explain the truth when the truth comes with a thousand warnings and caveats?

"I don't know. It's just, well…"

She extended her hand across the table, touching mine. I recoiled before thinking, as if contacting a hot stovetop. She glanced at my hand, but my burns weren't visible, nor were they from an abundance of touch. I felt bad but not in the way she expected. I eased my hand forward, resting on top of hers.

"Let's just say my mom and I found different ways to cope." My plate was empty, so I shifted my focus. My hand lifted to point. "Say… I know I can't change my past, but I do know I can improve my future… let's get dessert."

Her face froze, stuck between hurt and sympathy. I couldn't say I blamed her. She wanted to hear more and deserved even more. But instead, she shook her head. "You boys always have a one-track mind."

I twitched my eyebrows. "But of course. What else is there in life besides sweet food and sweet girls?"

She stood up from her chair. "No need to go overboard with the sweet talk. I already like ya."

I smiled and pushed in my chair, then held out my hand to let her go first around the shady tree. It was a clear path to the dessert tray. A few people looked up from adjoining tables, but most continued enjoying their own meals, their own conversations. Public yet personal. Like a wedding. Or a funeral.

As we walked side by side, my hand slipped around hers. It felt satiny and strong yet oddly delicate. We knew where we wanted to go, yet our walk was unhurried and paced. With so many choices ahead, some of them had to be good.

We talked long enough to close the place. I asked a ton of questions, partly to learn but mostly to avoid giving answers I didn't have. My goal was to focus on her, but in trying so hard I failed. I still couldn't tell her what I'd done or where I'd gone. I just couldn't. But I thought about it. Constantly.

I drove her home that night and walked her to the front door. Perhaps I was a gentleman after all. We walked so slowly, our feet floating above the porch steps. Again, my hand brushed against hers, so I held it. Some things only appear unplanned to the casual observer.

I kissed her. It was quick yet intimate, as if hoping for more would bring her closer. Her lips were soft, her back arched and smooth. She was leaning in just as much as I was. It surprised me, yet it didn't. Deep in my heart, I knew she liked me, but I couldn't get it out of my mind that she was the only one who did.

Chapter 13 – Shawn

October 1, 2003

I dashed into the auditorium with minutes to spare. Kids were everywhere, the place louder than a preschool playground. Out of the bustling gang of kids, I easily found Harry. His cheesy grin and goofy wave made me laugh, the reason why I was reluctant to come but also the reason I was happy I did.

"Look, he's here." I could just about hear Harry as he tapped Sebastian on the shoulder.

I maneuvered my way down to the front where my group was seated. They all looked up together, wickedness in their eyes. Skeptical, I searched for a whoopee cushion on the pew. None to be found, so I sat next to Peter.

A hand on my shoulder startled me. "Nice to see you, Shawn." Mike's white shirt reflected the colorful glow bleeding through the stained glass. He wasn't wearing a tie.

I strained my neck to look up. "Great to see you, too."

"Did you and the boys enjoy last week?"

I wiped my mouth, unsure of what to tell him. On one hand, the truth would make us all look bad. It was a disaster, through and through. On the other hand, a white lie would only stain my record.

I decided on the latter. "Oh, it was a blast." I stole a glance at the boys, but none looked at me. They were all chatting up a storm as if so much to tell since school finished only three hours before. "Although shortened by, um… distractions."

"I wanted to talk to you about that." He scratched the bridge of his nose. "Some other mentors approached me afterwards. They were concerned about you and your group."

"What do you mean?" My eyes widened, a courageous attempt at acting surprised.

"I just hope these kids aren't too much for you to handle. I know they're... rambunctious. Perhaps I asked you to do too much too soon."

I knew he would backtrack on this experiment. He realized his glaring mistake and hoped to replace criminal #1 with parent #24. I was in way over my head. I should have just walked away, never to be seen or heard from again.

But I didn't. "No, no. It's fine. I can handle it." My words, thoughts, and actions flew in different directions, and I didn't know which one to believe.

"Then okay. Try not to distract the other groups." He patted me on my shoulder, unsure of what to say next. "Enjoy this week."

He glanced at my boys like he knew something I didn't, then walked down the aisle before I said something I'd regret. My stubborn hand waved instead.

It was the settling part I didn't like, the feeling that others would have done a much better job than me. *I have one opening left, and I'm having a hard time filling it.* Not exactly a vote of confidence. I might as well have been a cardboard cutout.

My eyes drifted between my boys and the wide-open double doors, off in the distance yet getting closer by the second. The boys sat there — silly, annoying, and oblivious to the world around them.

For whatever reason, I stayed.

The music abruptly stopped, so Mike addressed the group. "Ok guys, let's get started. Quiet down, please."

There were no parents there except mentors. And me. Mutiny would have been easy with any planning and organization. Good thing the kids had neither.

Mike started talking about something, but it was difficult to listen above the hum of constant chatter. I swear the boys were louder than the girls. Loaded with enough words and giggles, you'd think they were from a different planet. They either had no limits or ignored what they knew, which didn't appear to be much.

My dad used to have friends over to watch Broncos games — a few guys from church; I don't remember who. They talked, but it only seemed to be about football and work. There was a transformation that occurred somewhere between being a boy and being a man, and I wasn't convinced it was for the better.

But I had to figure it out. Something was missing, at least for me, and it was the kind of feeling where I cared deeply about something. My dad always reminded me I had the gifts of aggression and passion, but they both got lost between distant memories and now. If only my dad was still around to remind me how I got them in the first place.

"Tonight, I wanted to talk about *respect*," Mike started, figuring the attention of half the audience was tolerable. "What does that word mean to you?"

I laughed at my mom's prophetic statement, however snarky and over-critical it was.

Four kids raised their hand.

"Ok, Zach."

"It's when you shake your opponent's hands after you whooped 'em." Everyone giggled, and Zach smiled at his yet another accomplishment.

"Well, that's one way. What's another? Dean." Mike pointed to the red-haired boy in the third row.

"You admire someone so you treat them well."

"Yes, exactly. Respect is about treating others the way you want to be treated. Who are some people God intended for us to show respect to?"

"Teachers."

"Pastors."

"Firemen."

"The President."

"All great answers. People who God placed in our lives to teach us something, to guide us through tough times. How about your mentors?"

If I believed I was placed by God, I'd buy it. But I wasn't. Respect was earned, not sold at a store or, worse yet, handed out by a free-wheeling pastor.

"It depends. Sometimes." Harry shouted out then glanced at me. I swore a little devil sat on his shoulder.

Come to think of it, I could always get my dad to talk about woodworking, the one non-family topic that always interested him. I was never allowed in his workshop — too dangerous for a curious kid — but he'd quite often bring it to me. The birds he carved, the mountains he burned with his pen. He was a master at creating something out of nothing, a craft I wish I knew.

And I was his only audience. My mom didn't care, and he never sold any or gave any away. No clue where they ended up. Knowing my mom, she tossed them all in the dumpster next to his fishing rods and the clothes from his closet. What I valued was not what she wanted to keep.

"Well, it should be all the time, shouldn't it?" Mike's leather-bound Bible folded over his hand. "Romans 13:1 says we're subject to governments established by God. Somebody said the President. What if we don't like him... or her? What if we totally disagree with what they do? With some adults, that happens no matter who's in office. Should we still respect them?"

The kids shouted out, some yeses, some noes. Half the kids couldn't even name who the president was, let alone what he or she did. For all the kids knew, they all retired as chunks of wax at Disney World.

"Yeah, we should. But it can be tough to do. Showing respect for people you don't like can be very difficult — people you disagree with, the teacher who gave you lots of homework, the kid who stole your backpack. In Matthew 5, Jesus said we should respect and forgive our enemies. Pretty daring stuff in his day. Still is today."

My mind drifted back to that Sunday, when my father left for a walk that lasted forever. Whittled into my mind with a carving knife, the wound still fresh. Gray button-down shirt, blue Dockers. His hands were loosely in his pockets, he glanced around but mostly straight ahead, and the upward motion in his step appeared as if he'd fly.

He took it all in: the birds, the cars, the people.

Who knew one of them could kill?

Mike continued. "So, what about your parents?"

"Yeah, what about them?" yelled out a girl in the first row.

Mike's hand swiped in front of his mouth. "Well, we should listen to them and do what they say, even if we don't like it. Ephesians 6:1-2 tells children to obey their parents so that you may live long in the land."

Mike's 'respect for your enemies' message had nothing to do with me. Nothing against Mike, but the thought of ever forgiving the man who killed my father was beyond my imagination, above the stratosphere of respect. The Bible says, 'an eye for an eye.' I totally agreed.

Curiosity swept across Peter's face as he raised his hand. "So, if we obey our parents, then we'll live to be really old?"

I almost laughed. At least he was brave and curious.

"It means your parents know what they're talking about, and they know what's best for you." Mike's finger extended. "And that leads to a long and healthy life."

There I sat in a church where the path to heaven was paved with acceptance and floodlit with forgiveness. I heard it so many times as a kid, to the point where I actually believed it was true.

Why did I listen to my father? He told me to ride home with my mother. But what if I hadn't listened? What if I had walked home with him? I would have dashed in front of the car and pushed him out of the way. Or better yet, I would have taken the hit and been the one to die.

But neither happened. Instead, we both walked alone.

•   •   •

The boys took their seats in the corner of the fellowship hall. I sat with them but stared outside. The sun was setting, painting the sky with a citrusy red. Sunset was earlier every day, and the effects were obvious: dormant grass, aspen trees lit with a blaze of gold, and a damp coolness keeping the fire in check. Fall was definitely a time for change.

"What do you guys think about honor and respect?" I didn't care to hear their answers. Asking eighth grade boys about respect was about as fruitless an activity I could think of. But I went with it.

"I don't know," said Zach, "the whole respect of your enemies sounds like a terrible idea to me. Why respect them? Doesn't seem fair."

"Well, you've never hurt me, but I still don't respect you," responded Harry.

"Quiet, bookhead. I'll only respect you if you start playing a sport."

"There's more to life than sports."

Zach laughed. "Maybe in your little world."

"Boys, boys." I felt more like a referee than a mentor. "Can we focus on our topic, please? Show a little respect here."

"Ah, that's funny. I get it." Sebastian smiled.

I briefly laughed, then glanced at Peter who was raring up with a question. Something about his mannerism told me he wanted to speak. My entire body tensed.

"So, Mr. Shawn. Should we respect our enemies?"

I again glanced out the window, noticing how the massive oak swayed in the wind. Leaves and branches moved ever so effortlessly, shaking randomly yet with an uncomplicated smoothness. Odd how something so big could be affected by something so slight as a breeze.

"Mr. Shawn… are you there?"

My head snapped back. Peter pushed up his glasses to the bridge of his nose, staring me down like a hotshot prosecutor.

I didn't have the heart to lie. "No, it's not fair to show respect to someone who's offended you. But not everything in life is fair." I paused, the boys all squinting their eyes in confusion. "What I mean is, you don't always have to treat others the way they treat you. Just because they're buttheads...uh, I mean jerks, doesn't mean you have to be."

They all looked wide-eyed and giggled. The other groups were all consumed by their own conversations. At least they didn't hear this time.

"Eh... still don't like it," Zach admitted, rubbing his hand along his gray sweatpants. Was this kid always dressed for an athletic competition?

"Well, I don't like it either, boys." I felt so inadequate. How could I explain to these vulnerable, gullible boys that respect for enemies was a bunch of hoo-ha? A lack of adequate words was just the beginning. "In fact, I hate the whole concept."

The boys glared at me as if my revelation was ground-breaking. To them it probably was. To me, it was only an admission, one I sure wasn't proud of.

Sebastian finally broke the silence. "Then... how are we supposed to do it?"

"Boys, I... I don't know." My finger patterned across my eyebrows. "I wish I had all the answers, but I don't." My collared work shirt rubbed against my neck. The only thing I knew was the realization of what I didn't.

"And here we thought you did." Harry smiled.

"Yeah right..." I focused on Peter, his expression droopy and falling fast. The poor kid was changing his expectations right before my eyes. "So why show respect for your parents? Is it just to be nice?"

Peter sat up, sullen yet engaged. "The Bible tells us we have to, whether we want to or not."

"Don't you think there are people who God placed in your life for a reason?" I reiterated what Mike had said ten minutes earlier. A fascinating talking point, whether I agreed with it or not.

"You know, it does make my life easier if I listen to my mom," added Harry.

"Do you listen to your dad, too?" My words decelerated with intuition as my brake. But I said it all.

Harry cringed his shoulders, avoiding words above him. "If I ever see him, I do. But it's been a while." He looked up. "Tell us about your parents, Mr. Shawn?"

There was a crisp smell in the room, like someone had lit a match then snuffed it. It was the fresh scent of poplar etched by my father, or the radiating smell of our neighbor's fireplace as we tossed a baseball until dark. I can still see the ball suspended in midair, the anticipation of catching it making my feet patter and my mouth run dry. But it's the smell I'll always remember.

Grace was right. The best memories only happen once, which is better than not at all.

"Well..." The clock ticked, a gentle reminder of the painful pace of time. "I live with my mom, and my dad died four years ago."

The boys were completely quiet. Wonderful yet awful.

"How did he die?" asked Peter.

"Peter! You don't ask someone how their dad died!" yelled Zach.

"No, no... it's okay. I can tell you guys. He was hit by a car not far from here. This was the last place I saw him. At church." I pointed to the floor because I didn't know where else to point.

"And he died from that?"

"Yeah, he did." I twisted around myself and scratched my back, just short of an embrace. "The driver was going 50 down Main."

"Oh my goodness! Was he drunk or something?" asked Zach. All the boys laughed, this odd form of expression where they couldn't think of any other. I felt sorry for them.

"Actually, he was." My head fell, shrouding myself from the unknown. Harry avoided words, the others avoided uneasiness. Me, I wasn't sure what I was avoiding.

Their eyes were so innocent, so full of promise and hope. In some ways, I dashed it all. They now understood that actions have consequences, and hate could be both. Indifference was never an option, at least for me.

"So, when Pastor Mike talks about loving my enemies, I have a specific person in mind. Believe me, I get it. I see the importance. But putting it into practice is something else entirely. I... I just don't think I could ever respect him, let alone forgive him. I just can't."

Chapter 14 – Aidan

Dear Aidan,

I hope you and your mother are doing well. It's been a while since we've last spoken. Hopefully, you still remember me as one of the boys your father mentored.

When your mom contacted me out of the blue and asked me to write this letter, I wasn't sure what to say. Honestly, I had to convince myself to write it. I wanted to respect your father for who he was, yet still tell the truth. I'm too honest a person not to. There is so much between me and my past, and time is the easy part.

First off, I wanted to tell you I'm sorry about your father. I know it's been a long time, but I just had to say it. Maybe it was for me as much as it was for you. So many losses to deal with, from time to life to everything in between.

I had a complicated relationship with your father. He was definitely a 'what you see is what you get' kind of guy. I respected that. He opened up about who he was and how he felt about things. Most people don't do that. He told us he was insecure, had problems forgiving, and took on a role that was way over his head. I was suspicious from the start.

But with honesty came a problem: it exposed him for who he was. None of us is perfect. I get that. When we see the inside of someone's heart, we realize their inner being is not always good. I hate to break it to you, but your father was far from perfect.

When I found out what he did to the guy in the alley, I was done. Our relationship shattered into pieces, never to be the same again. It was beyond saving, just like him. I tried to forgive him, but I couldn't. It was past my limits. Sorry for my honesty, but that's the way I saw it.

Before I met him, I wanted to know people I could strive to be like. People without holes, warts, or skeletons. People who were living, breathing creatures, modeling exactly who I wanted to be. Unfortunately, I didn't get that from your father.

My parents were the phoniest people I knew. They were the world's best actors, and church, school, and work were their stages. Everywhere but home. They fought all the time, enough to make my ears bleed. I feared my father would hurt someone, and eventually he did.

So, when your dad told us his personal story, I was floored, and not in a good way. Believe me, I was well aware adults had flaws, but I didn't understand why someone would share them with others. It made no sense.

He was yet another mark on a dartboard for me to avoid. I needed that, yet I didn't. It only put me one step closer to refining who I didn't want to be. I hoped for something more, someone to admire and teach me right from wrong. He definitely taught me one of those.

You may wonder why I'm wasting my time telling you all this. I want you to be a better person, one whom others respect and imitate. Learn from your father's mistakes. Be brutally honest, but only with yourself. That alone takes courage.

Your father would be proud of you. I hope that provides encouragement. I also hope you find a true mentor to follow. If you do, you've struck gold. Consider yourself lucky because it's pretty rare.

I continue to send happy thoughts your way.

Sincerely,

Peter

• • •

"Wow, did Peter hate Dad?" I shifted to one side and crossed my legs. This box was becoming the most uncomfortable seat ever.

"I wouldn't say *hate*. That's not a very nice word." My mom looked at the entire length of my legs, thinking as always about how much I'd grown.

"So, okay. He didn't like dad very much." While she looked at me, I peeked into the dark corners of the attic. My body shivered. With no definition or depth, whatever might be hiding over there was already doing its job.

"Let's just say they had their differences. Peter grew up in a tough household, and I think he had unreasonable expectations for others." She scratched her cheek, revealing a redness I hadn't noticed before. "I would have thought the opposite."

"What do you mean?" My stomach rumbled. I desperately needed food.

"Peter had a void in his life. We all want someone to look up to and admire, someone to strive to be like. I had hoped your father would have filled that role, but apparently he didn't." She was slouching, her shoulders falling toward the floor.

Peter's letter still clutched in my hand. "Then why'd you keep this thing?" She frowned but I continued. "I mean, what purpose does it serve for me to know that someone hates... I mean, dislikes my father?"

"I have to admit, Aidan, I was just up here a few weeks ago when you were at school." She rubbed her arms as if she was cold. "I almost threw it out."

"Why didn't you?"

"I don't know, to be honest. Perhaps I thought it was better for you to figure it out yourself."

"Figure out what?"

She sighed. "I didn't want to censor things. It didn't feel right. If we're gonna do it, then let's do it." Her head tilted to one side. "Of course, I wanted to wait a few years." She said it calmer than I thought, finally agreeing this was a fair idea. Or so I thought.

"Do what? Read the letters?"

"Yeah, that's part of it. But reading is just the beginning." She hunched forward, her eyes circled and droopy as if she was about to sneeze.

The dusty attic. The letters. The reports.

For the first time, I realized I wasn't alone. She hoped for something out of the letters, too. They described a past she knew, that she lived! But that didn't mean she couldn't learn something. "You mean, like interpreting what it says?"

"That's also part of it. I guess there's a story behind each letter, each report, like pieces of a jigsaw puzzle. It's not worthwhile unless you have all the pieces."

"Do we?"

She laughed. "Definitely not."

I wanted to know everything. I had to. There was no turning back. There must have been more to take from Peter's letter, whether or not he hated my father.

I almost gasped. There it was in the middle, staring at me. "What did Dad do to the guy in the alley?"

She stood up, stretching her hands above her head as if reaching for the ceiling. I let the letter drop to the floor.

I waited. No answer. "Mom! Peter couldn't forgive him, so it must have been awful." My arms waved in the air, partly to get her attention, partly to brush away the dust and smell of the cramped space. I clenched my teeth. "What did he do?"

She glanced out the octagonal window, but it was so dirty, I didn't think she saw anything outside. My impatience grew.

She finally spoke. "That's why I didn't want you to read these. I'm just not ready to talk about that."

"Then what…"

"Did you hear me, Aidan? I can't…" She marched toward me, hands extended. I flinched. "Don't you see? That was his terrible mistake. He did something he shouldn't have. He was so young, so mad, so… alone."

"You're never honest with me!" I yelled. I was thirsty for so much more about my father, starving in many ways.

I needed it all.

She looked surprised. "I am honest. You're reading the letters, aren't you?"

"Yeah, but…" My hand swooped down and swept up the remaining papers, the jigsaw pieces grasped in my hand. I walked to the stairs, hoping that leaving the attic would make my headache go away. "I'm eating lunch."

She followed my footsteps. "What would you like me to make?"

I paused then glanced back at her. "I'll make it."

"Oh my." She stretched out and placed her hands on my shoulders. I liked how that felt. "There really is a God."

I hit the first step. "Sure, Mom. Whatever."

Chapter 15 – Grace

October 9, 2003

Shawn drove us along the Peak to Peak Highway, a gorgeous road that wraps around the mountains. Fall colors were at their best: the yellow glow of aspens mixed with oranges and reds from maples and oaks. Toss in the evergreens, and it was a spectrum to behold.

"Fall is awesome." He glanced over his shoulder, his shirt sleeves tight around his wrists as he firmly held the wheel. "The changes in colors. The cool, damp air."

"You're such a romantic."

"Look what you've done to me!"

"Oh, really?" I angled my legs toward him and mistakenly sniffed; his car smelled like an oil field.

I wasn't one of those women who liked to change men, or at least I didn't think I was. But we both needed to figure out who he wanted to be first.

We edged around a sharp corner, Saint Malo suddenly in sight. Most of the camp buildings were set back off the road surrounded by a sea of pine trees with a surreal mountain backdrop. A statue of Jesus loomed over the road on an outcrop, guarding the gate with a raised hand as if directing traffic.

"I love that church." I pointed ahead to the Chapel on the Rock. "I always figured I'd get married there."

The church was by far the most famous part of Saint Malo. It sat right near the road, so it was impossible to miss. And honestly, no one would want to. It's beautiful.

"A little early to be figuring that, don't ya think?" He glanced at me, his right elbow twitching as he grasped the steering wheel.

"That was before I met you, bub."

The small chapel rested on a sturdy rock, surrounded by a moat like a fairy-tale castle. The stones were all sizes and shades of brown, with tall stained-glass windows and grand stairs leading up from the parking lot. The metal railings and rounded oak door were the only clues to where the church ended and where the rock began. The place was a legend.

"Wasn't the Pope there a few years ago?" He said it so nonchalantly, I thought he was joking. We talked about many things, but never religion. Although, back then, I considered the Pope more pop culture than religion.

"He even blessed the place, if you believe that kind of stuff. Should withstand anything!" His elbow continued twitching.

As far as blessings, I wasn't sure what I believed. Life seemed too haphazard for a random godsend to make any sense, let alone have any impact. My family never went to church, but I did believe in a higher power who paid attention every now and then. Whether I ever had to rely on him or her was a different story.

The road twisted and turned past camps and houses and motels. Most had cars out front with smoke billowing from chimneys, a few boarded up to prepare for winter. Everything was small in perspective, as Mount Meeker and Long's Peak cast their shadows below.

"I'm surprised there aren't more people up here," He maneuvered the car into the rutted, gravel lot by Lily Lake. Only one other car was there.

"So am I." The sky was a cobalt blue with hazy, gray clouds rolling in over the ridge. Did I miss the forecast? With Colorado, it never mattered since change was the only consistency.

"My parents and I took road trips up here all the time. Rain or shine." He shifted into park then sported a mischievous grin.

"I bet you enjoyed that."

He angled toward me, his knee propped up in the middle. "There'd be a ferocious storm that'd dump boat loads of snow with this dastardly wind whipping across the road. But my father navigated our car with ease." His hands flailed in the confined space of the car, almost hitting my arm. "Oh… and these wild beasts popped out of the woods and threatened us with their gnarly teeth, but my father slayed them with daggers he kept in the trunk."

I laughed. "Either you have an over-active imagination or dreadful timing when choosing road trips."

"Hmm... good point. Maybe both." His eyebrows flashed up and down like an old vaudeville actor. He seemed so playful, so spirited. Not to say he wasn't always, but something seemed different. I liked it.

We exited the car, quickly realizing we hadn't planned for the weather. I always forgot about altitude.

"Brr. Want your jacket?"

I crossed my arms and shivered. "I probably should. Thanks."

I threw on my light blue jacket, hardly enough to fend off the wind. Anything more intense — like wild beasts with gnarly teeth — was his job. I was always a sucker for chivalry.

We walked along the path, the crushed rock ricketing like a carriage. The serene lake reflected the surrounding peaks, which were big enough to be sliced in half by a layer of fog.

The sky was immense, even bigger and deeper than the mountains. I bathed in it. "Love and rainstorms, both so short-lived with lasting effects on everything they touch."

"Oh my. Who's the romantic?" His entire body shook.

"At least I admit it." I pointed at his thin white T-shirt, outlining his narrow yet muscular frame. "You could use a jacket, too." His arms trembled and twitched, speckled with hair and goose bumps. Bulging veins ran along his forearms, flowing from his biceps.

"Nah, you'll keep me warm."

He grabbed my hand and pulled me close, our walk now synchronized. My head leaned toward his chest, which expanded and contracted with heavy breath and a pounding heart. He bent down to kiss me, quick and sweet, like he always did. I loved the mountains.

We walked across the narrow, wooden bridge, the path to Lily Ridge to our right. There was no one else in sight.

"Ever come up here alone?" His words broke my trance.

"I've been coming up by myself lately. A loner in my old age, I guess."

"Oh, you're far from old."

"You'll have to let me know when I am." I grabbed his icy hand. "I actually look forward to it."

"I look forward to it, too." He spoke softly, briefly glanced at me then watched a family of ducks swimming by the edge, keeping our pace.

"So, what do you envision your future to be, Mr. Shawn?"

He dragged his feet and kicked a few rocks to the side. He finally answered. "I don't know. I'd live here for one. Can't picture myself living anywhere else." He paused. "Of course, I'd be married to a trophy wife with above average kids."

I punched him hard.

"Ow!"

"You deserved that."

"I did…" He rubbed his shoulder. "So, what's in your future, Miss Grace?"

"Well, I'd also stay here. I'd be a passionate nurse helping others clumsier than me." I smiled. "I'd have one husband, two homes, and three kids. A white picket fence around our yard, and two gardens in the back where I'd grow flowers in one and vegetables in the other. Oh, and my kids will adore their father."

He laughed. "Wow! Sounds like you've figured it all out."

"I'm a girl. I dream about stuff like that."

"Well, life would be boring if everything went as planned." His pace slowed, shoulders slouched and curved. His attention focused again on the ducks.

"Hmm. Maybe you're right. Sometimes." I still thought dreaming was worth the effort, a hopeful form of planning. But I also knew Shawn was in a different place in life than I was, transported there by time and events.

We rounded the backside of the lake, awarded a gorgeous view of Long's Peak, still mostly enveloped with a thick fog. The top peeked out, almost floating in the thick air. Snow blanketed the nearby trees, a spotted mix of dark green and pure white. The view was remarkably peaceful.

I massaged his arm, enjoying the tautness of his muscles. "I love when the mountains cloud over then reappear with fresh snow. Ever wanna climb that?"

He watched his steps closely along the uneven path, avoiding the stretches of deep slush. "Nah, it'd take super powers to scale that thing. I'm not much of a daredevil."

We walked across a long wooden bridge suspended above a grassy marsh. Ducks and geese swam amongst thick grass and cattails, avoiding the ice patches like tiny bogs.

"So, what would your superpower be?"

He grinned. "That's easy. I'd fly. Soaring above the clouds to see for miles on end. I'd see the whole world at once." His smile diminished as he glanced toward me. "And maybe everything would finally make sense."

"Sounds like you've figured that out."

"I'm a boy. I dream about stuff like that." He winked.

I was skeptical. To me, dreams reveal what's yet to come, not disclose what's already there. But I didn't want to dash it before it even started. It was his dream.

We took our final steps around the lake then stopped at the old picnic table near the small dock. He jumped on top and sat down, his legs spread and angled outward. His lean torso angled back, resting against his hands. Arms locked, stomach almost concave.

In one swift motion, I yanked the front of his shirt, gripping it firmly in my fist. I leaned against the table then pulled him toward me. We kissed. Different than others. Passionate and warm. Intense.

I closed my eyes. My hand reached around his waist, pulling him close, tightly against me. My jacket fell to the ground, no longer needed. His baseball cap landed nearby.

There was no snow, no wild beasts to attack. Our legs became entangled, our busy hands grasping for a place to rest. I didn't know where I ended and he began. We both led, followed, discovered.

I grabbed his hand, and we headed up to the ridge. The winding trail teased us with stunning views that we shared with no one else. The sun peaked out, but we barely noticed.

His movements became tentative, unsure of what to do, almost reluctant. I tried to reassure him, but it was obvious his motions were hidden behind something.

"It's okay, Shawn. I love you."

If love meant affection and caring and acceptance, then that's what we had, that's what we did. Everything became knotted into a shared existence, a survival of sort. He was there for me, my only shield from the cool, damp air.

Eventually, the fog lifted off the mountains, revealing their snowy peaks. Neither of us saw them. We didn't have to. They were insurmountable, but that didn't mean we couldn't climb them.

Back then I believed it all. I was a romantic, through and through. Hopeful yet foolishly naïve.

I still believed in dreaming, just not planning. That's when I got in trouble. Whenever I thought I had life figured out, that was exactly when I was proven wrong.

Chapter 16 – Shawn

October 15, 2003

It was a frigid morning, coldest that fall. I sat in the living room, watching snowflakes drift to the ground. My mom sat across from me sporting a newly awakened look with sunken eyes and matted, untamed hair that most women would hate. I almost felt sorry for her.

"Nice slippers." I envisioned her kneeling on the floor, throwing things over her shoulders to find those pink slippers, deep in the bowels of her closet, way back by the skeletons.

She didn't answer. Her hands swept in front of her as if aimlessly pushing away thin air. Her entire body slanted forward. She didn't have a cigarette and looked almost lost without it. But it would have taken decisiveness to get one.

I placed my book on top of the coffee table, right between a big, leather-bound Bible and a hardcover of *Dreamcatcher*. Two large stains on the wood were partially covered by the books. No ashtray to be found.

"How's what's her name…" She looked up.

I rubbed my eyes with tight fists. It was way too early in the morning to be totally shocked. But I was close.

"Grace." I said it loudly, hoping it'd sink in. I had told her about our first date. Her reaction was a resounding ho-hum. But at least she remembered Grace's existence, albeit not very high on details. "She's really cool. You'd like her." I pointed at my mom. "She's a lot of fun to be with…" I decided to say it. "like Dad."

She barely acknowledged me, angling back in her chair as if evading our lackluster conversation. She wasn't doing anything, perhaps not even thinking. As for me, my thoughts drifted elsewhere, away from what I didn't care for. At least in some ways, my mom and I were similar.

It was mid-October at Trout Haven in Estes Park, cool and overcast, smelling of dew on leaves and damp pines. Elk plodded all around town, even down Elkhorn Avenue, just as slow and widespread as the clouds in the sky. My dad and I stood on the large, flat rocks by the shore and threw on jackets when it rained. The rocks weren't slippery, only those with small patches of moss. We avoided those.

The rain showers came and went, but I figured everything else would last forever. He taught me how to tie the hook to the line, how to cast as far as I could throw, and what depth was ideal for biting. I threw as far as I could, never once letting go of the pole. It was firmly in my trusted hand, just as much as I was in my father's.

But I still didn't know what I was doing. I cast my line so many times until I finally got it right. Sort of. We caught a few fish that day — or I should say, he did — enough for a fine dinner. But we threw them back. My father said that wasn't why we came. I believed him.

He told me some hilarious stories that day. Like back when he was 19 and lost a round of Sheepshead to his buddies and had to go streaking around the neighborhood. The instant flashes of motion-detecting lights made it the fastest run he'd ever done.

He laughed so hard when he told the story, I thought he'd fall off the rocks. He was holding his stomach, eyes closed, tears rolling down his cheeks. Come to think of it, it was the last time I ever saw him burst into a laugh where his entire body shook. I loved listening but joined in anyway.

We cried from too much laughter, the only decent way to cry. My father could always find fun in everything he did, even in the simplest of fishing trips. And it wasn't necessarily in the words spoken or the actions taken. Those were mere consequences.

My head snapped back. My mom was staring at me.

"Nice to hear," she said, as deadpan as ever. It was clear that fun was a lost art in my family. Where did it go?

This time, I didn't let it pass. "At some point we need to talk about him." I put my feet up on the coffee table. "If we don't, he'll be dead forever."

"Shawn!" She yelled, her breath searing and rotten. "What in the world?" She stared in my direction, but her eyes drifted toward the coffee table, my feet the latest object of her scorn.

"Don't you see? I want him to be alive, to be here, in our conversations, which are as dead as he is." My raised hands pointed to the here and now, where I was but where I wasn't convinced I desired to be. "I want to talk to him, about him. To listen and catch up."

"That isn't going to happen." She reached for her pack, yanked one out and lit it. "Why would you say such a thing?"

"You don't get it." The peace of the snowfall having no effect on either of us. "It's been four years! I wanna talk about him. I'm ready."

"I'd love to as well… just not right now."

"Bull crap."

"Shawn, please. Don't be so unreasonable." Her hand trembled in a chilling up and down motion. My father was the last topic in the world she wanted to discuss.

"Then when?"

"I don't have a timeline." Her deep breath was full of smoke and frustration, but not enough words to make sense. "And don't force me to give you one because it would be wrong." Her voice was convincing, her eyes were not.

My feet hit the ground as I exhaled a lungful of displeasure, my endless supply never fading. I didn't want to be mad, but what I wanted never meant much anyway.

My emotions and trust of others were more up and down than a drive through the mountains. I didn't know what I needed, from them or from me. Something had to give.

"I'll be here waiting," I mumbled just loud enough for her to hear. No reaction.

I tried to disconnect from my expectations, but I couldn't. She'd get lost in her own little world, and I'd sit back and watch. Helpless. I hated the cycle, but I hated breaking things more. We were both too fragile for that.

• • •

The phone rang. My body jolted. I dashed to the kitchen, my bare feet pounding on the linoleum floor. I caught it before the next ring. "Hello."

Airy and quiet.

"Hello?" I glanced at the sink, still layered in dirty dishes and pans plastered with food scraps. More frustration was the last thing I needed. I looked away.

Stupid prankster. The phone flew towards the receiver when a faint voice spoke. "Morning, Shawn."

I was awake enough to realize who it was, entirely the opposite of who I thought. "What time is it, Phil?" I rubbed my eyes again, wondering why in the world he decided to further ruin my morning.

"Sorry if I woke you, man. How ya doin'?"

I stretched my arm toward the ceiling, extending for something just out of reach. My stomach tightened, desperately for food. "I sure wasn't expecting a call from you."

Actually, if anybody would call, it would be Grace. To hear her voice, telling me everything about her life in intimate detail. How she ran the same five-mile loop to blow off steam in the evening. How she adored cheese puffs and obsessively licked her fingers when eating them. How her pony-tailed Biology professor biked to class every day. Anything. I could have used some of her.

"Well, we haven't talked in weeks, so I thought I'd check in." His words were bouncy. A fake cheeriness. My ears ached from the vibrations.

"All's well…"

Silence. I had nothing to add.

"So… what have you been up to?"

"Not much."

Silence.

"I thought maybe you'd wanna talk."

"About *what*?"

"Whatever you wanna talk about."

"Well that helps. Why would I wanna do that?"

His deep breath echoed my frustration. "You know, this isn't going anywhere. I just wanted to tell you I'm sorry about what happened. You know me… I don't always think before I speak."

"Good to know we agree there." I rubbed the top of my head, my hair oily and shaggy. I desperately needed a shower before work.

"No hard feelings, right?"

"Oh no, not at all." I sounded like one of the boys, my voice swinging in a defiant tone. It was my turn to take a loud breath, my chest expanding outward. Apparently, it was the only part of me willing to budge.

"What's gotten into you? Get that freakin' chip off your shoulder. I mean, if you'd rather not have any friends…"

My body fell back against the wall, my eyes shut. This was going nowhere fast. "I always want friends, just good ones."

"What does that mean? You only wanna hear what you wanna hear?" I dropped my head as his question was so loud and punctuated, it cut through me. I bled guilt. "What are you expecting from me, from anyone? You have to be a friend to have a friend."

I exploded. "So I'm not a friend? Suddenly, it's my fault?"

"No, I... I gotta run. It was nice talking with you, Shawn. Have a great life."

"Wait, I…"

Bang! The loudest sound in the world. Our conversation ended before I even knew what hit me. I slammed the phone on its cradle then headed back to the living room. I fell into the chair and fumbled to find something to read. *Dreamcatcher* caught my eye first, so I grabbed it.

"Is everything alright?" My mom had this motherly, tilted-head look as if she'd pat me on the shoulder and tell me everything was going to be okay. It was incredibly odd.

I slouched in a mix of defiance and defeat. "Just peachy."

"Who was on the phone?"

This was one time I wished she stayed in her own, little world and avoided mine. "Phil. We discussed a few things, that's all."

"Wanna talk about it?"

"Not really." I flipped to a random page and glanced at the words. They made no sense.

"Shawn, I think…"

"I said I don't want to." I tried hard not to look up. My anger was boiling, and it would have vented through my eyes.

Her hand shook. "What happened? You used to be the best of friends." Her voice was so smooth, it could have been mistaken for passion. "I don't like seeing you so mad." It was more than I'd heard from her in a long time, as misdirected and meddling as it was.

My head snapped back against the headrest. I gripped the armrests, further tightening my muscles. "We haven't talked since our fight." I dropped *Dreamcatcher* on top of the Bible, aching my back in the reach. "I hope to never see him again."

"Never's a long time to hold a grudge."

"That's hilarious." Do I listen to her because of her vast experience, or point out the log bulging out of her eye? I was stuck, in more ways than one.

"Then what happened?"

My neck swelled. "Tell me what a friend is, okay, because I don't know anymore." She should listen to me because of my vast experience, my friendships measured in half-lives.

"You didn't sound like a friend." She mumbled.

"So you're blaming me, too? Oh my goodness… why does everyone blame me for this? What did I do? Phil's the one who started it." I rubbed my forehead with hard strokes.

"Whatever happened to turn the other cheek?"

"You ask a ton of questions, and it's really annoying." I had waited a long time for her to listen and care again. Why did I hate it so much now that she did? "I'm supposed to sit back while someone mocks me? I don't think so."

"Sometimes you have to," she muttered.

"And you got so skillful at it after Dad died."

My mom stared at me intently as if translating what I said. But there was nothing to interpret. She knew what I meant.

She crossed her legs. "Not something I'm proud of." Her speech slurred as she sucked on her flaming cathartic. "It's been a long road."

"And when does that road end?" My hand brushed along the armrest, the matching cover dangling over the side. I pulled it back and straightened it.

"This isn't about me."

I laughed at the absurdity. "It's entirely about you. And me. And Dad. Don't you see? This is us. This is our life. This is who we are." Her neck pulsed, her hand trembled. She had no clue what I meant. "Mom, we have to figure this out."

"Figure what out?" Her eyes squinted, telling me just how oblivious she was to all of this. It was this life we had to figure out, whatever was left of it, and there was no turning back.

I slanted forward, distinctly hearing a loud creak from deep inside the chair. "I think we should head to church this morning."

I scratched my head back and forth, wondering why I said it. Maybe I liked being out of the house or seeing my boys. Or it was the music, the community of it all. Something. I didn't know why. But it meant something.

"What? Where'd that come from?" Smoke rose from her ashtray fading into the air. "I can't."

"Can't what? Turn the other cheek?" I thought of my mother's indirection, her lack of confronting anything. For me, church was also a solution, the only one I ever knew. Which didn't make it a bad thing. "It'll be different this time."

"Too many issues to work out."

"Waiting for life to be normal? Don't mean to be rude, but you'll be waiting forever for that." It rolled off my tongue, but I still meant it. "You told me that the day after Dad died."

Come to think of it, it was the last semi-inspirational thing my mom ever said. I wiped my eyes again, pressing hard against them, blurring the room and everything else. I blinked.

She stood up and scratched the side of her head. "I wish you wouldn't listen."

"A little late for that." My chin rubbed against my shoulder as she marched toward the kitchen. In multiple ways, she was hopeless.

But I had to try. I whittled a piece of wood unsure what form would come out of it. I had to be careful. If I carved too much, there'd be nothing left.

Chapter 17 – Shawn

October 15, 2003

Only a few cars were in the church parking lot, so I parked up front then headed inside. The snow that fell in the morning evaporated by midday. For all the worry, the forecast had been wrong. Welcome to Colorado.

The place was eerily quiet. The lights were dim with a yellowish tint, and none of the kids had showed up yet. My shoes sounded like hands clapping as I found a pew front left. I removed my jacket and draped it over the back.

Footsteps approached me from behind.

"Hey, Shawn."

I turned around to see who it was, but the suit and tie gave it away. "Hey, Mike. Just waiting for the kids to show up."

Mike sat in the pew behind me and rested his arm on the back of the wooden pew. "Mind if I join you?"

"Sure." I tensed. My mind raced, thinking of what I could be in trouble for this week, or whether he was pulling the plug on this mentoring experiment. What I wanted this week was becoming very different from what I wanted last week, and in some ways, it confused me.

"Quiet in here, huh?" He glanced around the hollow auditorium. His small talk made me even more unnerved.

"Too quiet. How do you get any work done?" I angled back, my left arm draped over the hard, wooden pew.

Mike laughed then rubbed his hand around his mouth. "I play music in my office. I don't like silence, either."

I could relate. Music had always been my favorite method to control the world around me. I could play what I wanted, and it was soothingly predictable. But the boys' home outlawed it, right up there with cigarettes and girly magazines. I never thought I'd have such a craving to listen to the radio, let alone a CD of my choice. But that's just the thing. They didn't want me to have choices because the ones I'd made had been so poor.

Mike looked ready to explode with his question. "How's your mother doing? I've wanted to catch up but haven't gotten a chance to call her in a while."

I sat upright. I actually wanted to talk about her. "Funny you ask. We were just discussing my dad this morning." I scratched the back of my neck then returned my arm to the backrest. "At least I tried to."

"And she didn't want to talk about him?" He crossed his arms, bunching up his sport coat around his elbows.

"She never does."

A few kids started walking in but stayed in the back. Sebastian stood next to his taller friend, Caleb, laughing like little kids, probably about something silly.

"Everyone grieves differently, Shawn." Mike said. "She's just not ready to talk about him yet. But you can't push it. It might take a while."

"Yeah, well, it's been four years!" I stiffened, realizing I was repeating myself. But I'd keep it up until someone listened. "In some ways, it's like yesterday… But that's still a long time. Isn't that enough? Let's move on for God's sake."

He didn't react. We both turned around and watched kids come in at a steady pace. A few started walking toward us.

Mike leaned in, his face not far from mine. "Are you ready to move on?" He patted me on my shoulder. "Sure doesn't sound like it." He stood up to greet the kids.

I balled up my hand into a tight fist and struck the wooden pew. There wasn't going to be an answer, at least one that I wouldn't regret. I grumbled, turned, and faced the front, the only thing I could face at that moment and not get mad. But all I did was further prove his point.

·   ·   ·

Mike jogged to the front of the church. "Quiet down, kids. Let's get started." Always a hopeless battle.

As Mike spoke, Sebastian kneeled on the floor to find something he had apparently just dropped. Zach kicked him hard in the ribs. His grunt was loud and annoying.

"Guys! Get up, Sebastian. And Zach, don't kick him." My finger pointed at the victim then the accused. This was not starting well.

"It was an accident." Zach shrugged his shoulders and smirked, looking guiltier than ever.

I hated that word. He didn't even know what *accident* meant, nor did anyone else. Because it didn't exist. Everything in life was intentional. A motive lurked behind everything — either known or hidden, with somebody knowing what was coming. If not God, then someone else.

There was no such thing as an accident.

"Let's continue our discussion of the Ten Commandments." Mike spoke above the commotion. "Can anyone tell me what the fifth commandment is?"

Peter raised his hand with a corny smirk smeared across his face. He answered when Mike pointed to him. "That's the one about sex."

It felt great to laugh, but I did for a different reason. How simple life was, back when sex was a joke to giggle about. It was such a foreign concept to the kids, like music at the boys' home. The more someone told me I couldn't, the more I wanted to do it.

Mike wiped his mouth and shook his head. "Actually, that's the sixth. But thanks for the lead in for next week. Anyone else?"

For me, sex was something that rattled my faith, an intricate trust that someone else's advice was applicable to me. Worse yet, I had no one to talk to about it. I knew what Phil would tell me, and that's exactly why I didn't ask. I also knew I wasn't the only one to struggle with it. I was told it was a gift I couldn't open, which seemed cruel.

A blonde girl with glasses sitting in the first row raised her hand. "The fifth commandment is 'do not kill.'"

"That's right, it's to not kill. The New King James version says, 'do not murder.' That's closer to the original Greek. There were many wars that happened in the Old Testament, but this was different from that."

A short boy in front arched his back upright, almost willing himself to be taller. "That's obvious. Of course we shouldn't kill anyone."

I sat motionless, gazing at the sunset shining through the stained glass. The white light refracted into a spectrum, leaving nothing untouched. Blue painted the walls, green shaded the pews, and red splattered the floor.

"On the surface, it does appear obvious. But John wrote that to hate someone is the same as murdering them: 'Whoever hates his brother is a murderer, and you know that no murderer has eternal life abiding in him.'"

I wiped my brow with my fist, which I unknowingly kept clenched in my lap. To say I was dreading small group was an understatement.

Zach grinned before he even spoke. "Can I say that I hate John? He shouldn't have said that…"

Mike stepped forward down the aisle, scratching his head then motioning towards Zach. "We can't fault John. Jesus said that whoever murders or insults his brother will be liable to the fire of hell."

A cold harshness slid down my spine. My boys were listening to Mike even though they pretended not to. Harry glanced at me, and we briefly smiled, the only warmth I felt. That was good. I preferred a slight chill. Much better than being liable to the fire of hell.

• • •

The boys and I marched upstairs, this time finding a stack of chairs in the back corner that we disassembled. We slid the chairs along the floor, screeching on the polished linoleum.

The boys made a poor attempt at sitting in a circle — angling many directions and way too close together. Before I knew it, Zach punched Sebastian in the shoulder after he threw a spitball at Peter. Harry just laughed and ran around the group pretending to play duck-duck-goose.

"Ok, guys," I pleaded. "Let's settle down."

Sebastian grunted while rubbing his shoulder, but the others got quiet. Thank goodness.

"So what can you tell me about the fifth commandment?"

"I don't like Abigail," confessed Harry. "She's so annoying and copies off my tests. She gives me the creeps."

"Harry, you shouldn't hide your true feelings." Sebastian wrapped his arms around himself, forming a one-man hug. "Tell her how much you love her."

Surprisingly, Harry didn't react at all.

"Not killing is easy," said Peter. "But the hatred part sucks." His face twitched as he scratched his nose, a distraction from his eyes. His deep, cobalt eyes told me everything. Peter had remembered.

I had so much to confess, confronting head-on everything that Mike just discussed. I was a man with three lives: one expired a while ago, and two existed in parallel. Very few people knew the one, but at least I admitted it existed.

"I'd say the fifth commandment is the most difficult to keep." My mind was a jumbled mess. What to say, what not to say. "You know, it's funny… Our minds play funny tricks on us. There are things we want to remember but forget. Yet other things we want to forget but remember as vividly as yesterday."

None of them looked up. Sebastian finally broke the silence. "Has that ever happened to you, Mr. Shawn?" He pushed up his glasses and continued rubbing his shoulder.

"Yeah, it has. A few times, actually." I scratched the top of my head. "But one time in particular."

My shiny black shoes pounded on the sidewalk as my dad turned to wave goodbye, his broad smile all his own. The people around us were dressed more for spring than winter: short sleeve shirts, flowery dresses, light jackets.

Strands of cirrus clouds floated across the sky.

Perfumes and car exhaust marred the air.

A pile of dirty snow was plowed into a corner of the lot.

A distant car horn honked.

The church bell rang.

My dad walked away, listening intently to a nest of robins in a nearby maple. His right hand clutched the morning's program, rolled tightly as a magic wand. People were everywhere, but I heard the birds, too, above all else.

It was a gorgeous February day, bright and bursting with promise. The sun tricked me into enjoying the warmth, convincing me it'd be a day to remember.

I wished I never believed it.

I told the boys everything, including things I didn't even know I remembered. It could have been a much simpler story. With any other outcome, it would have been.

The boys edged forward, balancing on their crossed legs. They were all so attentive, so eerily quiet.

My story didn't end. Only the words. "I should have known what would happen that day. I should have prevented it." My damp eyes blurred my view. "I blame myself. I shouldn't, but I do. That's why I almost…" I stopped myself. Sharing had its limits. "It's pretty unbearable, guys."

My life was always defined by other peoples' definitions — what music to listen to, where I should live, what I should do and think. But did anyone know the real me? I wanted to move on, to be someone different, yet I had no clue how to do it. I was stuck, and the past never eased its grip.

What did *move on* mean, anyway? If it involved completely forgetting the past, then I wanted no part. I wanted to remember my father and the way my mom used to be. The fun times. I wanted to remember us, the way it all used to be, and I hated myself for not appreciating it when it happened.

But there were also mistakes, and unfortunately, I had to separate myself from it all. I needed to confront the truth of my past just as much as I wanted to forget it.

And to get there, I had to own it.

That scared me more than anything because it wasn't just me who was at stake here. It was everyone else.

Chapter 18 – Aidan

Dear Aidan,

I hope you and your mom are doing well. I think about the two of you often, and I pray you are safe and healthy.

You are an amazing kid who has the world before you, and believe me, it's a kick-butt world out there with so many adventures to explore. Luckily, you have a wonderful mom to help you navigate it.

I continue to have the utmost respect for your father even through it all. He was an awesome guy who helped us figure out some of life's issues and reinforced a lot of what my parents told me (even though I didn't believe them).

I have to admit, it wasn't always that way. I went through a stretch where I didn't appreciate your father very much. Certainly, he had been through a lot, but he made some awful mistakes in his life. I didn't know what to take from that.

However, over time I learned a more important lesson: I can control who I am by what I do. A big part of that is finding things larger than me — volunteering at the homeless shelter, playing in the worship band at church, doing stuff I'm passionate about.

But I had to be honest with myself. For example, I didn't know I wanted to play the guitar until a friend asked me and I tried it. Your father was masterful at that. He told us about things he did, like mentoring and forgiving, that ended up defining who he was.

I'll never forget the session where he told us about the day your grandpa died. With such gut-wrenching emotion, it broke my heart. I was 13, so I wasn't about to cry. But I sure wanted to.

He told us every detail about that day, from memories to emotions. But the saddest part was what didn't happen. He wanted to soar above the town, spot the speeding car, and swoop down to snatch his father out of the way. He wanted to be the hero. He wanted to fly.

And that was the gift I received from your father, to not only dream but to act on it. It sounds weird, but it's actually amazing and downright life changing. I wouldn't be who I am today without people like your father in my life.

He didn't get to save his own father, but he ended up rescuing so much more. He taught me to act, to create memories, and to hold onto them forever.

So, what do you do with this? Make the most of your life! Try new things, and don't be afraid to make mistakes. Don't ever sell yourself short because of who someone else thinks you should be. You're bound to make blunders along the way, but that shouldn't prevent you from achieving the greatness you're capable of.

Say 'hi' to your mother for me. Let me know what I can do to help. You can call me anytime as I'm only a few miles away. Don't hesitate to keep in touch.

Your friend,
Sebastian

•   •   •

I placed the letter next to my plate then took another bite of my sandwich. A slab of grape jelly hung from the corner of my mouth, so I wiped it off then licked my finger. "Who's Sebastian? I don't remember him."

"He's a quiet kid." My mom grabbed a Frito then paused to finish her thought. "Or I should say, he was. I haven't seen him in a while." She threw the chip in her mouth.

The letter covered my silverware and angled against the woven placemats that always sat on our kitchen table. "Why did Dad have to share about Grandpa's death with the kids? I mean, weren't they like, my age?"

She finished chewing then wiped her fingers on the napkin draped over her leg. "Your father was always different than me. It helped him figure things out… by talking about it, that is. And the boys better understood him."

"Makes sense." I wiped my chin. "Yeah, doesn't sound like you at all." My dad told people what he thought and how he felt. I liked that.

"I don't think he planned it. He never thought he'd ever mentor, really. But it was good for him." She bit into her sandwich. Jelly poured out the back onto her plate. I always make it that way — a slobbering mess.

"Ok, then what's the flying part? He didn't mean that, did he?" I put my sandwich back on my plate and took a drink of milk. My upper lip felt damp, so I wiped it with my finger.

She chuckled then tossed another chip in her mouth. "Not literally." She finished chewing. "It was his superpower, or at least the one he wished he had."

I didn't like a movie unless it included a superhero. Otherwise, who cares? Heroes vs. villains. Good vs. evil. Overcoming the ruthless forces of darkness to save the world! No other story's worth telling. Period.

"That's cool. I like that."

She finished her sandwich, mostly dark brown crust, then delicately wiped her mouth with a napkin. I was happy I had some left, enjoying every gooey bite.

"What would your superpower be?" she asked.

I didn't have to think about that one. "Easy, I'd be a chameleon, changing into anything I'd want to be. I'd just have to think about it, and poof! I'd instantly become a bear or a snake or whatever I'd want. And I'd go anywhere I wanted, too."

She watched my mouth, both unmoving for seconds, then grabbed another chip, gobbling them up faster than a teenager. She was always obsessed with Fritos, and I never understood why.

I had forgotten about my whole running away idea, at least not until I mentioned the going anywhere I wanted bit. I was too captivated by open letters and an even more open mom. But just because I stopped thinking about it didn't mean it couldn't happen.

"What's yours, Mom?"

She continued staring at me, wiping the corner of her eye with her index finger. "I've had to think about that for a long time." She placed her napkin next to her plate. "It took me a while to figure it out."

"And…" I stopped chewing.

"Well, it's similar to yours, and to your father's, but in a different sort of way." She glanced at the letter then back at me. "I'd time travel." She grinned. "And I know exactly the time and place I'd travel back to."

Chapter 19 – Shawn

October 26, 2003

I don't know what came over me — a sickness, a wanting to right a wrong. I honestly don't remember. But I attacked the sink, that mountain of putrid plates and disgusting dishware. Armed with Dawn and a thick bristly brush, I cleaned, one helpless dish at a time.

I scrubbed and scrubbed until the skin on my fingers was irritated and raw. My legs ached from standing so long, and the soap kept irritating my eyes. But I ignored the pain. I was determined to clean the entire mess, no matter what it took.

It was one of those never-ending, accumulating piles where any previous attempts to clean were slower than the piling on of new ones. We had to eat, but cleaning became more of a one-at-a-time, self-serving endeavor.

I couldn't help but think of the day I left the boys' home. My mom had pulled into the driveway with a cloud of dust, signed me out at the front desk, briefly smiled at the attendant, then drove me home in utter silence.

She only provided a car to ride home in, nothing more. And even that reeked like one giant ashtray on wheels. What was I looking for? I didn't know. Maybe we'd catch up, talk about life, argue about politics, discuss the merits of country music on plant growth. Anything.

She was my family, although I had lost track of what that meant.

It was one of the least memorable days of my life. Not because of what happened, but because of what didn't. If thought-provoking conversation was kick-started by notable activities, then neither of us had anything to say. We both stared at the road ahead, wondering where it would take us.

We were strangers. I knew I had changed — I was an adult now, whatever that meant. And it was obvious she had changed, too. A trance shrouded her like a veil — not a bride's but more like a cadaver's. More than half of her had already died, and the fraction that remained was reluctant to live for anything.

I regretted ever leaving.

I was certain my father felt the same.

And that was where the dirty dishes came in. Super-glued spaghetti stains that barely budged and milk that transformed into something unrecognizable. It all needed attention, but worse yet, no one cared.

And that's why I did. I was fed up. I wanted to see them gone. The grueling task of cleaning house required an attention to detail I'd never had. It was about time I found it.

So I cleaned. And the sink was a great place to start.

My mom scuffled into the kitchen, her shoes scraping on the floor. If she ever scared anybody, it sure wouldn't be from sneaking up on them.

"Good morning." I rubbed my eye with the back of my hand. Soap sprayed on my already damp T-shirt.

"Humph." Or some guttural noise. She eyeballed me, clearly wanting to ask about my task at hand. But she didn't.

I glanced over my shoulder as she opened cupboards. "Mentoring was good, by the way." I was ready to talk about anything, even banjos and begonias if it came to that.

"Oh…" She fussed with the grinder, however late in the morning it was.

"We're covering the Ten Commandments." I bent one leg to balance then wiped back my hair. "You know, that slab of rules written by the big guy in the sky."

She shook her head. "Nice."

I pointed my finger in mock accusation. "Don't be jealous and steal Billy's pencils, especially on a Sunday. And don't lie to your parents when you get caught."

She mumbled. "Great attitude."

"Thanks!" I twisted my body and smirked.

"They're reminders for people who don't think they need them." It was her turn to point at me. "Like you."

I scratched my cheek, popping bubbles in my hand. The unshaved roughness was harsher than the scrub brush. "What does that mean?"

"You'll see." There was my mother, speaking like she knew what she was talking about. "So, what was the topic this week?"

I threw the brush into the sink and draped the towel over the faucet. I had done enough attacking for one day. I reached back and rubbed my neck — kinked from bending over the sink so long. I sat down at the table, my legs tight and achy as I stretched.

I perked up. "I told the boys about Dad."

"Huh?" She flopped down into the soft, padded kitchen chair, a contrast to her rigid, inflexible self. The coffee maker gurgled in the background, the saintly smell of grounds wafting in the air.

"I told them everything that happened the day he died, and they actually listened." I leaned in. "I also told them how I obeyed you and Dad but wished I hadn't."

"You make no sense. Is anything off limits?" She reached for the pile of mail stacked on the table. Her hand shook side to side, enough to blur away age spots. It was too much, too fast, just as I intended.

"But I had to. I wanted to." My arms wrapped across my chest as I took a deep, heavy breath. "And I'm the better for it. It was amazing, like… I got rid of something."

"I'm glad you feel that way." She glanced over at the coffee maker, willing it to be done. But it continued with its mid-form gurgles, teasing her.

"You don't?"

"There are things too personal to share." She stood up and took big, looping steps to the counter. "Aren't you working today?" Her voice was raspy as if she needed to clear her throat. She stood over the sink, either admiring my handiwork or considering driving me back to the ranch.

"No, I'm off." I brushed away her distraction disguised as a question. "Some things, yeah. I'm not gonna tell anyone I'm growing hair on my back."

"That's TMI…" She grabbed the half-full pot and filled her mug. Liquid poured from above, landed on the burner, and sizzled. "There's also your family life, things at home that no one else should know about."

"Why not? Are you too private, or does it make you feel too uncomfortable, too… vulnerable?"

She grabbed her mug and headed toward the family room. She passed by me, her eyes as hazy and indistinct as her coffee. "I'd rather not talk about it."

"That answers my question." I glanced over my shoulder. As she reached the other room, I stood up and followed her. "Mom, we should go to church this morning. You don't even have to talk to anyone."

"Where'd that come from?" She flopped on the couch, her head sinking downward. She sat motionless for an eternity. "It's not that I don't want to talk to anyone, it's just certain things. I mean…"

"Well, then feel free to chat with the entire congregation if you want to." I balanced against the archway, my right hand circling outward. "Let's go…" I was trying to convince her, but she wasn't the only one who needed convincing. Decisions were easier when I had the upper hand.

"It's so much more than that. Things you wouldn't understand. Things that adults…"

"…make a big deal about when they shouldn't?" I rolled my eyes and crossed my arms. "And by the way, I'm one, too. It doesn't have to be like that." I took a step toward her. "All I know is this church thing has become important to me. Don't ask me how. The mentoring, the message, the meaning."

She stared at the table, desperately grasping for a distraction that was in reach.

"I want you to join me."

She wasn't as surprised as I thought. "I… I just have too many issues." It was only one, but who's counting.

"Lord knows that… precisely why you need to go. What better way to resolve them than to confront them?" If I said it, then I must have believed it. But my words were always firmer than my beliefs, especially when I wanted to be someone who I wasn't.

"What if I don't want to?" Somewhere in this conversation — or maybe this life — our roles had reversed. It was both funny and sad.

"You sound like a little kid. Let's go." My head snapped toward the door, making sure she knew what *go* meant. I had become the reluctant leader of this family, and I wasn't yet convinced that was a good thing.

She exhaled a long, deep breath, better than holding it in until she got her way. "I could never get ready in time."

A clock hung behind the couch. "Church starts in an hour. More than enough time. I'll even make breakfast."

"I guess miracles do happen, even when you don't go to church." She stared at the solitary contents on the coffee table then sat back in her chair.

I knew she wouldn't attend, but at least it was progress. I bent down to straighten the blanket on the chair. "Imagine what would happen if you went?"

Chapter 20 – Grace

October 30, 2003

Shawn pulled his beat-up Mustang into the Denver Botanic Gardens parking structure, clunking into a spot on the first floor. It made a chorus of noises — none of them very promising — and many of the knobs for heat and radio were long gone. When his car would completely disintegrate was anyone's guess.

I leaned over and kissed him, my fingers resting on his knee. "Looks like a gorgeous day."

"Sure does. Great choice."

We walked across the street and entered the gardens. He unfolded the map, and I balanced against his chest. "How about this one?" I pointed.

He laughed. "You would want to see the Romantic Garden first. Let's head to the All-American. God, country, family. Let's start from the top."

We left the entry building and headed down the brick and stone walkway towards the vast gardens. The café was to our right with two couples sitting around an outdoor table enjoying the warm sunshine. Neither of us was hungry, so we turned left and strolled down a crushed stone pathway guarded by flowerbeds on both sides. Flowers and shrubs stood at attention like a mini-parade, their last hurrah before winter hit.

"But you skipped over God." Our pace increased, forcing a bounce in my step.

"Not really." He scratched his shoulder, his casualness sparking my curiosity even more. To me, religion was this unknown thing that absorbed people, unsure if it was a support group, a casual book club, or a self-serving cult.

We turned right and headed toward the hearty flowers that lasted well into fall. So many deep, dark colors: reds and blues and purples. It was as if they tried desperately to contrast the drab brown of fall.

"Shawn, can I ask you a question?"

"Do I have a choice?"

I ignored him. "I'm wondering if you ever think about God. I mean, does He exist? Or is He part of this elaborate scheme to keep kids in line?"

"That would be Santa."

"Ha, ha." I squeezed his hand. "Really, I'm serious."

"Oh, there's no doubt in my mind He exists." He glanced around as the paved path became crushed rock. Then he stared at the birds chirping in the sycamore, barely even acknowledging the nearby flowers.

"And…"

He scuffled his feet, staring downward as if focusing on the scratchy sound. "Oh, He's always there. But sometimes I wonder if He actually cares."

I brushed up against his shoulder. "Why would He go through the trouble of creating us then not care?"

We walked down a few rocky steps to enter the lower portion. A breeze swept across the grounds, creating a noticeable chill. Flowers bent to avoid the wind, then snapped back in defiance. We were the only ones there.

He finally answered, "I know it doesn't make sense, but it's the way I see it. It feels like this 'go' button was pressed then the operator let the ride run all by itself."

"Wait…" I angled away from him. "You said He's always with us then you say He left the building. What gives?"

"Well, maybe He's not the operator."

We continued walking to the end of the path, then took a right at the waterfall. It was the Gardens of the West, a huge collection of dry, arid landscaping that somehow survived the harsh, unpredictable climate. Purple sage and a rainbow of hydrangea scattered among rocks and boulders, watching the sea of grass from the shoreline.

"Can I ask you another question?" I reached over and grabbed his hand.

His muscles stiffened, his voice deep. "You're going to ask me no matter what."

We stepped up a rocky path to an arid garden littered with cacti and other hearty plants. They looked thick-skinned as if resisting any acts of God, regardless of who's the operator.

"How did your dad die?"

All the plants had spikes or prickles or thorns, dangerous and intimidating yet necessary for survival. Every plant for itself. They thrived only because no one wanted to go near them.

His step accelerated as he scratched the side of his head. "He was run over by a moron."

I glared at his mouth, his eyes too insensitive. "Seriously… what happened?"

His lips formed a weak smile, his Adam's apple shifting up and down. "Yes, seriously. That's what happened. He was crossing the street after church…"

"So, your family goes to church?"

"Yeah, we do. Or we did. And I do again, but that's a different story." He rolled his head.

"Sorry to interrupt. He was crossing the street…"

"And heading to the grocery store. Never noticed the drunk barreling down the road. Never saw him coming."

"Oh my goodness. I…I'm so sorry." What else could I say? I was lost for words. "Maybe it was better he didn't see him coming." I knew it was dumb right when I said it.

He let go of my hand as if dropping a hot coal. "And how is that better? He should be at home, reading the newspaper, weeding the garden, pairing socks. Something. Anything. Better than this."

I stepped away. My arms crossed my chest, shielding myself from my own icy stare. "And what *this* are you referring to? Because we don't have to do this, you know. You can go home and drown in your misery if you'd like."

"Grace…" He closed his eyes, then spoke softly. "You know that's not what I meant."

"Then what did you mean?" My leg extended, and hip flexed, a helpful place to balance my hand.

"Maybe my mom and me. Maybe it's other stuff." His eyes were red and gleaming, drowning in complexities. He looked away.

"Like what?" I eased my shoulders, giving myself permission to keep walking. A gust of wind blew between us like a tunnel.

"I don't know! It's just been some tough years, okay? I made some mistakes and I wanna move on." His arms flailed, open and outward. "I want to live my life with you, with my mom. I just want to look ahead, so I don't have to look back. I don't care to focus on the past."

I wrapped my arms around his shoulders and kissed him. "You don't have to. Forget everything that ever happened."

"But that's not possible! I can't forget."

His words ran laps around me, the unspoken as much as the spoken. "I can help you try to forget." My intentions were full, but my promise was empty. I wanted to listen, to be there for him no matter what. But my role was so ill-defined at that point.

"Why would I want that… to forget, that is?" He shrugged. "The past is how I got to where I am now."

I felt like we were having two simultaneous conversations. I didn't know which one to respond to. "Where are you now?"

"Happy. Content. For the most part."

"Where are you not content?"

He squinted as if pushing away the hurt. He wiped his eyes. "I don't know. Something heavy is dragging me down, and I'm not sure what it is."

I rubbed his shoulders as we headed toward the Conservation Garden which highlighted the rare and threatened plants in the area. They flourished but only from constant irrigation and pruning. Apparently, if someone didn't help them, they'd cease to exist. A harsh reality, but maybe they didn't belong where they were in the first place.

"Do you think everything happens for a reason?" I asked.

"You know, you ask a ton of questions…"

"I do, don't I?"

He chuckled, a quick, deep staccato. "I wish they were all good." He shuffled his feet. "The reasons, that is, not the things that happen. Or maybe both."

"There's a difference?"

"Definitely." He answered abruptly but didn't elaborate.

I paused and waited. Nothing.

"Have you had something where you thought, 'Yeah, this was meant to be?' Where you knew without a doubt someone planned and orchestrated the whole thing."

"You mean, besides meeting you?"

"Oh my. Yes, besides that once-in-a-lifetime accident."

His shoulders cringed as if reacting to something I said. Again. Nothing. He kicked a loose stone off the path and into the underbrush. "Did I tell you I've been mentoring kids at my church?"

I stopped walking. "I didn't even know you went to church until a few minutes ago. No, you haven't mentioned that." Another gust flew my hair over my eyes. I brushed it aside. "I get the feeling there's more to you than I know. I guess I haven't asked the right questions."

"It wasn't intended as a slight." He sounded sheepish, making me sorry for my reaction. But I needed to know.

"How many kids and what age?"

He looked up and sighed. "Four middle school boys. All whacko, but sometimes fun and always insightful."

"You're a perfect fit, then."

"Gee, thanks." He responded quickly with a low rhythm, but then elaborated. "I just wished they listened more."

"Why would they not? I'm sure you have a lot to tell."

He laughed. "Yeah, and some of it's actually good."

We entered the Romantic Garden — finally! — our loop making a full circle. Roses bloomed in all sizes and colors, some rested in huge, terracotta pots, some planted in rows, all arranged in small, intimate groups.

I couldn't help but look at the lily pond at the end of the aisle with its floating, green Pac-Mans. It was making me hungry, even though I didn't typically eat ghosts. There were other ways to eliminate those.

I held his hand. We periodically glanced at each other, sometimes with smiles, sometimes with laughter. Words were obstacles, so we avoided them.

The sweet aroma of roses and evergreens.

The loud, unpredictable sounds from the active city.

Distant hurriedness drowned out by nearby peace.

The soft breeze.

The warmth of the sun.

Overwhelming yet satisfying.

• • •

We headed across York Street to the parking structure, waiting for a pair of cyclists with matching jerseys and black tights speeding down the road. Both had cast-iron calves.

"In the mood for some ice cream?" His mischievous smile told me his answer. Not sure why he even asked.

"Sure! Sounds sweet."

"Ha ha, very funny." We maneuvered between cars parked in the structure. "There's a new place that just opened over on 16th Street called Little Man. Been there yet?"

"Nope, sounds… height challenged."

"Oh, far from it. You'll love it."

We hopped into his car and drove past Cheesman Park to pick up Speer. The pillars from the pavilion overshadowed the barren trees. The lunchtime rush hadn't started, so traffic was light. This was the part of Denver to see it all: Pepsi Center, Coors Field, and loads of restaurants and bars. LoDo was my favorite part of Denver.

We parked down the hill past the fenced baseball diamond then dashed across the street to avoid a few oncoming cars. I suddenly noticed our destination. "What in the world?"

"It's Little Man." He paused then pointed. "Oh, and it's also the world's largest milk bottle."

"That is so cool." My mouth hung open as we walked across the street, always a sucker for the new and different.

The place was a gigantic, old-fashioned milk jug with openings at the bottom for serving customers. The gray vessel towered over the nearby buildings, surrounded by black tables and chairs. The vintage red and white awnings and striped uniforms topped it off like cherries on a sundae.

We stepped up to the line with only an older couple in front of us. The lady held her hair in a scarf and wrapped herself inside her long, wool coat. The gentleman wore a black fedora and dark brown jacket. Meanwhile, Shawn and I wore short-sleeved shirts and shorts.

"What would you like?" Shawn asked me. The older couple finished their order and stepped to the side, her scarf gripped in her hand.

"Don't know yet. So many flavors, so little time."

We approached the register, my forearms resting against the cool metallic countertop. The guy taking our order looked about 30 with a scraggly beard, tired eyes, guilty smile, and as thin as a ski pole.

Shawn chose the Milk Stout Chip while I dared to try the Fluffernutter. "Nice. I'm proud you can say that."

"I'll take that as a compliment."

We stepped away and grabbed a small table for two in the back. The black chairs were dense, rock solid against the sweeping winds along the Front Range.

"So… how's your mom doing?" I wanted to unravel the mystery of Shawn. But I also realized my questions at the garden became an unintended grilling. I eased off.

A few cars drove past.

"Doing pretty good." He folded his arms across his chest. "Actually… I'm trying to convince her to come to church with me, but I swear she's more stubborn than I am."

"What's holding her back?" I crossed my legs and wondered when my invitation would come, if ever.

They called us to the counter, so we grabbed our waffle cones and sat back down. He wrapped his head around the side and took the first lick. And the second. Then finally answered. "She was uncomfortable after my dad died. Felt like she was being watched. And judged."

"How'd she know that?" I licked around the top of my cone, the sweet dessert rapidly becoming a smooth cream. The warm sun was now my enemy.

"More perception than reality. But I've felt it, too."

"Why would anyone judge you?" I became a translator, his words either having double meanings or no meaning at all. "I mean, I'm sure they felt sorry for you and your mom and just wanted to provide comfort after your loss. But it wouldn't be judging."

"It is if you take it that way." He maneuvered his head again, catching drips before they fell.

"Then don't. Ignore them. What do they know?"

"Easier said than done."

I bit off a sloppy chunk. "I guess so. At least you were there to help her through it all."

He scanned the neighborhood then stared towards downtown. From a distance, Republic Plaza — tall and silvery, reflecting the bright afternoon sun — looked like a stack of Legos. Same color, perfectly aligned. The whiz and whir of cars reminded me I-25 was just beyond the hill.

Melted cream rolled down his hand, landing on his shorts.

"Shawn? Earth to Shawn…"

His glossy eyes watched my feet before finally looking up. "I wasn't there in a way I would have liked."

I squinted, weary from my ongoing excavation to find the real Shawn. "What do you mean?"

"Hard to explain…" He took a quick lick.

"You can tell me."

"Some other time… when it's right. Tell me about your family." His words fast and monotone.

I let it go, even though I was unsure when the right time would ever be. "We get along fairly well, although my brother's a lazy bum. Maybe all brothers are like that, I don't know. My dad's a big guy, but he's more of a teddy bear than a grizzly. And my mom? She's a busybody who'll run circles around you if you're not careful."

"Hmm, sounds like a typical, dysfunctional family."

"I wouldn't say that. But we are typical. And pretty boring, to be honest."

"I'd take boring any day. Sounds wonderful."

Our lives were different — that was obvious, including our outlooks. But which one caused the other? I loved him for who he was with no doubt in my mind. But it was difficult to see life the way he did, how boring could possibly be good. I guess it depended on what made life eventful.

"Good to hear. Then you agree. Dinner at my house tomorrow night."

His eyes grew wide, eyebrows raised towards the deep blue sky. "Wait… Isn't it too early for that? You sure you wanna introduce me so soon?"

He was full of surprise and wonder and expectation. Right where I wanted him.

I laughed. "It's beyond soon and you know it." I reached over and kissed his moist, ice cream coated lips. "I'm ready. Ready for anything."

Chapter 21 – Shawn

October 31, 2003

I couldn't decide what to wear so I paced near my closet, pulling out various shirts and pants like an online dating site. I was terrible at it. Every pair was a mish-mashed disaster. I finally chose a green polo and khakis, looking more like a conceited golfer than an insecure teenager.

I drove to her house and stood on the front steps, ready to press the doorbell while considering ding-dong ditch as a promising option. I adjusted my shirt and tucked it tightly into my pants, then yanked on my collar.

This whole 'meet the parents' thing could end in so many potential disasters. An argument with her brother over who's better, the Broncos or the Chiefs, would reduce to a fist fight. I'd choke on the pecan pie, forcing a Heimlich-induced nightmare. Or I'd trip over their couch, break my nose, and lie helplessly in the middle of their living room with her entire family standing over me shaking their heads.

Ding dong.

But those were small potatoes compared to them discovering the real me. They'd see right through my façade, realizing I was a total phony. That was my real worry.

I adjusted my shirt again, looking down to check that my belt was tight enough.

Third loop. That's the one.

Or do I use the second?

What if I eat too much and my stomach bloats?

Are they rearranging furniture?

Stashing away bodies?

Sweat collected above my upper lip. I wiped it away and threw my hands in my pockets. My keys jiggled.

Their front door finally swung open. Grace stood there in black jeans and a silky purple shirt, holding the side of the door in one hand, their German Shepherd in the other. She bent down to pet the dog, who looked like he'd jump me if she ever let go.

"Hi Grace." She smelled amazing, like a meadow of flowers. I almost forgot about the potential disasters.

"C'mon in. We were just getting dinner ready."

I eased through the doorway and leaned forward to give her a kiss, her lips moist from a cherry balm.

"Don't you look spiffy."

"Thanks. I wouldn't miss this for the world."

"I should warn you… we're not having Fritos."

"And here I thought… Well, see ya." I spun around and started to head back to my car. She let go of the dog and reached out to grab my shirt. She reeled me in and kissed me again. The dog stayed put.

"You guys need a room?" came an annoyed mumble from the living room.

I marched into their house with hand extended. Based on Grace's description, it was obvious who he was. "Hi, I'm Shawn. You must be Todd."

He stood up with a loud groan and shook my hand, his enthusiasm resembling that of a doorknob. "I'm Grace's evil twin." He slouched but was at least six inches taller and a hundred pounds heavier. His baggy sweats and loose, frumpy T-shirt made me wonder if he'd gotten up all day.

"Agreed on one point, but we're definitely not twins." Grace picked up a half-empty Coke bottle from the coffee table and a bag of potato chips that crumpled in her hand.

Loud footsteps bounded toward me from the kitchen. Her dad's shadow covered the room, her bear comment finally making sense.

I extended my hand, hoping it wasn't sweaty. "Nice to meet you, sir." I hoped his massive hand didn't crush mine, but his handshake was rather weak. His thinning hair didn't do much to cover his baldness, and his upper eyelids drooped as if he was tired, bored, or both. We stood only so close, his protruding belly like a personal space deterrent.

"Welcome! So nice to meet you at last." His voice was loud and deep. "We've heard so much about you." He paused. "And it's all true, I'm sure."

I smiled. He beat me to the punch. "Nice to meet you too, sir." *Didn't I just say that?*

"You can call me Jack."

"Hi, Shawn!" Grace's mom peeked her head out from behind the kitchen wall, flashing a smile, her graying hair wrapped tightly in a bun. Noticeable laugh lines radiated from her eyes, balancing just above her reddened cheeks, I'm assuming from kitchen warmth.

"Nice to meet you, too, Mrs. Liddell." All I could think of was how motherly she looked, this tenderhearted, cookie-baking lady who attended PTA meetings whenever she could escape her knitting.

"Call me Jill. Mrs. Liddell makes me sound old." She disappeared back into the kitchen.

My eyes met Grace's, and she smirked. She knew what I was thinking. I wiped the edges of my mouth and cleared my throat. Her typical family was apparently also a nursery rhyme.

"We'll be eating soon," echoed a voice from the kitchen. "Sit down and get to know each other."

"Have a seat." Jack motioned toward the enormous blue sectional that Todd breeched like a humpback. I almost laughed as I sat next to him, hoping he didn't break out into song.

I ignored the litter of crumbles on the cushion.

"So… Grace tells me you're working at a pet store." Her dad started with the obvious but not entirely in the form of a question.

I shifted to my right, hearing a crunch below me that sounded distinctly like Fritos. Only I would know that. Grace smiled but was clearly confused.

"Yeah, I am," I gauged his question: small talk or prospective boyfriend interview? For now, I assumed both. "But I do plan on heading back to school soon."

I neglected to mention my definition of *school.* I never thought it was a big deal I didn't finish high school. But it felt like an elephant in the room.

How many large beasts can fit in this house?

"Oh, that's good. Any thoughts or plans on what you'd like to do?" Jack watched me closely with a hunched back and squinted eyes, looking more like a hungry lion than a safari big-game hunter. At least until the proverbial gun collection came out. But there was no mistaking his intentions. The interview had begun.

"Well, I've considered being a veterinarian." It sounded nice, but honestly, I never thought about it before. My future was only recently unlocked, so planning for it was way out of my thought process.

"That'd be noble. You have a passion for animals?"

His question caught me off-guard, as if I didn't know what a veterinarian did. "I guess I do," was my simple answer, approaching the truth in this funky gray area. Or perhaps it was because this conversation centered around the animal kingdom.

It was funny how my life experiences controlled what I liked and disliked, from my passions to my problems. I naively thought it'd be the opposite.

"And he's amazing with them," added Grace. "Just the other day, he tamed a wild ferret. Brought him to his knees."

I spurted a few coughs before covering my mouth. Jack and Todd sat stone-like, making me wonder if they lacked hearing or humor. It was an awkward conversation going nowhere, but at least I felt more at ease.

"You must work out a lot," commented Todd.

I had no idea if he was serious. "I do," wondering if Todd ever picked up a weight in his life, besides himself, of course. "Been going to Snap for a while now. Helps me keep my sanity... at least what I have left."

"Dinner's ready!" yelled Jill.

I sprang to my feet and eased toward Grace, grasping for her hand. We walked toward the dining room through a large archway.

The table was neatly arranged, with floral-patterned dishes and sparkling silverware covering a pure white tablecloth. The centerpiece vase was filled with blue marbles and yellow flowers that added to an overall color theme. It was remarkably homey.

Grace's mom held two hot pads in her hands like oversized gloves and bent over the table to place the last dish in the middle.

"That looks delicious."

Todd rolled his eyes. I couldn't say I blamed him.

"Why thank you. Please... have a seat."

We all sat around the table, with Grace's dad sitting at the end and the rest of us randomly selecting chairs. They instantly passed around food and plopped it on their plates like porridge from a pot.

If any family should say grace, it would be hers. She shrugged her shoulders.

"I hope you like poppy seed chicken." Her mom glanced at me while spooning some on her plate. "I wasn't sure what to make, but Grace said you're not picky."

"Oh, it's my favorite. My mom makes it all the time."

Even Grace rolled her eyes at that one. I scooped two spoonfuls of chicken on my plate and passed the warm dish to Grace, our hands briefly touching under the hot pad.

"How's your mom doing?" asked Jill. "Grace told us about your father. That must have been difficult."

I was having too much fun to take offense, but I considered it. Her sympathy was acknowledged, but why'd she have to say it like she did? Difficult made it sound like a college entrance exam.

I moved on. "She's doing well, all things considered." I didn't know how to describe my mother, the unexplainable, remaining member of my family. "She started a new job a few months ago, a part-time secretary at a law office. She likes it. Do you work, Mrs. Liddell?" I deflected her question with my own.

"Not outside the home. At least not since Todd was born. I was a teacher for ten years before we had children. But I wouldn't have it any other way." She beamed. "I love being a mother."

It wasn't just what she said but how she said it — a floating melody, as motherly as hair rollers, striped aprons, or fireside book reads. She became a stereotype only because I was so unfamiliar with what a real mother actually was.

"Ever want to go back to teaching?" asked Grace.

I sliced the chicken and took a sloppy bite. It was amazingly tender, coated with this yummy, soupy topping that dripped down my chin. I wiped it off then licked my finger.

I totally lied about my mom cooking it. It was too good for that to be true.

Grace was right, she does have a boring family.

And I was insanely jealous.

"No, not really. I did my time. I couldn't handle the kids anymore. They're too much to deal with nowadays."

"What grade did you teach?" I asked.

With her hair crammed into a bun and chained glasses hanging around her neck, she still looked the part. Thank goodness she didn't have a ruler to bang on the table.

"I taught eighth-grade English." Somehow, I knew it was middle school. Don't ask me how. "My goodness… seems like such a long time ago! So much has changed since then: the schools, the kids, me."

Todd gnawed on his food like a dog, and their dad looked ready for a nap. Grace's mom talked and nibbled from her plate. This family was also dysfunctional, as much as any, I guess.

"Funny you say that." I finished chewing and stared at the ex-teacher with knowing eyes. "I've been mentoring some eighth-grade boys at my church for a few months now. They sure can be a lot to handle."

I continued eating while Grace's parents glanced at each other, exchanging head turns. "Grace hadn't mentioned that. You must be brave. That's a very difficult age to deal with."

I pictured the two of them trudging up a hill, the pail banging against Jack's thigh. I wondered if she ever told the story to her class.

"Yeah, no kidding. They haven't listened to anything I've said, but it's always wrestling time." I unexpectedly felt this deep-down pride I didn't know I had — mentoring those boys even after what I'd been through. I looked away to avoid blushing. But it was real, and it felt good.

"Well, if there's anything I learned from teaching, kids listen more than you think they do." Jill paused to take a forkful of chicken but didn't eat. "Everything you say, everything you do, they're watching. You may not think they are, but they are."

"I'm not so sure with these boys. They're different: different generation, different breed, sometimes I think a different planet." I chuckled, but no one joined me.

But I wasn't uncomfortable. I dug even deeper into myself, feeling like I was the only one who could handle my group. They were rude, immature, frustrating as all get out, yet entirely in need of a mentor who'd been through more than they had. The challenge of it was appealing if not rewarding, however maddening it was at times.

"I wouldn't count on it." She smiled awkwardly. "You've taught them more than you'll ever know."

I didn't know how to answer, so I didn't. She had never met my boys but was evidently familiar with the species. My brain was clouded by skepticism, but her attempt was admirable.

Grace stabbed some vegetables off her plate, so I did the same. They were hard and undercooked but seasoned just enough to make them delicious.

•   •   •

"Thanks for the wonderful meal, Mrs. Liddell," I turned toward her. "May I be excused?"

Her perplexed look was as if I'd asked to run outside in my boxers. "Of course! I haven't been asked that in decades." Her whole body shuddered.

Grace and I grabbed our plates and headed towards the kitchen. The door swung behind us and nearly smacked my behind as I rushed forward.

She turned around and smirked. "Poppy seed chicken is your favorite? Really?"

"Well, yeah. It's not a total lie."

"Aha." She reached out to rub my nose. "There's some brown I see. Let me…"

"Oh, cut it out." I slanted back to avoid her swiping hand.

She placed her dirty dishes in the sink. "Say… wanna go for a walk, Cutie Pie?"

"Since when did you ever call me Cutie Pie? I haven't been called that in decades." I stacked my plate on hers.

"You need to get out more." She grabbed my hand and pulled me towards the door. I playfully went with it. She wrapped herself in her sweater, and I draped my arm over her shoulder.

We walked past four or five houses until we reached a large open space. Trees were almost bare, cars drove blocks away, and fireplaces burned nearby. Everything slowed. We strolled on stillness.

"I think they liked you."

"Oh, come on… I don't believe you. Your dad had a droopy frown the entire time, and your mom adores everybody she comes across."

Grace giggled. "Now that's true, I'll give you that." She scratched her chin. "But that's the way they are. They're always like that."

"Then how do you know they liked me?"

"Oh, I just know. Trust me."

"I do trust you."

"Well, if that's the case… Close your eyes."

She said it so fast, I wasn't sure I heard her correctly. "What?"

She abruptly stopped walking and motioned toward my face. "Close your eyes. You said you trust me."

A few trees peppered the nearby landscape, but her house and neighborhood felt like a mile away. There was no one else around. The lake off in the distance reflected the moon, glowing like a jagged landing strip.

"I don't know… I…"

"Oh, c'mon. You'll love it," Grace said with a mischievous, enticing smile. "Trust me."

"You keep saying that."

"And you keep relenting."

The moon was full, its reflection shining like a laser maze.

"Ok. But no funny stuff."

"Depends what you mean by funny…" Her eyebrows flashed. My entire body shook.

She leaned forward to kiss me. Her one hand raised over my eyes, her other moving downward, rubbing my chest then resting comfortably on my abs. My muscles tightened. My legs felt warm.

She whispered near my ear, "Follow me."

"Do I have another choice?"

"Not really."

She grabbed the front of my shirt and led me in the cool darkness. At first, I moved tentatively as if teetering near a cliff edge. My feet swooshed on the damp grass.

"Where are you taking me?" I yelled, apparently confusing my crippled senses.

"Shhh…" Her hand briefly covered my mouth.

The more I trusted, the faster we went. We ascended a hill, my stride even longer as the ground felt closer. I instinctively extended my hand, reaching out for something that I knew was there.

Our pace quickened as the ground became level, my rhythmic breathing more pronounced. The lake was far below, houses even further. So my instincts told me. I began trusting them.

We stopped. Her hand let go of my shirt, my heels pushing upward, my arms swinging in small, fast circles. She stood next to me, her breathing a welcomed reminder.

"You can open your eyes now..."

I slowly opened them, hoping for the full effect of whatever it was I was supposed to see. The air smelled fresh. No sounds. Just us.

"Wow!" The only thing I could say.

It was a light show of epic proportion. The city. The sky. Laid out before us. I could reach out and touch it all with one swoop of my hand — the streetlights, the stars, the windy roads, the Milky Way. All meshed into a fine tapestry: light and dark, coolness with warmth, closeness, vastness.

It made me wonder what I'd been missing.

Perhaps contrasts could co-exist after all.

"I used to walk up here all the time when I was a kid. The depth of the sky is so humbling but looking down on the city is so... empowering. It's nothing, yet it's everything. Different from life."

"Do you still come up here?" My eyes traced the band of stars, leading to somewhere I'd never been.

"Not for a while. I've been so busy, running around between school and work... and you." She brushed my cheek. "I almost forgot about this place."

My mind drifted further than my eyes, contemplating everything I thought I knew. I stood over it all, the world below my feet, feeling light, approaching free. I wondered why things happened, how everything came to be, and where God was with all of it. I thought big. No answers, just questions, and in no way limited by the massive sky around me.

She was right. This was different.

"Do you dream up here?"

"Oh, I dream everywhere, including up here. Mostly, I dream of the future, where I'm going to be in five, ten, twenty years. I've always been a dreamer, lost in tomorrow."

"Tomorrow? What's wrong with today?"

"Nothing at all."

My hand slid around her hips, and I pulled her toward me. Her back felt as comforting as a silk sheet. She rubbed my neck, kissing me with a deepness I'd never felt before. Our hands moved in all directions, discovering each other in ways we'd never touched and places we'd never gone. Her scent was intoxicating, as rich as leather and as sweet as honey.

Our two worlds collided only because she was mine. My dad lived only in my memories, my mother stuck in her own. There was no one else. But at that point, there didn't need to be. We were defining our own existence. Just the two of us.

Her hand reached out to encourage me, my body shaking but eventually soothed from her caressing. We took it slowly, like rubbing sticks to ignite a flame. Her body felt firm like granite, my movements detailed and deliberate like an artist.

I picked her up around her waist and we landed softly on the ground, our bodies now completely intertwined into a oneness. My actions said everything I didn't know how to say. I couldn't speak, anyway, even if I wanted to.

My muscles ached as we climbed a seemingly impossible mountain. Together. I sensed how she felt and knew what she wanted. It was eventful yet natural — like young birds learning to fly — a daunting yet intimate ritual.

How could I see her or the sky above me, and not think that someone was in control of the universe? And how could I recognize my feelings even though I'd never felt them before? Again, only questions.

Honesty had forced me to admit my problems and worries, while trust made them someone else's burden. I just wished I hadn't misjudged so severely. Not just her but everyone. Then the impact would not have reached so far.

Chapter 22 – Shawn

November 5, 2003

I walked down the steps but felt like I traveled back in time. The basement of the old Methodist church looked like a snapshot of the 1970s with burnt orange walls and a dull, beige carpet. It was a large open space yet felt as damp and secluded as only a basement could.

At least some light entered the place. Small, rectangular windows lined the tops of the opposite wall, partially covered with grungy curtains donated by someone who didn't want them anymore.

Protruding from one corner was a large area separated by a thin wall. The large opening had a spacious white counter covered in pots and pans, making it obvious what the area was for.

My sweaty hands rubbed down my pants, my chosen alternative to praying. I tried to focus on everything except myself but failed miserably. All I could think about was what I had done. Four years was a long time ago, but it felt like yesterday.

Will anyone recognize me? Will they point fingers, scream obscenities, pick up rocks and stone me to death? I didn't know. But I had to do this. I had to confront this.

"You must be Shawn." She offered a vigorous handshake, trembling my already unsteady arm. "Nice to meet you. I'm Gail, the pantry director. How many kids do you have coming tonight?"

She looked in her forties with shorter blond hair pulled back in a clip, revealing a tired but content face. Her creases and wrinkles appeared more like badges of honor than punishments of age.

"I'm guessing all four will show up." I placed my hands in my pockets, unsure what else to do with them. "I hadn't heard anyone will be missing, but you never know with middle schoolers."

"Oh, that's a perfect number. How old are they again?"

"They're in eighth grade. Lord, help us all."

"He does, doesn't He?" She smiled. "Perfect age to learn a few things about helping others." She sounded so much like Grace's mom, it was uncanny — that soft, instructional tone where I learned something new but didn't feel like an idiot.

"They're great kids... most of the time." I rubbed right above my eyebrow as I struggled to describe my boys. They were definitely mine, but words to describe them were few and far between.

"I'm sure they are, especially with a nice, young leader like yourself." She wagged her finger at me as she walked back to the kitchen. "People should be coming soon. Let me get a few things ready."

She darted around every corner of the kitchen, driven to get done whatever her mind scrambled to think of. I couldn't keep up, so I looked out the far windows, the sunny day turning gray and overcast. Pots and pans clanked, echoing across the basement, announcing a meal and with any luck, scaring away my demons.

While she prepared everything, I greeted the kids as they arrived. I ran up the side stairway, the door heavy and metallic like a dungeon entryway.

The boys would be reluctant to do this service project, even more than me if that was possible. But I hoped their parents dragged them out of the house, pulling ears or using whatever means necessary.

A black Suburban with dark tinted windows pulled into the lot and stopped two spaces from the door. A bulky dude resembling a Secret Service agent stepped out. With a protruding belly and a round face, he was a caricature of an out-of-shape has-been. His stiff back and outstretched arms were topped with a gaze that'd kill. I was surprised he fit through doorways. The guy was a square.

He motioned for Peter to come out, but Peter appeared distracted, reluctant, or both.

"Nice to meet you. I'm Mr. Olson." His monstrous, calloused hand extended, looking like one of those oversized Hulk fists.

At what age would I be introduced by first names? I was trapped between two worlds, not a part of either.

"Nice to meet you, too." I lied.

The passenger door finally opened.

"Thanks for setting this up. His mom and I were just saying he should volunteer more." He scratched his barreled chest and glanced over me, a nice reminder who was taller.

"It sounded like fun, and yeah, maybe they'll learn something from it."

"Well, appreciating what they have would be a great start." No matter what he said, his voice sounded like a freight train.

I crossed my arms, my body twitching. "Something we all need to work on, I guess."

I felt like melting. His stare was that intense. Peter lumbered toward us, his reluctance on full display. Mr. Olson grasped Peter's shoulder as if clutching a calf. "This should be fun."

Peter glanced up toward his father and nodded his head, never making eye contact.

"Thanks for dropping him off. We'll have a blast, won't we, Peter?" I patted him on his back, his shoulders loose from slouching.

"Guess so," Peter mumbled.

Silence. His dad laughed awkwardly. "Ok, bye guys."

He sped out of the driveway. Peter never looked up.

"Ready for some fun, buddy?"

He dragged his feet on the pavement then picked up a jagged stone. He tossed it in the air a few times, catching it with his right hand. When his dad turned the corner, he threw the stone as hard as he could, striking the side of the brick building. It landed at our feet.

"Yeah, it'll be a blast."

I rubbed his head then pretended to tackle him from behind. He struggled to smile. From what little I knew about his family, I felt sorry for the kid.

The other boys showed up, each dropped off by their moms. When the third and final Honda Odyssey pulled up, I laughed.

"Let's get started, guys." I felt like a prison warden. Each boy had a 'do we have to do this?' look on his face as if he was about to grab a pickaxe and split rock.

I remembered what it was like and acted the same way. It took me years to figure out the importance of stuff like this.

We walked down the stairs, and I led them to the kitchen.

"Hi, boys! Nice to meet you. I'm Gail." She wiped her hands on her flowered apron and offered a handshake to the boys. They all looked up, speechless.

Harry glided over, making certain to be first. Not that he had much competition. "Nice to meet you, Ms. Gail." He shook with one hand and yanked on his belt with the other. He stepped back and continued fidgeting. Gail brushed her apron and half smiled. People always reacted to Harry in the same awkward manner that he acted toward them.

I shifted my feet and rubbed my blushing cheeks, hoping no one noticed. Anticipation was toxic. My heart pounded and sped ahead, but nothing changed. I'd hounded my mom to defy her demons. Perhaps I should have listened.

"So, you're probably wondering what we're doing tonight." Gail glanced around, getting no reaction at all from the boys. "First off, we're the Society of St. Andrew, a wonderful ministry that has impacted millions of lives worldwide. We've been feeding the homeless here for over ten years. People come from all over the area to be fed two nights a week. For some, it's their only nourishing meals. Tonight, we hand out pre-packaged food, and you wonderful men are here to distribute it."

Homeless. That's one way to describe the man in the alley I stumbled across. *Hopeless* is more like it. Not only did I do nothing to help, but I made matters worse. I took something that no one else valued.

"Where do you get the food?" Zach massaged the side of his head, the most unsure I'd ever seen him.

"That's a great question." She stared into his questioning eyes, as mesmerized as anybody. "We pick it up from local restaurants. Did you know tons of food get thrown out every day? We work with local restaurants to pick up all that food, label and store it, then hand it out to needy families."

"So... you pick food out of dumpsters?" asked Sebastian.

"No, not usually." She winked. "We pick up the food before it gets thrown out. The restaurants cannot legally hand it out, so we work with them to do it."

"That's just dumb... that restaurants can't do it, that is," added Harry.

"Well, it's a long story as to why that is, but people are thankful we're here to help. So, let's get started! Our friends will be arriving soon so we'd better hurry."

My heart was a ticking time bomb. I folded my arms across my chest hoping pressure might smother the fuse. It didn't help. Not at all.

He slept, barely covered with a filthy blanket.

We followed Gail out the back entrance to her white Chevy truck parked near the door. Bulky, cardboard boxes were stacked on the back bed, so we made multiple trips into the kitchen. The large counter was completely covered.

He reeked of booze and weed.

I counted boxes as a distraction: 24.

"What's this?" asked Harry, pulling a hard-plastic case off the top of a box.

"I'm glad you asked." Gail angled her head down to read the label. "Looks like spaghetti and meatballs. Let's separate out the main courses from the side dishes like potatoes and vegetables. We'll also have breads and desserts."

He probably hadn't eaten all day.

Each box was full of plastic containers, individually wrapped in cellophane and labeled with stickers. Most items were frozen. The boys and I divided them into four piles.

He was as desolate as the alley where I found him.

The room spun. I was ready to faint.

"What in the world is fennel-cabbage slaw?" asked Zach. "Looks disgusting."

"Well, to some people, that's a meal," responded Gail. "Better file it under vegetables."

I own what I did. Reluctantly.

Zach laughed. "Why don't they just buy it? Not that anyone would buy something such a disgusting purple."

I hoped that others forgot.

"Well, it requires money to buy food." Her hip flexed, pressed by her hand. "Many of these people cannot afford to purchase such a meal. I'm assuming your parents buy you food for which you are thankful?"

Touché. Zach had the oddest, most confused look on his face. He stared at Gail, devoid of snappy comebacks. His eyes deflated, glancing at his feet.

The boys unloaded the boxes and continued stacking the containers in the kitchen. The short windows along the opposite wall grew their anticipation. Legs shifted, kicking away patience, the shuffling bottoms of pants and dresses. There were many shades of black and blue, but no red.

He was deeply bruised and bled profusely.

I wondered if I knew any of them, or worse yet, if any of them knew me. I was a minor when it happened, so my name wasn't in the newspaper. But people talked. Word got out. The passage of time was my friend; memory was the enemy.

I dashed out the back, looking for something to do and luckily found the last box from Gail's truck. I headed back to the kitchen. We sorted as quickly as we could, with the boys needing constant help and direction.

But I couldn't even help myself. This was dizzying, overwhelming, and head-throbbingly painful. I ran to the bathroom and lost everything I had eaten that day. I wiped my forehead and glanced into the mirror. Cold water splashed onto my face, dowsing the paleness.

I returned to the kitchen and stood in the back. Anyone with a keen eye could notice I resembled the ghost I was trying desperately to avoid.

Gail removed her apron and glanced around at the boys with a knowing smile. "It's showtime!"

She walked over to the large metal panel and yanked it upward along its tracks. The sudden noise startled the boys, while I stared at Gail wondering how she did that.

An orderly line of adults had assembled, looking in as much as the boys were looking out. The people at the front steadied themselves with hands on the counter, resembling the upper halves of those waiting outside.

I caught a glimpse of Zach, an awestruck boy lost in his uneasiness. He looked terrified. He stared at the first person in line, a tall, thin gentleman with an unkempt, gray beard and a grimy, brown overcoat that had seen better days, most likely by someone else. He reeked of cigarettes and gasoline, an explosive mix.

The man looked up and shot a smile at Zach, but Zach turned away.

Gail stood by the counter and entered the man's name into her MacBook. She beamed at him, greeted him as Tom, then patted his arm with the most genuine touch.

She printed out a receipt and handed it back to Sebastian: '1 adult'. So little, yet so much. "Can you help this fine gentleman with some food?"

Sebastian grabbed a plastic bag and placed a single-serving entrée, a vegetable, and a small dessert into it. He handed it over the counter.

"Thank you," the man gruffed, smelling like a car exhaust. He walked away, cradling the bag in his arms.

The second person in line was a short, stocky woman with long, black hair. Her dress appeared raggedy and dated, and her gnarled hair was swept back in a ponytail as a poor attempt to contain it. She tottered back and forth.

"She lives in a cardboard box under a bridge," whispered Zach toward Sebastian. Zach giggled while Sebastian glanced over at me. I tapped Zach's shoulder, but he didn't look up.

The slip of paper came back: '2 adults, 3 kids.' I handed it to Zach. "Can you find a dinner for this nice lady?"

Zach stared at it. "I... I don't know what to do."

"You have two sisters, right?" Sebastian asked.

"Yeah, what does that matter?"

"Well... what would you and your family eat for dinner?" Sebastian continued. "That's what we're putting together for them: a dinner for their family."

Zach scanned the room as if waking up from a daylong nap. He barely moved. Harry pushed his shoulder and grabbed a plastic grocery bag.

"Zacheroony... C'mon, buddy. What would your family like to eat for dinner tonight?" Harry asked.

Zach blushed. "We... we already ate."

"No, no, no, dimwit."

"Hey!"

Gail was having a pleasant conversation with the lady at the counter. She didn't appear in a hurry, but I knew she was.

"If you could pick out a meal from this wonderful cornucopia before us..." Harry's hand swept over the counter. "What would you choose?"

Zach rolled his eyes and lined the taut muscles of his stomach between his fingers. "Well, I like chicken."

Harry pushed a few boxes out of the way and found one marked 'Chicken Marsala.' "How's this?" he asked. "Now... how 'bout veggies, bread, and dessert?"

One by one, they chose the rest of the meal, including whole kernel corn, an entire loaf of whole wheat bread, and a chocolate lava cake from some upscale place downtown.

"Go give it to her," I placed my hand on Zach's shoulder and nudged him forward.

His outstretched hand draped the bag over the counter, his eyes meeting hers for the first time. Zach's shoulders softened, and his eyes blinked heavily, driving any girl crazy in any other setting.

But this was different. He stared down the beam of a movie projector, showing a feature he'd never seen. The bright lights. The hum of the rolling reel.

I also saw a theater. Cold and dark, with popcorn kernels strewn across the floor. Soda cups tipped over and scattered into far corners, underneath seats and tucked behind rows. The seats were black and worn, distant memories of Hollywood blockbusters. It now showed a documentary, but the place was empty. Not a single soul came to watch.

I felt more vulnerable, yet also more at ease. Not because no one else watched or cared, but because I did. I realized why we did this, and I forgot about my past, at least for that brief moment.

I had ended a life. I was guilty of that.

But I also started a new one.

"Thank you," the lady whispered. She walked away with a hurried gait, off to somewhere.

Zach stood motionless. His melted silver eyes fluttered repeatedly then stopped, focusing on her as she marched out the door.

Chapter 23 – Aidan

Dear Aidan,

I hope all is well, my friend. As always, it was great hanging out with you last week. I swear you grow an inch every time I see you. What does your mom feed you, string beans? Sorry, stupid joke.

I must admit, it's odd writing this letter — partly because I see you so often and partly because no one writes letters anymore. But mostly because of our ages. However, we've never let that get in the way of growing up together. You guys have taught me so much this year, I sometimes forget who's mentoring whom!

Today marks the fourteenth anniversary of your father's death. I don't want to dwell on it too much, only to use it as an opportunity to tell you about him. To understand his role in my life, you have to understand more about me. I've told you some, but not all.

I was your age when I met your father. He was our group's mentor for our confirmation program. We were introduced in the beginning of the school year, and he mentored us for about four months. It was odd to have a mentor who wasn't a parent. Honestly, the only adults I knew were my parents, coaches, and more coaches.

Like it or not, we all play roles. Mine was the arrogant jock. I constantly cut people down and made fun of them yet praised myself to no end. I'd always focus on my own accomplishments, and believe me, there were many. I was the star for every team I played on.

But looks were deceiving. My self-esteem was at the bottom of the barrel. My father was an overbearing perfectionist who always expected great things from me. Sounds nice, but it was awful. He yelled whenever I messed up, and whatever I did wasn't good enough. I was never allowed to fail, which was why I never learned how to succeed.

It was at that point in my life when I met your father. Not only was he always supportive and encouraging, but he was always there. He listened, he encouraged, he led us in volunteering, and most importantly, he cared. And he did it not out of obligation but because he wanted to. I had never witnessed that before: someone who actually cared more about me than my success.

I know this sounds overly dramatic, as I only knew your father for such a short time. But it was such an important time in my life, when I was the lowest and least fulfilled. Did I know it at the time? Nope. We had just won the eighth-grade state championship in football! But I was hollow inside, caring about no one except myself.

The lightbulb flipped when your father forced us to volunteer at a food pantry. I had no desire to go and frankly, annoyed everyone with my bad attitude, including your dad. He stood in the back so ghastly white, I assumed he was sick and tired of dealing with me.

But I am the better for it. He taught us about love and compassion, about caring and respect. And we didn't just talk about it. We did it. We helped. We got involved. My life mattered when it wasn't about me.

Unfortunately, I never got the chance to tell your father any of this. It wasn't until much later did I realize how important it was to me. Don't get me wrong, I was thrilled to have a mentor and knew I needed one. But the impact of it all didn't hit me until much later.

For you, I have two requests. First, pick out three people who have made a positive impact on you. Tell them how much they mean to you. Tell them the amazing things they've done to influence you. And do it now while you still can.

Second, make an impact on someone else. Find an elderly neighbor whose lawn needs cutting. Help your teacher clean the classroom. Track down some younger kids and teach them something: at church, in a sport, anything.

May God bless your life and watch over everything you do.

I look forward to our youth group on Wednesdays as I have every week this year. You guys are awesome. See you there!

Your mentor and friend,

Zach

• • •

"Have I told you Zach talks about Dad a lot at youth group?" I clutched his letter in my hand, glancing at it as I spoke. I turned it over, the ink had almost run through.

Zach's handwriting was so messy, the other boys in my group could never read it — small, illegible characters smeared with a hand rubbed across the ink. We always kidded him about it.

"No, you haven't mentioned that. Hopefully in a good way." My mom placed her arm on the table and tilted in closer.

"Oh, definitely. Every time we sit down on the hard floor in the hall, he makes this funny grunt pretending to be Dad."

"That doesn't sound like a good way, Aidan." She placed her hand flat on the table.

"Oh, it is. Guys are different, Mom."

"I'll never argue with that." She sputtered a few coughs. "The way you and Josh and Eric talk to each other, you'd think you guys were mortal enemies. Seems rude to me, but I'm only your mother. What do I know?"

"Oh, a lot. Just not about guys." I smiled.

"Gee, thanks."

I held the letter in my outstretched hand. "Zach's mentioned the volunteering before: the food pantry, the nursing home playing games with the residents, oh… and they walked dogs for the animal shelter."

"Sounds like fun. They sure did a lot in four months." She crossed her legs, her hand smoothing out her jeans. "Say, you guys are doing a service project in a few weeks, right?"

"We're reading books with sick kids at Samaritan." I tipped back my chair. "Actually, I need to pick out some of my favorites to bring along." I twirled the letter, dropping like a helicopter.

She watched the letter hit the table. "That'll work great. I'll run in and check on my patients while you're there."

I bent my leg up on the chair and rested against it. "You'll laugh. My old books are back in the attic." It was already a whirlwind day. All the reading and discussing was making me exhausted. But we had to keep going. I had to know everything.

She shifted through the remaining papers — four left, two were hand-written letters.

"You'll have to head back up there. It'll be the heavy one." Her eyes shifted with her thoughts. She wiped a tear off her cheek.

"What is it, Mom?" I propped myself forward, trying to get a better look.

She pulled out one of the typed documents and handed it to me. The other three sheets landed flip side on the table. "I think it's time to read this."

I snatched it from her hand and glanced at the text at the top. My muscles tensed. "Oh my. Are you sure?"

She pushed the hair out of her eyes. "Yes, it's time."

Chapter 24 – Shawn

November 8, 2003

The clanging of the little bell announced my arrival to Grandpa's, a slice of Americana with padded booths, laminate tables, and the greasiest food on the planet. The carpeting was thin, the stools squeaked when patrons swiveled, and the faded upholstery had its day in the sun. Literally. The place was nostalgic without even trying.

I knew right away why Phil wanted to meet there. It was packed with people, too many witnesses for anything bad to happen. I spotted him sitting way in the back. I maneuvered through the crowd, not a single soul looking up from his or her tasty indulgence.

"Hey there, Mr. Corleone." I stood in front of the booth with hands in my pockets.

Phil looked up from his menu. "Hey!" He smiled, cautiously. If I didn't know him so well, I'd have thought he was glad to see me.

I removed my jacket and placed it on the ledge near the frosted window. I slid into the booth while watching Phil look at his menu. He had noticeable folds under his eyes and an unshaved shadow lining his face.

"How ya been?" I inquired.

"Busy." He looked up. "My old man finally forced me to get a job. About time, huh?"

"Should keep you outta trouble." A few short months ago, my comeback would have been very different. But I held back. Maybe I changed. Maybe he did, too.

The menu choices were daunting. My usual — two scrambled eggs, a mound of hash browns, a slice of ham, and sourdough toast — didn't sound as tempting as usual.

"So, what else is new?" I asked.

He tossed the padded menu board on the table, thumping as it hit. "Have I told you I'm dating someone?" He grinned.

"When would you have told me?" I swallowed hard, followed by an awkward silence. Thinking about my every word was not a dam-busting way to have a conversation. Momentum was hard with so much friction.

Our fight was a rain cloud hovering over our heads. Did I have anything against him specifically? Not really. Did he have anything against me? Probably. I was an awful friend.

"I guess we haven't talked in a while." He took a sip of water then wiped his mouth with his index finger. His slower movements aged him. "Jenny's pretty cool. She puts up with me, so she'd have to be."

I also placed my menu on the table, still unsure of what to order. I rubbed my temple, feeling the warmth of the nearby kitchen. The man sitting in the booth next to us spoke loudly with his hands, the eyes of the lady across from him were sloped and sullen.

There was nothing I could do but watch and listen. "That's great. I'm happy for you guys."

This small talk was irritating, but it was more my fault than his. Was there something else I was supposed to say? Forgiveness was not my strong suit — giving or receiving.

"You'll have to meet her sometime. She has a great personality." He chuckled, realizing his unintended cliché. "And she's hot!"

"She'd have to be for you to like her." Everything came out wrong, and I didn't know why. I wanted a fresh start. I really did. I just didn't know how to create it.

Phil opened his mouth then closed it. He sipped some water then finally spoke. "We met at work. We got to talking one day and hit it off. She likes my personality."

"Well, it's not your looks, that's for sure." The kidding was intended. Even he smiled. His penetrating eyes and chiseled face made women swoon. A long time ago, I stopped noticing the turned heads and halted conversations. He was just one of the guys. But it did allow me to fly under the radar. At least, I used to.

The waitress stopped by and took our orders, leaning against the table for balance. Her striped apron, tightly bound hair, and weary eyes made her the poster girl for overworked and underpaid.

I handed her my menu, waited for her to leave, then turned to Phil. We stared at each other, so much unsaid between us. "I'm also seeing someone. Her name's Grace and she's just amazing. I haven't stopped to breathe since I met her."

He smiled again. "You like her, don't you?"

"Yeah, I guess I do. Why do you ask?"

"Well, your hands are doing all the talking, Shawny boy."

"That's funny." I tried to peek outside, but the window was frosted over. So I stared at my hands, now resting on the table. "She makes me feel better about myself, you know?"

He propped against the backrest, his eyes piercing at me. He actually looked like he wanted to listen.

"The last few years have been tough." I rubbed the corner of my bottom lip. "I just... it's nice to have someone to rely on." I wasn't making any sense. Phil and I had known each other for such a long time, but this felt like the first time I'd opened up about anything. Why was it so hard?

"Well, don't rely on anybody too much. He or she just might let you down. Be your own man." He cocked his head upward, his distinct chin protruding outward.

I wasn't Grizzly Adams for goodness' sake. There were people in my life who were there for a reason: my mom, Grace, even Phil. I had to rely on somebody.

I realized he was not the only one who'd grown up.

The lady in the nearby booth was now on full out offensive. Her hands firmly against the table, her face a stormy red. I didn't have to know what she was saying, nor did I want to.

The waitress came by and slipped the plates onto the table. My dad would have said they were heaped with healthy portions, but that was exactly what they weren't. Phil's fries were swimming in some oily liquid, and butter dripped down the side of my Baked Rigatoni. They were heavy plates covered with even heavier food. We dug in.

"You know what…" Phil perked up, his mouth stuffed with a huge bite of hamburger. But he didn't care, nor did I. "We should double date. You, me, and the girls. They'd love it!"

"Not a bad idea." I took a bite then placed my fork on the table. I liked Phil, I really did. But I knew him too well — the school assignments he'd cheated on, the money he'd stolen, the countless hearts he'd broken, the grudges he held. It was a laundry list I never intended to keep. "Whatcha doing tonight? Grace and I were already getting together."

"Where ya headed?" His eyes were lined by thin creases near his temples, as honest as I'd ever seen.

"No plans." I smiled. "Wanna hit Casa Bonita? Grace has never been there. And she calls herself a Coloradan." I huffed, faking a disgust.

His head almost hit the wall behind him. "Let's do it. I'm always up for cliff divers and crappy food."

"No kidding. Minus the divers, this place isn't too bad, either."

"Cool! Jenny's looking forward to meeting you." His arms rested on the table, straddling his plate. "I've told her a lot." His smile was genuine, but I couldn't look past what he said. It was so deep, so full of stories and promises and resentments. Everything he kept with nothing to gain.

We stared, waiting for the other to say more. In some ways, we did. He also knew what I was thinking. In fact, he knew me better than anyone: my strengths, my faults, my mistakes. Some he accepted, most he forgave.

But there was another, more ominous cloud that shadowed over us. And it was about time I stood up to it.

"Some of it might actually be true."

Chapter 25 – Shawn

November 12, 2003

I sat silently in the pew, in sharp contrast to my boys who were as loud and obnoxious as ever. They laughed, pinched, and kidded with such brutality, I'd have thought they despised each other. Nothing held back. Honest yet cruel.

Phil and I used to be like that. Every day in the summer, we'd ride our dirt bikes to Pioneer Park and hit the playground. Climb, flip, run, repeat. And all the while discussing nothing in particular — no hidden agendas, no hurtful words, at least none that lasted more than 24 hours.

I drove past the park the other day. The equipment was tiny with parts of it in desperate need of repair. I ducked to walk underneath the rusted poles of the swing set, and the slide was barely longer than my legs. I maneuvered under the monkey bar cage, my head almost hitting the top.

"Hey guys," yelled Mike from the front. "We have a full evening tonight so let's get started. Let's pray first." He cleared his throat, then said a prayer to open the evening.

The room hummed. Most kids focused toward the front, a few spoke in whispers, sharing secrets that no longer were.

"Can anyone tell me the seventh commandment?" Mike placed his hand on his forehead and slanted his head down. With the glaring lights, he could hardly see.

A boy in the back raised his hand and grunted. The kids around him laughed, but he didn't seem to care.

"Yes, Philip." Mike pursed his lips as if expecting a poor answer.

"Don't steal," the kid announced.

A tight clench twisted my arms. They burned from my hands upward. The stained glass was a distraction, so random yet so precise, the vibrant colors standing out more than the sturdy metal holding it together.

"That's correct," Mike pointed out. "At first, this appears obvious. Don't steal. But is it just about taking other people's things, or are there other reasons to not steal?"

A host of kids raised their hands, almost in unison. My boys appeared as disinterested as ever.

"How about back there." Mike pointed to the fifth row, still hovering under the glaring lights. "Jake."

"Because other people don't like it when you take their stuff, including my sister," said a boy with messy blond hair and an even messier smirk.

Mike smiled. "You're on the right track, Jake. In Romans 13:9, Jesus summarized the rest of the commandments with only a few words: 'Love your neighbor as yourself.'"

Simple yet so full of assumptions.

Mike paused to let it sink in. "What Jesus meant was if we love our neighbors then we wouldn't do anything to hurt them. That includes murder, jealousy, even stealing. Stealing can be rude and disrespectful, but first we have to own up to it. Has anyone stolen something?"

What if I don't love myself?

A few tentative hands raised. Their innocence minimized their theft to a simple share to a group. The simplicity of it was maddening. But I got it. I understood why they shared. Better than not.

There was such a separation between them and me, and age was only half the story. Mike called on a few, defenseless kids, who in that context seemed so much more. Mike's pointed finger didn't help.

"I stole some pencils at school."

"I stole answers from a friend's test."

"I took a friend's bike for a ride, and he didn't know it."

Mike nodded his head. "Thanks for sharing. So, what do we do if we steal from someone?"

"We tell them we're sorry."

"We give it back."

And how does that fix the problem? How does giving something back erase a mistake? By that point, it's no longer about the item. If somehow, we could neatly place things back where they were, that still wouldn't erase what happened.

What if giving it back wasn't even possible?

The room shifted and swayed like a ship setting sail. These kids were headed toward a distant land, a long and tumultuous journey for everyone involved. Unfortunately, I didn't speak from experience. I drowned before we even left port.

Maybe in their world it was true. Hand it back and everyone smiles. But in the real world, it was horribly wrong.

While confronting was necessary, giving back was next to impossible. But that didn't mean it shouldn't be done.

• • •

The boys trailed me to the fellowship hall, reaching the corner where we always sat. The window was fogged over from the damp cold. It was raining. I could feel it.

We all sat on the floor with an untouched stack of chairs to our right. The boys begged but I didn't relent. I shouldn't be the only one uncomfortable. Zach smiled as I groaned.

"So, what do you guys think about not stealing?" My words trailed off, barely sounding like a question. It was a word I hadn't used in a long time.

All the boys settled into their position on the floor. Peter reclined on his stomach, stretching his legs behind him. The other boys crossed their legs, making the shape of an 'X.'

"First thing, it's rude." Peter removed his raggedy baseball cap. "Why take something that's not yours?" He scratched his matted, blond hair then put the cap back on.

Harry spoke next. "Must not be happy with what he has."

I immediately saw glimpses of Phil — the lack of tact, the quick jump to conclusions, and the wherewithal to blurt it out without thinking.

"Either that or the devil made him do it," Zach added but contributed nothing. He nudged Harry, forcing him to fall on Peter. Did they always have to overact? Our group time would have been so much easier if they were puppets, where I controlled the strings.

Sebastian waved his hands in the air. "I liked how it was tied in with jealousy. If you're not happy with what you have, then you want what someone else has. And some people are just too dumb to go buy it instead."

My face reddened. I had enough of their pathetic guesses. They had no clue what they were talking about. "I'm glad you guys figured it all out. But I hate to tell you, you're all completely wrong."

They all had the blankest of looks. They didn't believe me, nor did I expect them to.

"How would you know, Mr. Shawn?" Harry asked.

"Because I have."

"What do you mean you have?"

"I stole something once. Actually, a couple of things."

Zach stared at me with a half-smile. "My dad said you went to jail for something."

I froze. Zach says a lot of things, mostly about himself. But I was not expecting that. Not at all. "I guess I did. Kind of." I wanted to own what I did. But these were kids. Young and innocent, at least far more than I was. Why tell them? Why ruin not only their view of me but of life? Honesty was one thing, restraint was another.

"What'd you do?" Sebastian spoke in such a soft tone, I assumed he didn't really want to know the answer.

"I stole from a store." I took a deep breath. "A liquor store."

Peter sat up and balanced on his knees. "What'd you steal?"

"Well... some money from the cash register." I sighed. "And some cigarettes."

"Why'd you do that?"

I leaned forward, crossing my legs and angling into our circle. I was ready to unleash, and I hoped they were ready to hear. "I was angry. Furious. I hated the world. But I wasn't jealous or unhappy with what I had. I don't know why I did it. Maybe I just didn't care."

"But something set you off, right, like you snapped?" Zach asked.

"Maybe I did. I don't know." I knew there'd be no going back, but maybe that was what I wanted. "Right after my dad died, I walked into the store on a night just like this one. I stole what I could as quickly as possible then ran out. The store manager chased after me, but I was a fast runner. Well, faster than she was."

Peter sat up and balanced on his knees. "What happened next?"

"I ran until I heard sirens, then snuck into an alley and hid behind a dumpster. That's when I noticed him."

"Noticed who?"

"A man lying about five feet away from me." I tried hard not to visualize him, but it felt like yesterday. Everything was so real, yet it wasn't. "He was trying to sleep, covered by a filthy, old blanket, his feet sticking out the end. He looked like he had fallen out of a chimney."

The boys sat up and stared. Harry gulped. Zach curved his back to lean forward.

"His bloodshot eyes were enormous as if I was the first person he'd ever seen. But they were slow to focus, looking toward me but not at me. His body swayed. He coughed. That's when I smelled the booze and the weed."

Peter laughed at my description but then gazed directly at me, which stopped him cold. I felt expressionless, but I was positive that wasn't how I looked.

Zach also leaned forward. "Wait… you were in jail for three years for stealing from a store?"

I scratched my head. "How'd you know that? And no, it wasn't jail, Zach. It was a boys' home, up in the mountains."

"Sorry, my dad just talks a lot. And listens, too, I guess."

I wondered who else knew, like it was this shared secret that everyone was aware of but no one wanted to discuss. "There was more, but I shouldn't tell you guys. I mean… it wasn't good. Far from it."

"What do you mean?"

"I mean I did some stupid things. Things I should've known better not to." My admission didn't satisfy them at all. In fact, it only aroused more curiosity.

"Did it have to do with the guy in the alley? What happened to him?"

I took the deepest breath, my heavy chest expanding then contracting with a lungful of air that gradually changed my appearance. "Yeah, it did." I shook. My mind couldn't focus, only on sights and sounds that I tried so hard to forget.

"Did you steal something from him, like his blanket?"

I laughed. "I wish it were that simple."

"Then what?" Zach asked.

I looked around the spacious hall. The other groups were packed into the other three corners, as far away from us as possible. I had done so much in that room — the games we played, the overnight lock-ins we had, the church dinners we ate. The room held so much to me, like a time capsule of my life. It was only a space, yet somehow, it was much more.

I looked at the boys. So young, so full of life and potential and any future they desired. They were that age where everything was still ahead, yet they still thought they knew it all. I only knew because it used to be me.

Unfortunately, one day they'd wake up and realize they had no clue what life was about, what it meant. They'd lose the control they never had. That's when the world comes crashing down, with billows of dust obstructing their vision.

They probably knew what I was about to say next.

Except they didn't.

"I killed him."

The chatter from the other groups sounded like raindrops hitting a roof. Random yet pounding. I wondered what they were discussing, and whether their kids were engaged or helpless or terrified.

Both my hands were shaking. I'd never spoken those words before, and they horrified me. The boys had clearly never heard them. I don't know why I even said them. I craved honesty, and that I gave. But why? Weren't my words just one more thing I wanted to take back, to change and make right?

"I was so mad. A drunk driver killed my father days earlier, his funeral the day before. And here was this guy." I wiped my eyes, a wetness draping off my fingers. "I was ready to explode. I didn't know what else to do."

The boys and girls and mentors from the other groups were far enough away that they couldn't have heard me. They acted like they didn't, as if life was normal. Apparently, my dark cloud of influence only reached so far.

Peter said, "But you can't just do that."

"But I did. He was in such awful shape already. So, I ended his misery." I wiped my cheek with the backside of my hand. "Because there was nothing I could do about my own." My confession felt so unfulfilled. Incomplete. But hadn't I said enough?

Peter and Sebastian shifted away from me. Their hands balanced on the floor and their legs slipped backwards, leaning against the wall. I swore they looked differently at me, not recognizing what they saw.

"Did anyone find out?" asked Harry. "I mean… did you get caught?"

"The police came knocking on our door a few days later. When my mom opened it, I knew I was done for. My life had changed forever." I blinked slow and hard. "Exactly what I hoped for."

"What happened next?"

"I was tried in juvenile court and convicted of armed robbery and petty theft."

"Wait… what about the guy in the alley?"

I scratched my cheek. "I got off on a plea deal. That's what happens when they can't prove anything. There were no witnesses."

"But you just said…"

"I know what I said." I tried so hard to hold back, but I wanted to scream. Many things prevented me, yet it wouldn't have been any different than what I'd done every day since. "Justice is different. No one else saw what happened."

"That's not right." Peter spoke so quietly as if all air had left him. He stared at the floor unable to look directly at me.

"Well, that's the truth. Took a year to get through the courts, then they finally sentenced me to three years in a juvenile detention center. I call it the home, even though it wasn't. I hated the place but deserved to be there. Gave me time to think."

"What'd you think about?"

"Why I wanted to live."

The boys still didn't understand. Their stares were empty, their movements slow and halted as if wanting to bring up a question but not knowing what to ask.

That was my problem, too. I was paralyzed knowing that what I wanted couldn't happen. But what I needed, I got. Turns out, they were very different, and that was entirely a good thing.

I never understood my actions, why I thought one thing but did something else. It was a disconnect that ended up defining who I was, even though it truly wasn't.

I'd been thrashing about in the middle of a vast lake, hopelessly drowning.

"What do you mean?" asked Zach, the only one of the four still looking at me.

Little did I know, I could have helped myself, never realizing my feet could touch bottom.

"I wanted to be with my dad." I stared into Zach's eyes, burning with intensity. Overwhelmed yet focused. Full of warmth. I loved that kid. "And I would have done anything to get there."

Chapter 26 – Aidan

Case Number: 55397235
Date: 14 February 2000
Reporting Officer: Deputy Seiler
Prepared By: CPL Krenzke
Incident Type: Assault & Battery

Address of Occurrence:
Alley on 600 Block of Elm Street, Clearfall, CO 80543
Witnesses: None
Evidence: None
Weapon/Objects Used: None

At 6:42 a.m. on the morning of February 12, 2000, the body of a man was found in the alley behind an Ace Hardware store by the store owner, Mr. Anurag Dubey. After Mr. Dubey called 911, Deputy Seiler arrived on the scene at 7:06 a.m. to inspect the premises and assess the situation. The homicide division arrived on the scene at 7:27 a.m. The body was examined and found to have severe abrasions on the neck and torso and severe trauma to the head. This bodily distress was most likely caused by continued blows from a foot and/or hand.

The unidentified man appeared to have been homeless, as his body was wrapped in a blanket and lay behind a dumpster. No form of identification was found.

The body was sent to the Forensics lab for further testing and analysis. A blood test was performed, and his blood alcohol content (BAC) was found to be 0.26%, more than three times the legal limit in the state of Colorado. Marijuana was also found in his system. The official response from the coroner was that the severely high BAC contributed to the man's death, although this was not proven from further testing.

The evening before on February 11, 2000, Log Cabin Liquor, located on the 800 block of Elm, was robbed by a male suspect, later identified to be Shawn Stevens, a 14-year-old male from Clearfall (refer to case # 855397221). He admitted to the burglary and was arrested on February 13 on charges of aggravated robbery, petty theft, and unlawful possession of a deadly weapon. An investigation into any connection between the two incidences is ongoing.

Positive identification of the body or any additional pending charges will be reported to the District Attorney as they unfold.

•   •   •

My hands shook, my throat tightened, the kitchen steaming and uncomfortable. I stared at the report, unable to look up at my mother. Neither of us moved.

"Did he do it?" I asked through gritted teeth, creating a deep whisper that didn't sound like my voice at all. It was too full of rage for that.

"Do what, Aidan?"

I threw the report down, my hand banging on the table. "You know what I mean! The guy in the alley… did he kill him?"

She froze for a second then kicked her feet, staring at them. "Aidan, you have to understand…"

"I understand a lot!" The trembling in my hands shifted to my chest, my head. "Just answer the question. Is my father a murderer?"

"He was so much more than that."

I literally felt like exploding, breaking up into a million little pieces. "So you're saying he did it. Oh my goodness, he killed someone."

While my outward appearance could not stop shaking, my mind went blank. There was no doubt, both my mother and my father lied to me. She tricked me into believing he was worth admiring, and he fooled me into hoping he actually was. She looked down at the table, sullen and depleted, her tears falling onto her plate. She brushed her cheek then wiped her hand on her blue jeans.

"Why?"

She finally looked up, as uncertain and tentative as I'd ever seen her. "Why what? Why did he do it?"

"No, not that. You lied to me. You and Dad."

"We never lied to you." Her hand fell as flat as her words. "It's just a part of your father's story that you haven't heard. It's not like we purposely..."

"You kept it from me! I... I admired him." I thrust my hand against the table a few times. She closed her eyes but didn't flinch. "Now you tell me he killed someone? Seriously?"

"Aidan... he made a mistake."

"Made a mistake? That's how you pass off a murder... as a mistake?" I threw both my hands against the sides of my head. "That's so bull!"

"Please settle down." She reached out and touched my arm. I cringed and recoiled. "Think about it. His father had just died, and he was angry."

"That doesn't mean you go out and kill someone!" I stood up and shoved my chair against the table. They hit, metal on metal, a harsh clang. The table shifted.

"None of us are perfect. We all..."

"Yeah, but just because I do something stupid to someone at school doesn't put me in the same category as a murderer."

"No, it doesn't. But who decides that?"

"I don't know. I guess... Ah! This is so bogus." I shut my eyes, thinking of this family portrait that never was: standing in an alley, covered with filth, my dad's arm around me and his foot resting on top of a homeless man. I shook.

"Well, God thinks..."

"I don't care what God thinks." I mumbled.

"Aidan, really? Yes, you do."

"No, I don't. And I don't care what you or Dad think either." I bent over and balanced against the back of the chair with both hands. "This was my time

to get to know my father and find out who he was. Oh, that happened alright…"
I inhaled. "I… I don't know what to think."

"What you should think is…"

"Don't tell me what to think!" My entire hand pointed toward her then smashed the wall. The wall was thin, but the pain ran deep. I shook my hand then marched toward my room but abruptly turned and looked back. The intensity of my stare burned the back of my eyes. "Ok, what was your reaction? How did you take it when you found out?" My intention was to corner her as much as she did to me.

She stood upright and walked toward me. I backtracked a step. She stopped. "I wasn't thrilled. No one was." She paused for an eternity. "People wondered why he was even allowed to mentor."

I'd heard enough. I turned around and stormed up the stairs, slamming my bedroom door behind me. Homework papers flew off my desk. The lamp shook then steadied. My room spun in circles as I searched for something to rip to shreds. The first poster I saw was the victim, my hands the criminal.

My closet door swung all the way around and banged the wall as I reached inside and grabbed the blue and white Adidas bag I usually used for soccer. It fell limp in my hands, the strap hitting my thigh as I stomped over to the opposite side of my room. Each drawer had something I wanted, something I thought I'd need in the coming weeks. I threw them into the bag. Everything unfolded into an intertwining mess, so I stuffed the pack down with my hand, forcing it all to fit. The bag barely zipped shut.

I fell onto the edge of my bed, the bulging bag leaning against my leg. My face fell into my hands, a poor attempt at softening the sobs I didn't want her to hear. She'd attempt to rescue me, and it would fail miserably. For both of us.

Never again.

It was time to leave. Where I was going didn't matter. What mattered more was that I was leaving.

Chapter 27 – Shawn

November 16, 2003

"Time to go, Mom," I yelled up the stairs. "We'll be late." The second hand on my watch spun faster than a CD player.

"Yeah, yeah." She ran down the stairs, her flowery, red dress bouncing as her feet banged against the steps. She positioned her earring with both hands while stepping into her flats. I twirled the keys then walked out the front door and started the car.

We drove to church, mostly in silence. I was excited for her to join me, but my mind was still on my boys. I second-guessed myself, worrying that I shared too much. And I wasn't about to tell my mother any of it. No doubt, she would have agreed with me.

The bell tolled as we pulled into the lot, a not-so-gentle reminder that we were late. My mom nervously looked around, her hands constantly twisting the strap on her purse. She was either going to pee in her pants or run away screaming. I hoped for neither.

I opened the door for her, then outstretched my arm, holding my hands together with elbow out. "May I escort you, madam?"

She tentatively stepped out of the car as if the ground below wouldn't hold her and her burdens. She pulled together the sides of her long, black coat while hanging onto my arm. The coat mostly covered her long, burgundy dress, which I hadn't seen in years.

"This wind is awful," she yelled during a gust that did its best to silence her.

"Gives you a new hairstyle. I like it."

"Oh, cut it out." She swatted my arm. It was nice to see her playful, albeit mostly to hide her uncertainty. I didn't blame her. This was a big step for her, no matter how small it may have seemed to a casual observer.

As we walked into the entryway with hurried steps, a familiar voice came running toward us. "Mr. Shawn!"

I turned to look but already knew who it was. "Hey, Harry! How are you doin', buddy?"

"Couldn't be better. You never told me you had a sister." Harry looked up and smiled, the flap on his shirt hanging out like a flag in the wind. For all that had changed, some things had remained the same.

"You're hilarious." I rubbed the top of his hair, another victim of the wind. "This is my mom, but I'm not sure I want you two to meet."

Harry slapped my other arm. "Of course you do." Harry extended his hand. "Nice to meet you, Ms. Stevens."

My mom let go of her jacket to greet him. "Nice to meet you, too. Shawn told me a lot about you."

He pushed his glasses upward and just watched her. It was nice of my mom not to mention what I actually said about Harry.

"We'd better head in, buddy." I nudged him, throwing him off balance. He crossed his legs as he stepped, arms outstretched like a tightrope walker.

He strode alongside me with continued glances as we entered the sanctuary. We walked in together, my mom clutching her jacket with one hand and pulling her scarf over her head with the other.

"If you don't want to get noticed…" I leaned in, my mouth half open. "then you shouldn't sneak around like Mata Hari."

"Sorry, I'm just not sure I want to be here."

"But maybe you need to be."

Her half-smile was more out of agony than happiness. "You shouldn't listen to your mother so much."

Harry glanced at my mother. "Your son told us to listen to our parents, Ms. Stevens."

"That's wonderful, Harry."

I began to appreciate him for everything that he was.

"Nice to meet you again, Ms. Stevens." Harry bowed slightly then ran off to sit with his family. He didn't say much but sure told me a lot.

My mom and I took our seats on the end of a pew, about the middle of the sanctuary and far enough in that we could see around the big, wooden beam.

We stood for "Now Thank We All Our God," one of my favorite hymns as a kid. The organ sounded louder than usual with everyone belting it out in unison. The young lady to my right was a soprano in the making, while the old man in front of me was a full-fledged bull horn. True harmony at its finest, even though it was far from perfect.

I knew what my mom was thinking. The last time we attended together, most people totally avoided us. After my father's sudden death, most people just didn't know what to say. Worse yet, some approached us and maxed out the stupid-meter with thinly veiled condolences.

He's in a better place.

God wanted him as an angel.

My mom said it got worse when I left. I could only imagine, not to say I wanted to. But whoever said time heals all wounds apparently lived to be very, very old.

I wished I had been there. Even better, I needed to. I would have shielded her from senseless pitying and condescending eyes. But I wasn't.

During the last verse, Pastor Mike trudged up to the towering, white pulpit, his steps like an ailing backpacker. He placed his papers on top then breathed, heavy and deep.

I stopped singing. The more I watched, the more I realized something was terribly wrong.

My mom gave no reaction at all, besides swaying ever so slightly to the music. Knowing her, she wasn't thinking of anything outside herself. At that moment, it was for her benefit.

The last word was sung. The organ abruptly stopped.

"I welcome you in the name of Christ Jesus, our Lord and Savior." Mike's eyes glossed above the crowd while I squinted my own to figure him out. With such a lack of color in his face, he looked ready to faint.

"I'd like to tell you a story." He wiped the side of his mouth with an open hand. "After a grueling 48-hour shift at the fire station, Matt Grunwald hopped into his car and headed for home, something he had done many times before. As Matt continued down the Illinois freeway, his workday was taking its toll. He was exhausted. Without warning, he fell asleep at the wheel.

"His car swerved to the left and clipped the side of a brown minivan alongside him. The van lost control and hit the guardrail at a sharp angle, forcing it to flip on its side. The van smashed against the pavement and eventually came to a stop on the side of the road. The driver of the van and her 6-year-old son were killed instantly.

"The husband and father is a dear friend of mine." Mike grabbed a handkerchief out of his pocket then wiped his nose. My mother was as stoic as ever. He continued, "He's also a pastor. Like many of us, he initially responded with a mixture of anger and sadness at such a tragic loss. Appropriately so.

"But then he took a different approach. Rather than lash out his frustrations and hostility on Mr. Grunwald, he chose a path of forgiveness. He successfully argued to the judge to lessen Matt's sentence. Still to this day, they meet for lunch on a weekly basis. They continue to cherish an unlikely friendship."

Mike wiped his forehead and surveyed the crowd. Nobody moved or made a sound. Silence. A calm sea. Unfortunately, that's when storms inflict the most damage.

"Would you be able to reach out with such an unlikely hand of forgiveness? Can you make a bold leap with a continuous act of love? In 1 John 1:9, it says, 'If we confess our sins, God who is faithful and just will forgive our sins and cleanse us from all unrighteousness.'

"What a great example God shows. No matter who we are, and no matter what we've done, He has and will continue to forgive us. And Jesus followed the example of His father. In Luke 23:34, Jesus said, 'Father, forgive them, for they know not what they do.'

"When Jesus spoke those words, this was not forgiveness for a random, unintentional act. These people had every desire to see Jesus dead. It was a cold-hearted, pre-meditated killing of an innocent man! Yet He forgave them."

Mike scanned the crowd again, a weak attempt at making eye contact with his audience. He appeared to be looking for someone in particular, eyes shifting side to side. He never looked at me, or at my mother.

He continued, his words softer, more calculated. "As forgiveness and mercy have been extended to us, we in turn need to extend the same to others. We have no choice."

Mike grabbed his sheets and stepped off the podium, his footsteps pounding like a bass drum. I reached behind my mom and rubbed my hand against her upper back. The gap in her shoulder shifted as she wiped her eyes.

I felt sorry for her. Why church had to be so eventful when she came was beyond me. She craved normalcy but never got it. I still didn't regret bringing her, though.

Music for the next song started. I don't recall which one, but I do remember it was booming and intense, in sharp contrast to the silence I hoped for.

I closed my eyes. My vision clouded by memories but more real than ever, stored in a steel-cased vault I never cared to open.

The date was February 6, 2000. Also a Sunday.

We attended church that day, sitting close to where my mom and I were that morning. I was fourteen and halfway through my freshman year in high school. It bugged me to sit between my parents. I felt like a little kid, and, unfortunately, I acted like one.

My parents woke me up for early service, my shower was cold, and my mom wouldn't let me wear shorts. To top it off, I had to sit between them like I was an escorted prisoner.

Could it get any worse?

After the service ended, I walked out behind them, grumbling, while they discussed the day's schedule. It was sunny and 60, not a cloud in the sky. But I didn't care. After he forced me to go home and do my homework instead of hanging out with my friends, I called my father a control freak and told him in no uncertain terms to go to hell.

Don't ask me why. Please don't. Some things just can't be explained, whether I do them or someone else does. Words are always a poor technique for resolution.

No wonder they split at the bell tower.

He walked away down Mountain Avenue in the general direction of our house, while my mom turned to the left to head to our car. I asked to join my father, but he said no. I couldn't blame him. My mother told me to come with her.

It was my fault. Why did I drive him away, right when I needed him the most? Why did I listen? I should have gone with him, but I couldn't have it both ways.

I turned one last time to watch my father, his hands in his pockets enjoying a nice walk on a sunny winter day. His shoulders out, broad yet loose. He was trying to clear his mind of all things bad and painful and uncontrolled, including me.

He looked taller, which was funny to me now. I was looking forward to passing him in height. It was only a matter of time. In fact, he would ask if I'd always look up to him, but that lost its humor years ago. I didn't have an answer then, only laughter. But now is different.

That was the last time I ever saw him, my last day of resolve and understanding. Also of peace. And that was a peaceful day only because I've compared it to every other since.

I became consumed by hatred for the drunk who killed him. I wanted more than anything to hear the guy died a nightmarish death in his cell or was scorched in the incinerator. Anything.

Revenge was sweet, if only in my dreams.

I was an old piece of wood, weathered and hearty on the outside but rotted hollow on the inside. My woodworking father would have thrown me out and replaced me with a higher quality piece. 'Can't carve something so rotten. Never be worth anything,' he would have said.

My father always said he admired my passion, my strong desire to right a wrong. I always had that, even back to third grade when half the class cheated on a math test. I despised them all. My dad was the one who had to calm me.

He also warned me. While passion was noble, make certain to direct it for good. Use it to accomplish something.

That Sunday, as I sat with my mother, I decided to do something I never thought I'd do. I would obey my father, one last time. I would direct everything for good, like an unexpected gift plopped on my lap. As Mike said, I didn't have a choice.

But what kind of gift was it? What did it expect from me: a thought, an action, or both? I knew the outcome I wanted, I just didn't know how to get there. Whatever it was, I wanted to do it right then and there. But I couldn't.

The music abruptly stopped. The singing halted.

My mom was crying, and so was I.

I finally knew what I wanted, and coincidentally, it was also what I needed.

• • •

We walked out into the foyer, the entire congregation awkwardly silent. As we approached the double doors leading outside, I noticed Peter and Harry walking not far behind their parents. Peter's mother threw on a windbreaker, surprised by the gusts that erupted across the front lawn.

"Hey, Mike. Great to see you." I shook his hand as we stood right outside the doors. "Powerful sermon."

We both watched the swallows fly out of the bush just behind the door. Their wings fluttered, drowned out by the howl of the wind.

"Thanks. Great to see you, Ellen." Mike acknowledged my mother — no handshake, just a slight bow — then nudged toward me as if sharing a secret. "Say, can we chat later today? Something has come up." His eyes shifted, looking unfocused and distracted.

"Ah, yeah. Sure." A thick breeze swirled around the inner courtyard of the church.

"I'll stop by your house later if that's okay." His eyes were red with strands of creases below. "I'll be in your neighborhood and just wanted to chat." Mike was an awful liar. Something was up.

All I could think of was the last time he came to our house, that day in February. Maybe my mom was thinking that, too. Until recently, I would not have been ready, disliking the thought of him being in my house. It was nothing against Mike.

"That would be great. Does two or three work for you? I'm meeting Grace later."

"Let's do that. I'll be there around three. It won't take too long." He scratched the bridge of his nose.

"Can I ask why?"

The father behind me picked up his young daughter, the mom glanced at her watch.

Mike rubbed the outside of his pants and twisted to see who was next in line. "We'd better wait till I come over."

"Okay…" I put my arm around my mother as we walked down the sidewalk toward the high bell tower. My mom covered her ears, expecting the noontime tolling. I was surprised she remembered.

Clang.

I dashed ahead and caught up with Peter and Harry. "Boo!" I yelled, smiling as I tapped them on their shoulders. I rubbed Harry's hair, already a complete mess. Peter looked up and smiled.

Clang.

They both turned and laughed. Their eyes gleamed, telling me so many things at once. After everything they knew, everything I told them, nothing changed. How simple I was to write them off for their youth.

Clang.

They stopped abruptly in the cold, blustery wind. As I placed my hand on Peter's shoulder, the approaching shadow startled me, a long, dark profile that could only happen in winter. The pounding of footsteps didn't surprise me.

"Get your hands off my son!"

My hands reeled back as if touching a blistering campfire. Instincts always won, not to say they were right.

My head snapped in the direction of the voice. I instantly recognized him, bulky and out of control like a semi without brakes. It was Peter's father. He was a man on a mission, determined to act, too fast to think.

"Whoa, I was patting my buddy Peter. We were just…"

"You can forget the *we* part, nor is he your buddy." He spoke through gritted teeth, words without breath or thought. "Peter, come with me."

Peter rushed by his dad's side, leaving me alone and exposed, as vulnerable as ever. His dad planted his immense hand on Peter's nape, grasping his collar and constricting his fingers around the poor boy.

"Ow! Dad, that hurts." Peter tilted his head forward, attempting to avoid what he couldn't.

"Mr. Olson, what's up, man?" I instinctively stretched out my hands. He glared but didn't respond.

They walked away, his dad marching, dragging Peter. I tried to follow, but my mom grabbed a handful of my jacket, slipping down my shoulder. I snapped my head back in a mix of confusion and anger.

A crowd formed around us. The air felt hot, the cool breeze long gone. Peter's father swiftly turned and led with a pointed finger like a compass, however wrong his sense of direction was.

"I heard what you did." His hand inches from my face. "No kid of mine is going to learn anything from a criminal like you." The veins on his neck bulged.

"Don't you think you're overreacting? I mean, c'mon, that was like four years ago."

A stiff arm came out of nowhere and brushed between us as if keeping an elevator door open.

"Calm down, Bob." Mike sounded desperate to play peacekeeper. "Let's be civilized here. We just talked about…"

"I know what you said, Pastor." Bob had the deepest, most bellowing voice. "But that tidy solution doesn't always work."

I stood off to the side, not wanting to be caught in the middle any more than I already was.

"I think you're missing the point."

"If you had done your homework and performed the proper background checks, we wouldn't be in this mess. Criminals on the left, and children on the right."

I stood to his left but found no irony.

The crowd continued to stare.

Mike exhaled, his voice airy. "I did and yes, I knew."

Peter's dad protruded his finger again, unable to respond with words, confused and flustered with too much to say and with not enough words to say it.

I sniffed and instantly recognized the scent. It smelled like a burnt match.

"Goodbye, Pastor," was all he said.

The deep crimson on his face was shockingly dark. A flame kindled inside him, his blood was boiling. Irreplaceable damage to all, including himself. It was all too familiar.

His labels and assumptions were such a copout: defining me a criminal was as bad as calling them mere children. Only someone lazy enough to be unfamiliar with both would use them.

Part of me wanted to know how he got to that point, or if he even knew where he was. Was he oblivious, blind, or just looking the wrong way?

But there was one unmistakable truth that once again reared its ugly head. An unwelcomed guest, like an illness that came out of nowhere. My life, my way too eventful life, would once again never be the same.

Chapter 28 – Shawn

November 16, 2003

The sharp ringing startled me, even though I knew it was coming. My mother sat in the chair across from me, her fingers cradling a cigarette. She took a long, deep puff, then smothered it in the ashtray. Her hand swiped the air, a feeble attempt at destroying the evidence.

I lunged forward from my chair, walked to the front door, and opened it. "Hey, Mike. Come on in." I scooted aside.

"Thank you. Great to see you, Shawn." He stepped into the hallway, shuffled his feet on the thick rug, and handed me his long black overcoat and matching hat. The hanger clanged as I hung it in the closet.

He walked around the edge of the wall and glanced into the dining room. "Ellen," Mike greeted with a nod. "Nice to see you again."

My mom approached with a vague smile, almost as if genuinely happy to see him. "It's been a while. Nice to see you, too." Her hand pointed toward the couch. "Please, have a seat."

Mike sat down and fell onto the firm middle cushion.

I was always astounded how my mother could change at the drop of a hat, as if she had a whole repertoire of personalities at her disposal, none of them particularly real.

"Would you like anything to drink?" I stood in front of my chair, not ready to get down to business just yet.

"No, thank you." He strained his neck and took an extended glance at me, measuring me up for height or weight or something that might have changed. "I'm fine."

I sat down, calmly and unhurried, disappointed he didn't request slow-brewed coffee.

"Nice of you to stop by," my mom started. "I know Sundays can be busy for you." Her arms rested on her crossed legs like a Hollywood starlet. Her deep wrinkles, saggy eyes, and questionable persona told me otherwise.

"No problem. I do find time for the important things. No matter what day." No knock on Mike, but visits from pastors weren't always good things. They only show up when trouble strikes like EMTs or hurricane relief workers.

"Thank you for the wonderful sermon this morning. It was… inspirational." Her words were crisp and calculated, twitching her nose after she spoke.

"Thanks, Ellen. I appreciate that. Unfortunately, not everyone thought so." Mike's glare bounced off the floor then up at me. "I wanted to apologize for this morning. I don't know what got into Bob. His actions were out of line. I hope it didn't bother you too much."

The entire right side of my face made a slight upward motion: my forehead, eyebrow, and mouth. "I've been called worse things in my life."

"I don't think he meant what he said."

"The heck he did! Meant every word."

"Shawn!" My mom pounced, but at least I spoke truth. I still wanted to control it, if that was even possible any more.

"I've heard it before." I turned toward her. "He meant it all: words, harm, everything." I fell into yet another boiling pot of expectations. And it burned.

My mom fidgeted with her hands. "But how did he know? That's what caught me off guard."

A startling large man threatens to break my neck, hurtles damning words at me, and what catches her off guard was that he found out?

"Peter must have told him. What I said and all."

"And what exactly did you tell them?" Her hands were restless, her eyes as blurry as her intentions.

"I told them what I did." I rubbed my shoulder. "Everything."

"Why on earth did you do that?" She glanced at Mike as if hoping he disappeared. "I thought we talked about that."

"Yeah, we talked. But we didn't agree." I fell back into my chair, restraining my anger as best I could. It's what got me into trouble, but now was different.

"Ellen, I do understand Shawn's desire for honesty with these boys. And I respect that." He again turned toward me. Yes, it was honesty. And I was getting punished for sharing it. "Peter told his father. He called me first thing Thursday morning to discuss it, and he was, well, a bit irate."

A bit irate. That's like saying someone is mildly deranged, or slightly hysterical. You either are or you aren't. There isn't much in between.

"What did he want?" my mom inquired. "To vent or start a conflict? Because we've heard it all before."

"Well, yes and no. He did want to voice his opinion, no doubt about that." Mike's peacekeeping lingo just kept coming. "But he also had reservations about things from here on out."

"What does that mean?" I couldn't figure out where he was going with this and was losing patience fast. "Does he not want me to mentor Peter anymore? I mean, c'mon, that's ridiculous."

"He did mention that as a possibility, yes."

My eyes rolled into the ceiling. I figured not everyone would accept it, but this was a nightmare I never planned for.

"Why should he care what Shawn's done in the past?" My mother was as close to yelling as I'd ever heard. "That was four years ago, Mike. A difficult time for both of us."

"Mom, let's keep this on me, okay."

"But it's true, Shawn. We handled the situation in different ways." Desperation seeped through her words, proving her point more than the words themselves.

I clenched my teeth. I tried to interject to keep her out of it, but she did it anyway. Beads of sweat collected above my lip, my neck tightened.

"We've moved on," she continued. "He made a mistake, but can you blame him? It was forgiven. I forgave him. God forgave him. You said so this morning."

My eyes rolled upward again, only this time to capture the salty tears weighted down by time. I had never heard her say that before, and frankly, never thought I would. *I forgave him.*

"I understand, Ellen, and I wholeheartedly agree. But forgiveness can also be a personal choice," Mike said. "We'd love to blanket it across everyone involved, but people process things differently. It was the first time Bob had heard about Shawn's past, and he's not willing to forgive. At least not yet."

"He never will." I mumbled. Neither reacted.

"I'm going to have a talk with that man. Doesn't he live over on Wilson by the Morrison's?"

I laughed out of sheer instinct. My mother, for all her gruffness, couldn't even confront a fly let alone swat it.

"I wouldn't suggest that, Ellen. Actually, I'd strongly discourage it. Let them process everything in their own time."

My mom slid back in her chair. Her arms draped across her body as if protecting herself from a chill in the air. She looked in need of a blanket.

"So, what happens now?" I snapped. "Where do we go from here?"

Mike moved closer to me, falling deeper into the unsupportive part of the couch. "First thing, know that I don't regret my decision for you to mentor." He looked at me, but I turned away, embarrassed it had come to this. "I've heard some great things about what you've done, and I'm sure many of the boys... and most of the parents, agree. You've been a wonderful influence on these boys who are growing into fine young men."

"That's great to say but not true. The boys rarely listened. Yeah, they like my stories, but that's what got me into trouble. Other than that, nothing."

"I wouldn't count on that."

"Yeah, well, they've now learned how to be intolerant and unforgiving." I swallowed hard, my throat tasting like charcoal. "Great lesson from the parents."

Mike didn't respond. My mom was still motionless.

I continued. "So, what now? Am I excommunicated? Thrown into the fiery pit of hell?"

Mike's brow furrowed and creased. "I think you should take a break from mentoring for a short time. A cooling off period we'll call it." He bobbled his head as if we'd already discussed it.

"The only one who needs cooling off is Peter's dad!" I shouted. My temples felt like escape valves. Mike was doing a terrible job of proving his point.

"I just don't want any more conflicts."

"Oh, so that's what this is about." My mom was suddenly re-involved. "Keeping the boat steady. Maybe we all need to confront our past a little better and rock the boat."

I winced. She didn't mean it. Then why did she say it?

Mike moved to his right, falling deeper into the couch. He sat at eye level with my mother. "So, let me ask you, Ellen." He spoke softly, almost in slow motion, but I still couldn't prevent it. I even knew what he was going to say. "Have you forgiven the driver who killed your husband?"

It was an odd feeling — the room contracted but the space between us exploded. Real yet contradictory. Space and time collided into a thunderous bang that nobody heard but everybody felt.

I was now positive contrasts could co-exist.

My mother again sat motionless, barely moving to breathe. Did she not know what to say? Had she forgotten the question? Did she turn to stone? She was either trying desperately to remember or frantically trying to forget.

She moved with the gritty determination of someone who was slapped. She stood up from her chair and walked toward Pastor Mike.

I pushed myself out of my chair and stood next to my mother, our shoulders almost touching. It was ironic that without intention or planning, we essentially formed a wall at the same time my mother was about to burn a bridge.

"It was nice to see you," she finally said. "Thanks for stopping by, and we'll see you again soon."

I never knew what response to expect from my mother. Sometimes her spoken and unspoken words became a jumbled mess that meant more than it sounded.

Mike stood up with both arms extended. "Sorry, Ellen. I just wanted to confront what was needed."

"Well, there's definitely a time and a place for everything. You've convinced me of that. Have a nice day, Mike." She motioned toward the door.

I followed Mike into the hallway, grabbed his coat and hat from the closet, and handed them to him. We both watched my mom walk into the kitchen with slow, shuffling steps, her anger somehow both intense and lethargic.

"Let's keep in touch." He finally spoke, our eyes meeting. "I'll let you know when would be the best time to come back on Wednesdays. The time will come, and it will happen soon. I'll make certain of that."

"I'm sure you will." My hand balanced against the open door. "Thanks for stopping by. Maybe we'll see you again next week."

Mike walked out the front door then down the steps that I had just shoveled that morning. I propped myself against the doorway and waved as Mike squeezed into his brown Honda Civic, then drove away. I closed the door to keep out the cold air but continued standing in the entryway, torn between honesty and forgiveness.

Why couldn't I have both?

I also agreed with my mother. There was a time and place for everything. But to me, it was now and here. I had reached a point where I could never, ever go back. What's done is done. More importantly, I realized that was an amazing thing.

I also knew that would be the last time I would ever see Pastor Mike. Not sure how I knew, but I did. While predictable in some ways, it would be for very different reasons.

Chapter 29 – Shawn

November 16, 2003

"Where'd ya like to eat tonight?" Grace asked as she drove her Jeep down Alameda, her hands draped over the steering wheel, her eyes drifting between the road and me.

"Anywhere close. I'd rather not be out too late." I yanked the zipper on my jacket back and forth, not thinking at all about food. I wasn't that hungry.

We arrived at the restaurant and parked in the back lot, finding the lone open space. She maneuvered in, and I grabbed her hand as we walked down the dimly lit alley. The off-white building was a gritty stucco with chunks missing in places, and the rusted downspouts were twisted metal snakes. We maneuvered around it all.

"I didn't think there'd be snow left." Grace pointed at the pile of dirty slush stuck on the north side of the building, doomed to last much longer than it should have.

"Not sure if this alley ever sees the light of day." I squeezed her hand. "It last snowed like two weeks ago."

The place was packed. We grabbed the last booth in the back. She grimaced and massaged her calf muscle as she slid in. "My leg's killing me."

"Got a cramp?"

"Yeah. I should mention I ran five miles this morning. Gee, I hope it's not shin splints."

"There's a cure for that... Stop running!"

"Maybe I have a low threshold of pain. I don't know."

"Then why do you run?" I started thinking of all the ways we were different.

"Hmm... Good question."

The waitress stopped by, and we ordered our food. I went with my usual while Grace tried the Patty Melt, a slobbering of everything bad for you. We took off our coats and placed them next to us. The place was drafty but warm. Grace slid off her scarf and placed it on top of her coat.

"So, how was church this morning?" She asked as if we always talked about it. We didn't.

Eventually, I was going to ask her to join me, but my fear of rejection always won. Now it was a different fear — a morning and a place I had no desire to discuss.

"Well... it's been better." My words left me, and I felt deflated. It had nothing to do with my words, however.

Her eyebrows creased inward as she wrapped her hair in her hands and threw it over her shoulder. I drank some water and placed my other hand on the table.

"Boring sermon? Depressing hymns?"

"I wish." I found nothing else to focus on, no fascinating conversations or people to latch onto. Everyone else was a peaceful bystander.

"Then what happened?" Her head swayed with the cadence of her words.

I knew I was done for. Owning my past and being honest with her went hand in hand. So I let loose. "I'm no longer allowed to mentor." I was forced to either bluff or call the bet, and I stink at bluffing.

"What? That's horrible. Why not?" Her elbows rested on the table. I angled backwards, my arms crossed.

"Well, I was honest with the kids. I told them everything that happened."

"Huh?" She pulled at her sleeves. "That makes no sense."

"It would if you knew my whole story." I stole another glance around the restaurant. Everyone looked the same: old, overweight, and oblivious to bad food.

"I thought I did know your story. Your dad died, your mom cocooned. What else is there?"

I reached for my glass of water, even though I wasn't thirsty. The water was cool, the glass sparkled. Her six-word summary of my life was surprisingly accurate, except it left out one person.

"We discussed the seventh commandment."

"I don't remember what that is." Her head was steady, her jaw tight. "I hope for your sake it's not 'do not lie' and that you're breaking it right now."

I realized we hadn't discussed that commandment yet. Although, it would be covered next week when I wouldn't be allowed to be there. Dumb luck, I guess. "Nope. Been there, done that."

"Then what is it? You're beating around the bush here, and it's driving me nuts." Her eyes penetrated my every motion. She had me.

I had to go all in. "It's 'do not steal.'"

"Go on." Her hands swirled in the air as if rotating a small crank. She was getting annoyed, and I couldn't blame her.

I took another sip of water, gauging the conversations around us. Was it mundane stuff like football or the weather? Or deep, meaningful conversations that went somewhere? Was it even possible to tell?

"I never told you, did I?"

"Told me what?"

I shifted back, settling in on the padded seat. "Well, things were tough for my mom and me after my dad died. We dealt with grief in different ways. She spent most of her time either lying on the couch or locked in her bedroom."

"Your poor mother."

"That wasn't everything, though." My hands began moving. "I was the opposite. I spent most of my time hanging out with Phil, and we either hit parties or held our own."

"How old were you again, like 14?" She knew the answer yet still sounded surprised.

"Yeah, that's right." I took a deep breath, wondering how many reasons to provide, how many excuses to give. I chose none. "So, one night, after smoking a pack."

"You never told me you smoked."

"You never asked."

"Don't patronize me! I want the truth. No secrets."

Does anyone truly like secrets? They're just disguises for truth. Hearing them puts me on the inside of something that appears good on the surface. Like the popular crowd in high school — I told everyone I didn't like them, but deep down I desperately wanted to be a part of it.

"I sure won't have any after I'm done."

"Shawn, please."

"Sorry, this is tough for me." My eye began twitching, so I rubbed it. "We ran out of cigarettes, so we needed more."

"Seriously?"

"That's what happens when you're young and stupid." I smiled, but she was not amused. "So, we stole Phil's dad's pickup, and he dropped me off at the liquor store over on Elm. Some streetlights were burned out and the parking lot was wet and muddy.

"I walked into the store, headed over to the counter, and asked for a pack of Marlboros. She was stunned I was bold enough to walk into the store." I rubbed my eye again. "That's when I threatened her with my dad's pistol."

"What?" Her eyes were on fire, and her arms shook. She zoned out everyone else in the restaurant.

There was no going back now. "I grabbed the cigs and some money then made a run for the door. She tried to run after me, but I knocked over a display rack to cut her off."

She shook her head. "You're a jerk."

"I know. I deserve it all."

"That used to mean a lot to me." Her voice shaky yet intense.

"You have every right to be mad."

"Mad? You think all I am is mad?" Her hand slapped the table, the closest replacement for my face. "So, what happened next? I hope you got caught?"

"I did. Two days later." My world was caving in, and there was nothing I could do about it. I felt six inches shorter and getting smaller by the second. "I ran out of the store, but Phil was nowhere to be found. He ditched me."

"Can't say I blame him."

The waitress stopped by to drop off our food. She looked at both of us and smiled but quickly realized she was very much alone. Grace looked away, her eyes hazy and blurred. I was disappointed when the server left.

I reached for my glass but realized it was empty. "There's actually more to the story." And Grace deserved it all, whether she wanted to hear it or not.

Why was confronting the truth so hard? All I was doing was telling a story that already existed. But either I realized deep down who I was, or I feared what would happen if others figured it out.

"You've gotta be kidding me." She wiped her eyes, her look of surprise diminished with every tear.

I told her everything I remembered about the alley, from the sights and smells that infuriated me, to my despicable actions they caused, to the dirty green dumpster that allowed me to hide them. Cars and people were nearby, but nothing was close enough to realize what I was doing. Not even me.

My actions were impulsive. I became somebody who I wasn't, punching and kicking away all my hurts and problems. He was at fault for everything, only because he was there. I became powerful, taking control of my life yet losing it in the process.

But in other ways, it was all premeditated. I was a combustible mix surrounded by too many things flammable. The only difference between a small spark and an engulfing flame was my environment, and the day after my dad's funeral in the alley were the time and place for that to happen.

Looking back on it, I wasn't surprised the smell of alcohol enraged me. I needed something to drive my actions, and I chose poorly. But accomplices are never at fault. It was me. Not my environment. Not the booze. Me. I did it.

Unfortunately, I wasn't the only one affected. I was well aware of the hurt I caused. But there was nothing else I could do except tell the truth.

"This is so past forgive and forget. Not when you've intentionally hurt me. Not when you outright lied to me."

I was surprised she was able to speak. "But I didn't lie. You have to understand."

"No, you understand! I'm not the problem here. You are." Our food sat untouched on our plates. "Both actions and words can hurt. And you are guilty of both."

"Grace, please." My open hands reached out as if asking for a blessing that never came.

It was the first time I had ever seen her cry, so deep and intimate and revealing. I wanted to tell her it would be alright, that everything would work out. But I was through with lying. The problem was what was revealed. It was now separating us faster than I ever thought possible.

She stood up as quickly as she could, knocking over her glass of Coke. She grabbed her coat and purse and ran out the door. A few people looked up, but they had no clue what they were witnessing. The little bell rang. Everyone heard it, but only I knew what it meant.

She was gone.

I closed my eyes, preventing others from watching me. But I knew. Piercing eyes always radiated heat, yet their effects were only skin-deep. Inside I felt ice-cold, like a brain freeze on a hot summer day. Unexpected yet intensely painful. Regrettably, this would last much longer.

I suddenly remembered I lived five miles away, and my feet were my only mode of transportation. I hated the idea of walking, but running sounded even worse.

The irony was thick. Running was what got me into trouble. From what, I always knew. To where, I never did.

But this time was different.

Chapter 30 – Shawn

November 16, 2003

As I stepped out of the restaurant, I realized I wasn't quite sure how to get home. Driving, I knew, but walking was different. I was stuck with no one else to blame.

Dusk had settled. The crisp air smelled of melting snow, greasy food, and wood-burning fireplaces. It was too much for my worn-out senses, so I got rid of one, throwing the leftovers into a nearby trashcan.

I waited patiently at the light, even though no cars were in sight. At least I obeyed something. I crossed the street, walking carefully along the line bordering the crosswalk. It was straight and narrow, just what I needed.

I turned the corner onto Longs Peak, right past Bein Park where I used to play soccer, or at least, run aimlessly. I was awful at it, even scoring a goal once for the opponent. But that never bothered my dad very much. His encouragements were never gauged by expectations. He was always proud of me, no matter what.

But that was then.

I realized I was near Sebastian's house. A few Wednesdays ago, back when life was normal and wonderfully boring, I had dropped him off. As I turned the corner around the cul-de-sac, his house was the third one in, guarded by a huge maple tree.

I hesitated. Was it worth another lecture, another accusation, another confrontation?

The sidewalk was uneven, displaced by the deep roots of the tree. His house was a green two-story, with a short, upward sloping driveway. The basketball hoop that hung above the garage reminded me of a 'mine is better than yours' argument he had with Peter. At that age, everything was a competition, an insult, or both.

This was creepy. Wouldn't that be icing on the cake, getting arrested for snooping outside someone's house?

"Mr. Shawn? Is that you? What are you doing here?" A familiar voice shot out of the darkness.

"Yes, it's me." I sighed. He caught me. "I was walking in the neighborhood, so thought I'd stop by." I had reached the point where I hated to lie, especially to a kid.

"Do you know how cold it is out here?"

"Yes, I do. But thanks for letting me know." I shivered, as if talking about it made it worse. Funny how that worked. "What are you doing outside on a night like this?"

"Taking out the trash. It's one of my chores, but I don't like it very much."

I laughed. "Well, it's a grand idea to leave your garbage by the curb. Get it out of the house. Pronto."

He threw the bag in the trash cart then dropped the cover, letting it bang. He stood still for a moment, silhouetted by darkness, probably staring at me. "Huh? I take it out whenever it's full."

"Never mind." I raised my chin. "Good to hear."

"Did you wanna come in?" His voice shaking.

"I wouldn't want to intrude."

"Really, it'd be okay. We were just about to eat."

My stomach growled. I needed food fast. "Well… if your parents don't mind." It wasn't the food part I was worried about.

I tentatively followed Sebastian through the garage door into a small entryway packed with a washer, dryer, and a mishmash collection of boots and shoes. Some big, some tiny, one pair with Velcro flaps and decorated with Rugrats characters. Sebastian's stories of his annoying little brother came to life.

"Mom, Dad," Sebastian called out. "Shawn's here!"

Sebastian's father bounded around the corner. I instantly recoiled like a makeshift shield. I braced for the worst.

"Shawn!" His dad bellowed, a barrel-chested man with short, brown hair and a bounding smile. "Nice to see you here. We weren't expecting you, but you're certainly welcome to come in." He had this familiar look to him as if we had met before. I couldn't place where.

"Thanks, Mr. Cook." I breathed, partially relieved. "I shouldn't stay too long. I… I need to head home at some point."

"You can call me Brad." He shook my hand with a firm grasp, his sleeves rolled up around his elbows. "Did you have dinner yet? We were just about to sit down and eat."

I shrugged my shoulders. How do I explain I ate three fries and two bites of a burger, then threw out the doggy bags over by the park? "No, I haven't eaten yet."

"Well, you're in luck. Come on in."

I dropped my shoes onto the existing mountain of footwear then stepped into the dining room where they had gathered around the table. This felt so incredibly awkward and intrusive, almost as bad as being a Peeping Tom.

"Hi Shawn! I thought I heard you were here," said Sebastian's mom as she rounded the corner to place the remaining food on the table. "Please join us. I hope you like eggs and waffles. It's our Sunday night favorite."

I should have felt fully relieved, but I didn't. "I love waffles. Sounds… comforting." I leaned against a chair and crossed my legs.

"That's great! Feel free to sit next to Sebastian's brother, Ben. He'd love to meet you."

I sensed I was being watched. I met Ben's gaze, noticing his dark blue eyes just like his brother. His hair went every direction except down, and a river of syrup already flowed down his small, curved chin.

"Did you have fun playing outside, Ben?" I eased into the chair next to him.

"I did." His smile loosened the flow as drips landed on his shirt. "How'd you know?"

"Well…" I leaned over near him, their mother watching me out of the corner of her eye. "You just took off your hat, didn't you? I used to love playing outside… way back when I was a kid."

My dad and I threw more snowballs at each other than anyone in Colorado. I swear, whenever there was any snow on the ground and no matter where we were headed, he'd bend over to scoop up and form a launchable pack of slush. It'd fearlessly fly toward me, always hitting me on my chest or legs or some place harmless. That started it. My scoops were smaller, my actions slower, and my aim worse. But I still loved it. Even better were the hunts for the last surviving pile of snow kept hidden by summer shadows. It could sometimes take many curvy mountain roads to find it. We were always up for an adventure, with excitement defined by the act itself.

"Why don't you now?" His voice soft and nasally.

I chuckled at his simplicity. But he was right. *Why didn't I?* "I don't know. I guess I should play outside more often."

"You should. It's fun!"

Waffles flew off the griddle and landed on our plates, their aroma mesmerizing. Brad ran in and out of the dining room, tending to the griddle and reaching over to grab a bite or two off his plate when he could.

After everyone had one, he finally sat down at the table. He looked at me, just as I stuffed a huge bite into my mouth. "I wanted to bring up this morning, Shawn." He paused. I froze. "I'm sorry that happened. Bob was way out of line. He can be that way sometimes, so try not to take it personally."

I chewed my bite. It needed more syrup.

"I'm sorry, too," added Sebastian's mom. "Just know that we support you through it all. We've already said a prayer for you and will continue to. Isn't that right, Sebastian?"

Sebastian nodded, his face red, staring at his plate. The kid was stuck. Not just between his parents and me, that was nothing compared to what he witnessed that morning. Collisions always cause destruction, but now he had to choose a side. That's not right for a kid.

"Thanks for your support. I appreciate it," I finally responded, my bite mostly eaten. "But don't you care about what I did? I mean, I did some... regrettable things." The understatement of the year. It was awful. Painful. Almost unforgivable.

"Shawn, if we waited for the perfect person to come along and mentor our son, we'd be waiting a long time." She placed her hand on Sebastian's head then dropped to rub his neck. "Do you think we expect our boys to be perfect?" She paused, but I didn't answer. "Of course not. So, maybe they can learn from someone who's real, like them only older. I also don't want to be paralyzed by unforgiveness. Sometimes, it's best to move on."

She was crazy. They both were. You don't just let a murderer hang out with your kid. I considered standing up and yelling at them, setting them straight. How dare they have me hang out with their son? I didn't deserve the chance.

But I didn't stand up and I didn't yell. Even I didn't know who I was anymore. Within the span of seven hours, I had been called a worthless criminal and a supportive role model. Whom should I believe?

Brad watched his wife then turned to look at me. He grinned, almost laughing. "I'm surprised you don't recognize us, Shawn. We've been at the church a long time and helped a lot with youth events. Believe me, we've followed your story. I just figured we'd never see you again."

I can't believe I hadn't figured it out before. He suddenly looked like an older, paunchier version of one of the parents I used to know. He ran games at youth nights, served food at lock-ins, and basically volunteered in ways that others forgot. And Sebastian was just a kid, his brother, a baby.

Perhaps I should have done more trying to remember than struggling to forget.

I was at a loss for words. What could I say? I ate instead. Waffles were fresh off the griddle and smothered with maple syrup. All heaped onto my plate, completely satisfying yet wholly undeserved.

But while my mouth and stomach enjoyed, my mind did not. It was preoccupied with the one person in my life who understood and accepted me, yet I did my best to prevent exactly that.

I should have mentioned it all sooner, but the way it came out was even worse. Of course, changing my story was completely out of the question. I struck out on timing, delivery, and content.

It was all so perfect, so real. But was it honest? I smothered it with my truth, suffocating our relationship.

Why? Because I had to. I was a slave to my own inaction, and it was about time I did something about it.

Chapter 31 – Grace

November 16, 2003

I drove home faster than I ever had in my life, swerving at every corner, with limited control of my movements let alone the vehicle's. My eyes burned, and it ached to keep them open. Everything I tried to focus on was undefined and blurry, including the road. Driving was a terrible thing for me to be doing, but I had to get away.

The hurt in my belly was unlike anything I'd ever experienced. But then again, I had never been that close to anyone before. I trusted him, from my inner thoughts and desires to everything there was to know about me.

Of course, that changed in the blink of an eye. Or the telling of a story. My life had somehow transformed from this wonderful thing to an utter and total mess.

I banged on the steering wheel, furious at him. Not only did he do something awful, but he lied about it. He didn't tell me. Lie by omission was still a lie.

It came down to trust. Pure and simple. Did he not trust me to withhold something that important? Could I ever trust him again? Trust was a medal of honor, earned with respect and not handed out to just anyone.

I stopped at the light, slamming my brakes. The tires squealed as I fell back into the seat, my head purposely banging against the headrest.

He was too ashamed to tell me what he did, and that's a deep trait that doesn't change overnight. If we were going to continue, something was going to have to change, and it better be him.

I knew it was too perfect. Princes don't ride white horse!

I pulled into my driveway, ran to my room, and slammed the door. I fell on my bed, covering my face for protection against everything I knew.

How had it come to this? I didn't know who he was anymore. But then again, that was the point. I didn't.

I tightly wrapped the blanket around me, soft cotton with silky edges, and gazed at the glow-in-the-dark stars I had placed on the ceiling a long time ago. I'd stare into the night sky, wishing for love and friendships and happiness, all bursting with possibilities and limitless potential. But the stars weren't real, nor were their promises. As I lay there, I spotted three moons and countless Saturns. A parallel universe.

I closed my eyes. So many thoughts, so many questions. My head ached, the down pillow providing no comfort whatsoever. I thought of him, of life, of everything.

My mind softened and flowed.

Random noises.

Children laughing and spinning.

A rickety, old merry-go-round going around and around, ready to disintegrate any second into a pile of rubble. How did they not know?

They held on tight. Giggling.

I stood nearby and watched, shaking my head at their willingness to believe and trust in something they shouldn't.

But then it stopped.

I was all alone. And no one heard my muted cries.

• • •

My eyes opened slowly. They burned, dry and irritated. I had no idea what time it was, nor what day. My only hope was that I had left the day behind and traveled to some place far away, or at least tomorrow.

The alarm clock read 8:35. I blinked hard and rubbed my eyes, hoping it would change. But it didn't. Then I noticed the glare of the PM light. I hated that light.

I stood up, calves still aching from my run, and headed to the living room.

My brother hadn't moved an inch on the couch. "Where's mom and dad?"

He glanced up from whatever mindless show he was watching. "Uh, you don't look so hot."

"Where are our parents?"

"On a date. They went to...."

I ignored the rest, slipping into my shoes and dashing out to my car. Streetlights provided the only definition in the harsh darkness, shining off the road, revealing depth where there wasn't any. I sat motionless in the driver's seat, wondering what to do, where to go, whom to see. It needed to be someone who would understand not just Shawn but also his past, someone who would listen to all my grievances.

I suddenly realized who to talk to, and I had just seen him that morning.

•   •   •

I pulled into the driveway, hoping it was the right place. It had been a while since Shawn pointed it out, but I remembered, figuring it would come in handy someday. However, I assumed it would be under very different circumstances.

The snow crunched under my feet as I cut across the lawn. The walking path to my left looked clean and shoveled, but I didn't take it.

The doorbell clanked loudly, announcing my arrival like at a diner, which only added to my frustration. The door opened slowly, as if I had just disturbed his peaceful evening. Pastor Mike stared at me, looking as confused as I felt.

"Hi, I'm Grace, Shawn Stevens' girlfriend." I stood completely still, unsure what else to say, and annoyed by my self-inflicted title.

Mike's eyes twinkled as if expecting to see me. "Yes, I noticed you this morning. You sat towards the back. I always scan the crowd for visitors, even on a day like today." He sighed. "Please, come in. Can I take your coat?"

"No thanks. I won't be long." I stepped in, walking past an old-fashioned, wooden coat rack covered with a black top hat and matching overcoat. I wrapped mine tighter, wishing I had worn something heavier.

"Let's sit over here." He pointed to the living room past a waist-high bookshelf. The shaggy blue carpet was old and matted, and the shelves were packed with books. We sat on light blue recliners with a rounded end table between us. I brushed the wetness off my coat.

He broke the silence. "Did Shawn know you were at church this morning? I noticed you sat on opposite sides."

His face was noticeably harsher up close. A weak smile framed the wrinkles around his eyes, his cheeks veined and rutted.

"No, he didn't." I slouched my shoulders, feeling timid at my admission. "And I slipped out right before the end, so he wouldn't see me."

He lost his smile. "You definitely missed a lot after the service. Probably for the better."

I was too afraid to ask what he meant. "I could only imagine." But I tried hard not to. "Yeah, Shawn mentioned church a few times but never got around to inviting me. My family hasn't attended in a long time."

"Well, I'm glad you came. We would have never met, otherwise." His hand reached out as if intending to pat me on the back. "So, what else do I owe this pleasure?" His lips thinned, and his chin jutted out.

I always wondered what a confessional would feel like, where dark secrets were met with feigned interest. "It's not a pleasure, really." *How do I tell him? What do I say?* "Shawn and I had dinner a few hours ago, although it seems like weeks. In some ways, I wish it were."

My head swirled, and my body ached. I didn't know Mike at all, but he topped my list of people to talk to about Shawn only because there was no one else on it.

"He told you what happened, I take it?"

"I guess so… He told me what happened four years ago."

"Ah yes. That seems to be the hot topic as of late." He took in a deep breath. "So, what was your reaction?"

"I was furious!" My cheeks singed, heated from the inside out. "It wasn't just the fact that he did it, although that was awful, too. It was more that he didn't tell me."

"Sounds like he did tell you." His voice of reason was intended to be reassuring. It wasn't.

"Well, yeah, but not right away." My hands folded around each other. "He should have told me way earlier. I mean, don't you think I should know my boyfriend's criminal record?"

"And what would you have done then?" He paused and motioned toward the kitchen. "By the way, do you want anything to drink: ice water, soda, coffee?"

Both his questions threw me off. This guy was less of a walkover than I thought he'd be.

"No… no thanks. I'm fine." I shook my head, almost forgetting what we were discussing. But how could I? "It wouldn't have made me happy back then, either. It's more a matter of trust. He doesn't trust me with his past, and he withholds parts to please me. I was shocked."

"Shocked that he did it or shocked that he told you?"

I shifted my legs to get more comfortable, but it was hopeless. This conversation was making me dizzy. "Well, both. I mean, neither. I don't know. I just…"

I was even more of a mess than when I arrived. My hands braced against the chair, pushing upward as if convincing myself to leave. I knew this was a bad idea.

His arm balanced on the armrest, his hand reaching outward. "I'm assuming Shawn also told you about his father, about what happened."

"Yeah, of course he did." My head shook. "But I don't get why that matters."

"Did he mention his father died five days before the incident?"

"Well, no. He did say it was right around the same time." I didn't feel like I knew Shawn anymore, as if he was a passerby at Union Station and everybody around us was running to catch his or her train.

"Did he mention his father's funeral was the day before?"

"No, he didn't." I shifted again. Now I totally felt like an idiot. "But… he killed a man! I can't even tell you how awful that makes me feel." My whole body shuddered, the room was cold and drafty. I wrapped my coat even tighter.

Mike uncrossed his legs, his forearms rested on his thighs. The recliner creaked like the door of an antique. "Grace, I'm sorry you had to hear his story, and I'm sorry he didn't tell you earlier. But let me tell you something I've learned over the years." He wiped his mouth with an opened hand. "I speak with various people with different backgrounds, different stories, and different hurts and hang-ups.

"One thing I've learned is to put myself in the place of others. How would I react if I were in their shoes? Is there a reason why they act and say what they do? Is there a backstory I should consider?

"I truly believe there are reasons for everything. Not excuses, but reasons. Whether it be something we learned from an experience — good or bad — or the reason for that experience in the first place. But that requires an open mind, open to those experiences but also open to how and why people do what they do."

He paused for a long time, his words digging into me like a dagger, twisting and shredding my insides. But I didn't bleed. Anguish and uncertainty flowed instead.

"Grace, I would encourage you to be open to what God is trying to tell you. When I got a speeding ticket a few years ago, I realized I needed to learn patience — a costly lesson." He chuckled softly but abruptly stopped. "Consider not just how Shawn can grow but also how you can grow, too. Yes, Shawn did a terrible thing. But we must learn to march past that."

My cheeks felt slapped by the hand of someone I barely knew but trusted. I cleared the dampness from my eyes then wiped the underside of my nose. "Thank you. I… I just don't know what to do."

"Well, I've laid a lot on you. And so has Shawn. I would suggest you think about who he is and why he did what he did. We all need forgiveness."

"I know that." I sniffed then grabbed a Kleenex from the dispenser on the end table. I dabbed my nose.

"I guess we're all familiar with that whether we like it or not." Mike inclined back in his chair and blinked slowly to reset his eyes.

"But aren't there some things that are just so far beyond forgivable, that we shouldn't ignore?"

He glanced at the ceiling then at me. "We need to forgive anything that God forgives. Lucky for us, that includes everything." He reached back and rubbed his neck. "By the way, I'm sure Shawn loves you very much."

I brushed my cheek, unsure of what to believe any more. "If only I knew what to do with that."

"Well, you can begin by telling him how you feel." He stared, but I looked away, my feet shuffling on the carpet.

My eyes drifted from him to the floor to the table. I stood up, not knowing what else to do. The air felt damp, as if a thunderstorm had passed. My basic actions were no longer automatic, like breathing and blinking and moving my legs.

"It was nice to meet you, Grace," he said. "Keep warm out there."

It was all a daze. I don't remember if he stood up to say goodbye or folded open the newspaper and shooed me out.

I sat in my car, unsure how I got there or where to go. I left his driveway and made a sharp right onto Pierce but couldn't see far enough ahead to navigate. I wiped my eyes, only making matters worse. I didn't even know what lane I was in.

I had to stop. I pulled over into the nearby park and hit the brakes in the empty lot. My car spun but with more control than the rest of me. It finally stopped. My face fell into my hands, and my forehead landed on the top of the steering wheel.

My head hurt. Everything hurt.

I was suddenly aware of a deep-down nausea in my belly. My life was no longer normal, even though I'd lost track of the definition. So much had happened in so little time, no wonder I needed to stop.

But there was so much I didn't know — how to learn from the past, why I was stuck in my present, and what possessed the future. All three were cruel choices.

My car door flew open as I couldn't ignore the hurt any longer. I ran to the nearest light post, placed my uncovered hand on the frosty pole, and lost everything I had eaten that day. I wiped my mouth on my sleeve, still leaning forward as the nausea remained. Any trace of dignity remained with yesterday.

It had been years since I had done that. I hated it but remembered it, too. I was helpless with no foreseeable control of anything around me.

I closed my eyes, not wanting to see the stained snow nor anything else. I wiped my pale face and swept back my hair. I knew I looked pathetic but felt even worse. Too many thoughts to ponder, too many decisions to confront.

I trusted, and he failed. Miserably.

Maybe Pastor Mike was right. I was too harsh. I should view things from Shawn's perspective, consider why he did what he did, then give him a second chance. But that would require a cup of forgiveness laced with insanity, burning my mouth if I drank.

I opened my eyes. My entire body shivered. But it was from much more than cold air. Right there, in that unfortunate, compromising position, I realized what I did next had my life and someone else's dependent on it.

Chapter 32 – Aidan

Knock. Knock.

I was surprised it took her so long. Normally, my mother would pounce on me for anything I said or did. But this was different. Knowing her, she paced back and forth in the kitchen, scratching her head, wondering what in the world to do about her son.

I rolled over onto my back and propped my hands behind me. My shirt slid up, so I pulled it down to cover my stomach. I felt empty. The comforter was soft but not enough to protect me from my stiff, old mattress.

Knock. Knock.

"Aidan? Are you awake?"

I closed my eyes and tried hard to disappear. Poof. I vanished. My bed disintegrated and took me with it. The earth opened and swallowed me into a deep sinkhole. An alien spaceship offered me a once-in-a-lifetime opportunity at a different life.

But nothing happened. Her voice hung in the air, her shadow never moved, both sneaking into my room through the gap under the door.

"Aidan?"

"Yeah." I moaned.

"Can I come in, honey? I'd like to talk about this." Silence. "I also have another letter you might want to read."

It was my fault. I brought it on myself when I asked to read the stupid letters. I rushed it. *It was her fault.* Who knew she kept other things like police reports and secrets? I didn't understand her at all. *It was my dad's fault.* Whoever or whatever he was, he wasn't who I thought.

"Yeah… come in." My mouth tasted dry and rutted like a worn bike tire, my mind spinning for a purpose, a meaning, an answer. *Why me?* I couldn't shake any of it, including getting rid of her. She was more stubborn than I was.

The door eased open as she peered around it with the creepiest of mom smiles. My body shook. She leaned down to pick up the homework papers then placed the makeshift pile on my desk. Disappointment was plastered on her face. She walked over to my bed — tiptoeing across the poster remnants — her hand clutching some papers.

"Mind if I sit down?" She pointed to the end of my bed.

"Hmm…" *Could I even say no?*

When she sat down, the rest of the bed elevated slightly. I shifted my legs to avoid touching her, my hands still propped behind me. I felt more exposed than ever but couldn't find the energy to move.

"I'm sorry I didn't tell you earlier. I really am." She sighed. "But you have to understand, you weren't ready. Your father did some unfortunate things in his short life, and they're difficult to talk about."

"For who? You?"

"Yes, for me."

"Don't you think I'd wanna know?"

"Of course. That's why I requested the letters… and kept the reports." She reached over and rubbed my lower leg, then tapped it three times with her words. "So you'd know."

I felt a deep coldness inside me, hoping a shiver would help it escape. But it never came. Her eyes were fiery red, her cheeks blushed and warm.

We were opposites. No doubt.

She glanced over and noticed my duffel bag packed full of stuff that mattered more an hour ago. It lay lifeless against my closet door, another victim of my anger. I found the courage to heave it across the room when I realized I didn't have the courage to leave.

Her shoulders raised as she glanced between me and the bag. It was crammed full of clothes, now resembling a big, rounded pillow. She clearly wanted to ask why I packed it. But she didn't.

I sat up and crossed my legs, my shoulders hunched. "What's that?" I pointed to the papers in her hand, three of them grasped between her thumb and fingers, resting against her leg. One looked to be ripped out of a notebook.

She held them up then dropped them on her lap. "Two more letters, and another report." She leafed through the papers and picked out the one she was looking for. "Read this one. It might help explain more about your father."

I snatched it out of her hand, scrunching loudly as if I had balled it up to throw it. Did I really want to read another letter? I figured it couldn't get any worse.

• • •

Dear Aidan,

Your mother suggested I write you a letter. Why she trusted me, I have no idea. But I realized I do have some things to tell you, some random spouts of wisdom that only yours truly could offer.

First off, know that I'd give you the world if I could, or another place if you prefer. You've grown up to be a strapping young boy. You're attentive, passionate, and darn good-looking. And you're just like your father, which brings me tears of both joy and sadness.

God never gives us anything He knows we can't handle. I just wish He didn't think so highly of me. Losing my husband and my only child forced me to question everything. But I trust in His plan, whatever that may be.

It wasn't always like that. I felt abandoned when so many bad things happened and judged that I didn't stop them. I was both a neglected widow and a powerless mother. I checked out because checking in hurt too much. And I blamed too many people for my mess, including Shawn.

But he persevered. He taught me the courage to confront my demons, as he confronted his own.

Part of his struggles were his own doing. What he did still gives me nightmares. Where did I go wrong? As a parent, I have to ask that, and I do every day of my life. I wasn't much support for him, but he still didn't have to do what he did. I've tried to get my head around why.

I had always attributed it to misguided passion, or screaming for attention, but it was more than that. Those are solvable.

It was a deep-down responsibility for what happened to his father. He always thought it was his fault, as if somehow, he caused it. He also wondered if there was some way he could have prevented it. It was an awful case of survivor's guilt driven by an unwillingness to forgive himself.

He carried more than he could handle. Guilt was a heavy burden, his ultimate enemy and downfall. He took huge steps to make it better, but I'm not sure it entirely went away. Getting someone else involved only lessened the pain. To him, it was worth a try.

If I learned anything from your father, it's to have the audacity to be honest with myself, and with others. I have resolved many things with God and His church. Pastor Mike has been a source of comfort in my darkness. I still struggle with much, but at least I'm on the road to healing paved with honesty.

My encouragement for you is to be candid and sincere in all aspects of your life. Trust yourself and the people around you. Be there for your mother. Encourage her to tell you about your father. Shawn had his flaws and drove me nuts now and then, but we must remember him for who he was.

I love you with all my heart. You are a special boy who has a very special life ahead of him. Go forward with all the love and support needed to be whatever you want to be.

Love,

Grandma Stevens

•   •   •

My mom walked to my bedroom window, placed her hand on her hip, and glared outside at our neighbor's garden, at least what was left of it. The plants and flowers had died with the coming winter. Only brown stalks remained. But she stared for a while, never moving, as if seeing much more.

I dropped the letter on the floor. "Mom? What does audacity mean? And why did Dad have demons?"

She twisted her head back. "It's courage to confront what you need to. Your father learned how to do it, possibly because he had so much to confront."

"Like what?"

She reached up and outlined the frame of the window. Her fingers moved slowly as if expecting splinters along the way. But there were none. She rubbed faster, sliding back and forth along the side, her entire hand now touching it.

"Everything that he did as well as everything he thought."

Considering the age of this rickety, old house, that window had leaked buckets over time. The frame was too damp to be cracked or splintered.

"Was it his fault?"

She turned to stare at me, her eyes full of emptiness. "Was what his fault?"

"The death of his father. Grandma said he thought so." I held up the letter in my hand.

"No, it wasn't. And that's what he needed to confront."

I stretched out my legs. "How did he die?"

"You mean Grandpa? We talked about that earlier."

"No, no. Dad. You said it was sorta similar to Grandpa."

She wiped her eyes and closed the curtain on the window. Darkness rushed in. She walked back to my bed, glanced down at the remaining sheets of paper, and pointed like a teacher noticing my unfinished assignment. "That's the next one."

Chapter 33 – Grace

November 16, 2003

I dashed into the corner store, knowing exactly what I needed but no clue where to find it. Aisles flew past, item after item: toilet paper, potato chips, toothbrushes. My eyes drifted back and forth, up and down. Dizzying. The cashier and security camera glared at me. My anxiety intensified.

There it sat, next to the tampons, yeast infection gel, and K-Y jelly. I grabbed one and darted to the counter. The item swung back and forth, hitting the side of its packaging in rhythm with my steps. My hand shook as I handed it to the attendant with little control of my actions. I said nothing. I was nervous, embarrassed, and downright terrified.

I paid for it, barely looking up at the checkout lady. I didn't want to know what she'd say, let alone the smirk or scolding she'd give me. 'Aren't you a little young?'

I cared what she thought only because I tried so hard not to. She had no idea what I'd been through, what I'd endured. She could judge me all she wanted.

I sped home thinking about Shawn, about me, about us, unsure if the last part even existed. My hands gripped the wheel, the only part of me paying attention. My misty eyes distorted my view ahead even more than it already was. Luckily, the roads were clear.

I pulled into my driveway, parked the car, and headed straight to the bathroom. My hands trembled as I unpacked it, fumbling in my hands, my fingers intertwined into a garbled mess. Clink. It fell into the sink. I wiped under my eyes then rested my forehead on my hands. My deep breath felt like my last.

I attempted to read the directions but could hardly see them. Why'd they make the text so small? And this was to be read by an out-of-her-mind, vulnerable woman during the most life-altering moment of her life?

I threw the box on the floor.

I pee, and I'm done. Simple and foolproof, right?

I quickly did it, placed the stick on the counter, then slumped on the floor. My hands sweated, my heart pounded, my mind raced. I couldn't sit or walk or do anything, but I had to do something.

So I thought.

I thought about Shawn.

He stood before me, his legs taut, his muscular arms extended out. Distinct, handsome features carved his face like a Roman soldier. He was strong and loyal yet exposed for all he was. His deep eyes told me who he really was: a man who carried a sword by day and a boy who carried only himself by night.

Disheveled hair, smirky grin. His thin, wiry frame overwhelmed by his armor that clearly didn't fit. The army marched past and trampled him. His life hung on by a measly thread. It had spiraled before, and history was cruelly repetitive.

What would this all mean for my future, for his? How would Shawn react? Would he stand up like a man and take responsibility? Or would he run away like a little boy, deserting me and his child?

What would my parents say? Would they support me or kick me out on the street? They've always been there for me, but this was different. This was unprecedented.

My mom and I always had late night rap sessions, talking about school, boys, and everything else that seemingly mattered. Mugs in hand, legs crossed on the couch. How would that happen now? 'Teach me quick how to change a diaper because it's bedtime for the little one.' Basically, it wouldn't happen.

The longest five minutes of my life.

I stood up, slowly and painfully, my body aching as if I had just gone for another run. But this was much more. Legs, head, and heart, all wounded and hurting, hemorrhaging a mix of blood and loneliness.

The moment of truth.

I picked it up and held it tightly in my hand. I stared at it but didn't believe what I saw. Why was I surprised? It turned out exactly the way I thought it would.

My emotions stunned me. At first, I laughed. What else could I do? I was a modern-day Sarah, surprised and shocked, laughing at the absurdity of it all. But at least Sarah and Abraham desired what they got.

Or maybe I did. I didn't know.

What else was I supposed to think?

The test was faulty.

I'd raise the child on my own and get shaming looks in every gas station, every church, every restaurant I went.

I'd give the baby up for adoption, only to gaze at every child 19 years younger than me and wonder if maybe, just maybe that was my future walking away from me.

I couldn't do it. I just couldn't.

My head shifted back and forth like a rudderless boat. My body swayed in a clockwise fashion, but my head spun even faster. In the mirror, everything was still, but nothing was peaceful.

I fell onto the floor. My head landed in my hands, and the grief flowed harder than ever.

Ironically, I felt like a little kid — that helpless age where I thought I could do it all on my own, only to realize that was far from the truth.

Chapter 34 – Shawn

November 18, 2003

Cars and trucks flew by with a haunting consistency. Puffs of smoke trailed behind each, swirling in the backdraft. Continuous yet unpredictable noises. Some slowed when they saw me, acknowledging with a head nod or just a glance. But most zoomed on past, hardly knowing I was there. They certainly didn't know the significance of where I was. Not many did.

That was okay with me. I hoped to observe more than be watched. I hoped to be alone, but that couldn't happen. Not there.

I was deciding what from my life was worth saving. Everything was up for grabs. Everything.

That's what happens when you bet it all. And lose big.

Footsteps approached in the slush. I didn't look up.

"What are you doing here, Shawn?"

Was it the *doing* or the *here* part that surprised her? Sitting near a curb watching cars race by wasn't something I normally did. Come to think of it, Grace didn't even know what *here* meant. But I figured she'd find me eventually.

I wiped a tear from my eye, brushing my cheek, hoping it wasn't as blotchy and inflamed as it felt. "Just thinking."

I was never one who took time to think. The concept made no sense to me, as if thinking was something to schedule. But I did go to think, and that was the only thing I was doing.

Grace tapped me on my shoulder. "Are you okay?"

"Compared to what?" I continued looking ahead, my legs extended out onto the sidewalk, my hands straddled behind me for balance. My entire body shivered.

I didn't expect an answer, nor did I want one.

I figured she hated me.

She sat down next to me, wrapping her arms loosely around her legs. The ground was soggy and damp, but she apparently cared as little as I did. "I stopped by your house, hoping to find you. I did get to meet your wonderful mother. She suggested I'd find you here." Grace stroked her hair. "She seems... nice."

I laughed. "Yeah. Nice and loony." My jeans were dirty around the knee with too many holes and rips to count.

She didn't react to my comment, nor should she. My mom could put on a good show, especially for someone she didn't know. You had to spend a lot of time with her to find out who she truly was.

"Sorry I didn't get a chance to introduce you. I'm awful at that." I scratched my head. "Add that to an ever-growing list."

Cars streamed by. Some fast, some slow. Only a few drivers were laser focused on the road, but most were distracted by eating, drinking, or toying with the radio. The beverages looked harmless: water, soda, Slurpees. It was the people I worried about.

"I'm sorry, Shawn," she whispered.

For what? For being informed her boyfriend was a criminal? For listening to a story she didn't want to hear? For meeting me?

I should have been the one who was sorry. She was swept up in my life, with very little to grab onto for anchor or support. She was the innocent bystander who didn't see any of it coming, not that there was any way she could have. Life was always unexpected and trying to guess it was just a losing man's game.

"I'm sorry, too." Sorry I stole cigarettes, sorry I stole a life, and sorry I stole the false sense of peace she had from not knowing. I was also sorry I didn't tell her sooner. But it was all kick-started by revenge on my dreadful existence, which I would never be sorry for.

Cars passed in front of us in such a blur, I couldn't tell how many and which direction anymore. Grace was the opposite, sitting perfectly still, considering which direction of many to take. I couldn't blame her.

Then, she unleashed.

"How dare you, Shawn! How dare you throw a story like that at me without any warning." Her finger stuck in my face. "Infuriating. That's what you are. That's what you did... and what you didn't do." She shook her head. "You should have told me."

The slap across my left cheek didn't hurt as much as I thought it would. But I held it anyway, grasping the pain I deserved.

"I said I was sorry."

"You don't get it, do you?"

"Get what?" Of course, I only further proved her point. What more was I supposed to say or do? I didn't understand the process. I really didn't.

She sighed, her tongue clicking. "I don't even know you anymore. Who are you, Shawn? Someone who loves and supports, or this raging madman who murders in cold blood? How can I trust you?"

The cars thudded and splashed when they hit the pothole to our right. We missed the spray, but the noise startled me. Every time. I pulled in my legs, buffering against my chest, my arms grasping them like pillars.

Vehicles traveled over the faded stripes of the crosswalk as if they weren't even there. No one even noticed.

"Did you know my father died right over there?" I pointed with my entire hand. "The car struck him, and he landed over there." I barely pointed further, more of a wave. She'd get the idea. It wasn't the direction that mattered.

She stared at the road, following my lead. More cars, more thud, more blur and splash. "How did you and your mom find out?"

I tilted my head, keeping everything else except memories intact. "The police called our house. I... I remember my mom screaming, this all-out, blood-curdling shriek. The last trace of emotion escaped her. After that, she became pretty stoic. I kinda lost both my parents that day."

"What about you?"

I shook. My mind drifted across the last four years, thinking of people and places and words. I wiped my eyes, my lids feeling warm. Of all the conversations I had, of all the deliberate things people said to comfort or blame, no one ever asked: *what about me?*

"A mix: sad, mad, confused. How else was a 14-year-old boy supposed to process the death of his father?"

"Who were you mad at?"

"Everyone. I had to blame someone, so I figured I'd make it easy."

"But it's never easy."

We both stopped and listened to the birds in the nearby tree. A few sang in harmony. Most sang on their own. The fullness of it all was beautiful, yet so poignant and real.

"I feel like I'm compared against the life I could have led. Or at least blamed for not leading it." Random thoughts swirled in my head. "Like there's this alternate reality some place where I'm fishing with my dad or hiking in the mountains or just sitting on a park bench talking. We're smiling and laughing and utterly enjoying life. But, of course, that's not actually me. And somewhere along the way, I chose incorrectly."

Her eyes darted between the smoothness and blemishes and stubble that defined my face. "Do you feel guilty?"

My hands fell off my legs and my eyes burned, toward her and her question. "What does that mean?"

Her arms wrapped tighter around her legs. "Sorry, I'm not implying anything. I just wondered if maybe… maybe you asked 'Why him?' Or maybe there was something you could have said or done."

Her words were coated with the guilt she assumed I had. She had already made up her mind.

"What was I supposed to do? I couldn't stop him. I couldn't have prevented it. There's no way! How was I supposed to know?" My voice cracked. She was losing me. I had already lost myself.

She scratched her head, waiting for me to listen again. It took a while. Then she said, "I love you. I'm sorry. I forgive."

"Huh?" I looked at her for the first time since she arrived. Her eyes were droopy, her face sunken and harsh. I wasn't the only one who had been crying. We had more in common than I thought.

"That's what you should have said."

I smiled. A damp, teary smile. Her words rang familiar like a bell tower. I had heard them before from people I didn't like. But I remembered them anyway, engrained in me forever.

"That assumes I knew he was going to die. But you see, I didn't. You never know." I rubbed my cheek with my fist.

"Then I guess you have to say it all the time."

I laughed. I didn't know why, but I did. "Ok then. Past forgotten. What am I supposed to do now?"

"Forgive. Your father, the driver, yourself."

I opened my mouth, but nothing came out. The road suddenly became empty. No cars, no people, only us.

She was right, even if she got the order wrong.

She stared at the lettering on my shirt, unreadable as it shifted in the gusty wind. "You shocked me, Shawn. And what you did was appalling. It was way too much for me to handle, so I left. I wasn't sure I wanted to see you again. But we share so much, I just… I had to find you." She reached for my hand then patted it.

"That you did."

She found me alright, but that didn't mean I wasn't lost.

After a long pause, she said, "I forgive you."

Just like that, I guess. Words, feelings, actions. Some kind of combination. Pre-meditated yet quick. Simple yet complex. My life was an intricate blur, but I'd take it for what it was.

Again, I considered standing up and yelling at her. How dare she allow a cold-blooded murderer to sit next to her, to touch her hand, to kiss her. She had obviously lost her mind.

But I didn't stand up, and I didn't yell.

"I love you."

"I love you, too."

"I want to know everything about you, Shawn."

"Warts and all?" My hand shifted on top of hers.

"Of course."

I was embarrassed as if I said something wrong. My words were muffled and incomplete as if I stood in a chamber of rushing air, drowned out by my surroundings.

Unfulfilled. That was how I felt.

Grace, on the other hand, looked into my eyes. She bent forward and kissed me on my cheek. Her hand reached out and caressed a lock of hair that had fallen over my forehead, then she scratched my back with short, quick swirls. Her legs stretched out in front of us.

Deep down, I felt ashamed, as if someone had handed me a bow-topped gift, and I forgot to get anything in return. An awful feeling. I hated receiving solely because I couldn't give.

And I was terrible at solving difficult problems. Maybe it required too much patience which I didn't have. Or maybe I just didn't want to put the effort into doing it. But as a start, I figured I'd focus on the outcome, then eventually decipher the steps to get there.

"I have something to tell you, Shawn." She leaned in again, her lips almost kissing my ear.

It didn't take long, but she told me everything she knew about us, about our future. I listened closely, then smiled, wiping the last remaining tear from my eye.

I couldn't believe it. I was going to be a dad, a role I never planned for but cherished, nonetheless. My shame instantly disappeared, replaced with thrills and fears of the unknown. My heart jumped then sank into my chest like a rock.

I didn't know how to feel or what to say. How could I? It was all new to me. I looked at Grace then awkwardly glanced at her stomach. She stared at me, but neither of us said another word for a long time.

I couldn't wait to meet this child, to tell him or her all my hopes and dreams for them, for me, for us. I wanted to take them places they never thought of going and tell them things they never thought they'd hear. I wanted to introduce them to the world, yet keep them for myself. And saving the best for them, I wanted to teach them how to thrive.

Of course, that wasn't possible. At least not yet. If only my life could fast forward to how and where I wanted it to be. But that required patience. I had a few loose ends to tie before I could.

That's when I looked ahead, while at the same time looking back. I had to to learn. A few times in my life, I mistakenly foresaw my future as being certain and well-defined. But it wasn't. Not at all. I only fooled myself into thinking I could predict it.

I figured what I knew or thought mattered. That was my mistake. Turns out, I focused on the wrong thing. It was more a question of who not what that defined it all. That's what really mattered.

Chapter 35 – Shawn

November 28, 2003

The two-hour drive was boring and uneventful, giving me enough time to think about something I never thought I'd do. He didn't expect me, nor did I want him to. That way, if I pulled out, nothing would be lost. But I knew I had to do it, so I drove until I did.

If it weren't for the barbed wire on top the ten-foot fence and the armed guards staring down at me from the lookout towers with rifles clutched in their grips, the place was pretty. A high rock formation was just past the buildings, and I could see for miles across the mesa. But most people didn't go there for the view nor even by choice.

The visitor room was drab yet bright, with florescent bulbs shining down on the off-white linoleum floor. I sat down in a dull plastic chair surrounded by short walls that made it feel like a booth. My hands folded in front of me, waiting as patiently as I could.

When he finally came out, I could tell he had changed, at least physically. His eyes were sullen, his walk sluggish and hunched. He had lost weight, his potbelly nearly gone. But he appeared smaller, lacking definition, obviously not hitting the weight room as a free amenity of his luxurious stay. Maybe the food wasn't that good either, like they ate melon and cucumber slop heaped onto old, plastic trays. But honestly, I didn't care if it was.

"Hi." I was the first to speak as he sat across from me. His movements were slow and deliberate as if he was doing something he was forced to do. He scratched his recently shaved chin. I actually felt sorry for him.

At first, he barely acknowledged me, glancing around a room he must not have been familiar with. The overhead lights shone down like spotlights, revealing everything around us. Nothing could hide. He stared at me. I stared back. He remembered who I was.

"I hope you're doing well." It was a sorry attempt at small talk as I didn't quite know how to begin. While it all seemed like a dirty past between us, it felt new and unfamiliar. "I bet you didn't expect to see me here."

"Why no, I never thought I'd enjoy such a pleasure."

I leaned forward, my elbows resting on the counter between me and the thick glass barrier. "Well… I have something to tell you, and it's probably not something you expected to hear."

"Am I out on parole? Well, thank God. I never thought the day would come. Now I can finally see my kids." He smiled and sighed, clearly not the one among us who craved sincerity.

It hadn't occurred to me that he would have a family, that all of this would also affect him, his wife, and his kids. In the courtroom, my eyes were too fixated on revenge to even notice anyone else there.

"I forgive you."

I said it so fast. I had to before I forgot how to do it. Previously, I had been lost not knowing at all what to say or how to say it, but it became easy when I realized the actual words didn't matter.

His upper body hardly budged. We continued staring, his eyes less alert and more bloodshot than mine. His arms crossed. My hand wiped my eye. We looked at each other differently, at least I assumed he did for me.

And he was different. He was a man filled with hopes and dreams and regrets, willing to move on as much as he could, yet still grasping to memories. I saw him yet so much more, as the glass between us suddenly became a mirror.

Chapter 36 – Shawn

December 12, 2003

Grace and I headed up the steep path, the sunny weather cooperating more than I could have imagined. At that altitude, snow accumulated in sneaky places and lasted forever: the swells of rock piles, tucked next to tree groves, and in shaded parts of open fields. My dad would have enjoyed pointing them out. But the marked trail was fairly clear of snow and debris.

Except this one stretch. Jagged stones and flat rocks littered the path. Small ones moved with any misstep, the flat ones like stairsteps but prone to ice build-up. The sun made it even worse, blinding us if we ever looked down.

She slipped but caught her footing. "One more of those, and I won't be happy." She bent down to tighten her boots. "This is pretty, but I'm not convinced it's worth the effort. Couldn't we wait till spring?"

I winced. What was I thinking? She was pregnant with our child, but I had no clue how I was supposed to treat her. Do I pamper her for nine months or continue life as normal? Again, all new ground to cover. She agreed to the hike, but I questioned myself for even suggesting it. Maybe I wasn't ready for all this, even though deep down, I knew I was.

I adjusted my sunglasses and climbed up to the next ledge. I extended my hand behind me and helped Grace. She landed next to me, putting her hand on my shoulder.

I finally answered her question. "Spring is too late." Another thing I learned from my father: if it's important, do it now. The fact that the winter had been mostly dry thus far further proved my point.

She reached over and brushed dirt off my jacket. We both glanced back at what we'd accomplished. The trailhead was way out of sight, over two thousand feet in elevation below us. Trees and bushes were also long gone, replaced by a field of various rocks and dormant grass — brown and gray with specks of snowy white. Beautiful if only from secluded randomness.

"How much longer?" Her running put her in excellent shape — her breathing was a lot less labored than mine. And apparently, she wasn't far enough along to affect her stamina. But I couldn't blame her for asking. We were both still sucking air, and my lungs and calves were on fire.

I popped the top on my half-empty water bottle, took a sip, and wished I had brought more. "We'll be there soon. Trust me."

"I do. I guess." Her words floated as she gasped in the thinning air. She caught a breath, her chest expanding and contracting, then drank from her bright blue Nalgene.

"It's the challenge that's the fun part." I took another sip.

She didn't answer.

As we passed a frozen waterfall to our left, we both looked anxiously at what was ahead: a steep incline covered with remnants of a large granite slab. It was so steep; I'd almost call it a wall.

"You sure you're able to do this?" I knew it was a leading question, but I wanted to keep going.

"Of course. Why not?"

I was too afraid to point out the obvious.

We threw our bottles in our backpack and started upward, now scrambling more than hiking, climbing up and over each successive rock. We avoided the occasional snowpack to keep our footing intact. She didn't say anything, but she didn't have to. I knew she was losing patience, with me and with the hike.

I wheezed, holding in my excitement as much as letting out my exhaustion. The funny thing was I knew what I wanted to do but couldn't decide where to do it. Originally, it was the name that caught my eye: Chasm Lake. I liked the sound of it. And once I knew, I had to see it. And conquer it.

But I second-guessed myself. First off, Grace was expecting. Second, while the weather was good, the grade, complexity, and length of the hike was much more than I bargained for. Of course, in Colorado, every worthwhile destination came with a level of difficulty, yet the challenge only added to the experience.

As I stepped up from a huge boulder, I double-checked my pocket. It was still there, still radiating heat like a hot coal. I worried she'd figure it out, read my mind, interpret my actions. She'd know. And if I wasn't careful, it'd burn a hole where it sat. Secrets are like that.

We finally reached the top of the granite wall, our destination almost in sight. While they looked intimidating, the boulders ended up being not as insurmountable as I thought. We followed the trail, snow crunching below our boots.

We rounded the corner and climbed upward with very little marking for a path. Loose stones were scattered everywhere like large clumps of dirt. Perhaps they were all one huge rock once, thrown down and smashed into a million pieces.

My body told me we were close. Anxiety was a sense.

A few more tiring steps toward the sky, and there it was. The frozen lake was shadowed by the towering flat face of Long's Peak. But the lake itself was stunning: a flat sheet of glass with infinite cracks and small ripples like surprised waves. The stillness was breathtaking.

The eastern wall of the mountain was spectacular, one of the most recognizable and famous peaks in all of Colorado. And there it was, just ours. The top was rough and jagged, while the face was flat as if cut with a saw. People called it "The Diamond." I liked that.

We placed our backpacks on the ground and took sips from our water bottles. Grace and I glanced at each other, both panting and gasping for needed oxygen, its importance enhanced by its scarceness. We both looked out over the surroundings. Besides our breaths, there wasn't a single other sound. Birds flew overhead with graceful silence. The smell was fresh and untouched, almost as if no smell at all.

I leaned back against a large boulder and admired the beauty around me. The solid mountainous backdrop was in such sharp contrast to the fragile, frozen water. There were not many colors — just whites and grays and blues, but that made it even more moon-like and surreal.

Opposite the lake, a wall of snow abruptly stopped, hovering above the ice. Layers of recent storms were easy to spot. The mountain ridges were decorative shelves storing sprays of snow and rocks.

I finally caught my breath. "You're probably wondering why we came all the way up here." My hands levitated, pointing out the here and now. This time, location mattered.

She leaned forward and laughed. "Well, it's gorgeous, I'll give you that. And it's a hike I've never done before." She looked at me. "But yeah, I was wondering. Why here? Why now?"

I dwelled on my problem-solving ability — or lack thereof — and realized the solution I craved wasn't the hard part. It was the path to find it. I always figured it was too far away from me to find let alone achieve. But I was wrong. Turns out, my answer was four years in the making and right in front of me the entire time.

"Well, I have two things to tell you." I threw my glove on the ground and wiped my forehead with my bare hand. Both were damp and cold. "The first is something I should have done a long time ago."

"The suspense is killing me."

A sudden gust swept across the lake, across us. I reached out and held her, not letting go till it was done. We kept our balance. The sun slowly disappeared behind a light, fluffy cloud. Slate gray ones trailed not far behind, existent and threatening. But nothing was going to stop me.

I took in a deep breath, puffed out my cheeks, then pursed my lips. "Last week, I headed down to Cañon City." I took another sip from my bottle, then put my glove back on.

"The only thing down there are prisons." Grace shook her head. "What were you doing there?" She leaned over and ruffled through her backpack, pulling out a Clif bar.

"That's exactly where I went." My arms crossed my chest. "And I visited a Dean McFarland." I wasn't sure I'd ever say his name again, especially in such a beautiful, remote place like this. It sounded awkward. The last time I heard it was way back in Denver at a location I've tried so hard to forget.

"Who's that?" She took a bite out of the corner and chewed. She seemed so relaxed, so content with life. But I desired so much more.

"Sorry, I should explain." I leaned forward, placing my hand on her hip. She was totally confused. "He was the driver of the car who killed my father."

She coughed, almost spitting out her food. Her body stiffened. "What could you possibly get from him?" She covered her mouth.

I scratched my chin. "It's not what I got, it's what I gave."

"What was that?"

"I forgave him." I finally realized what it involved, this odd mix of actions and words and feelings. Tough to explain. But similar to many things, I knew it when I found it.

"You say that so nonchalantly." Grace adjusted her winter coat, wrapping it tighter around her body. It was getting noticeably colder. "He killed your father, Shawn."

"He did." My arms crossed tightly in front of my chest. "But I had to confront him. And more importantly, I also had to forgive him."

Her feet tottered as she leaned back against a rock. "Shawn… that's a nice gesture, but why'd we come all the way up here to tell me that? We could have done that in a warm coffee shop back home."

As if on cue, the temperature dropped about ten degrees. The swirling air became hard and abrasive against my face, my hands. Wind howled. Grace wrapped up her hair in a ponytail, brushing it out of her eyes.

"Well, he wasn't the only one in prison."

Grace swung her head, shuddering with agitation. I knew because I felt it, too. "Why?"

An excellent question, one I asked myself repeatedly. Why him? Why my father? Why me? My suffering from the event became so entrenched, it literally became me. Because of that, I accepted it. No more.

I finally realized the simple answer. "To get past my past." Moving on and remembering could coincide. I could do both. I didn't have to forget, and even if I tried, I'd be miserable at it. Yet even with memories intact, I could find other ways to define who I was. That was powerful.

There was no one else around for miles. Yet I didn't feel alone, nor would I have if Grace wasn't there. But that wouldn't make any sense. My seemingly never-ending road to recovery was finally ending, and she had to be there.

Oddly, I instantly thought of my mom, beaten down by circumstances beyond her control. My simple act of forgiveness would add to her list. She wouldn't understand it, nor particularly appreciate it. Not at all. And that was okay. Eventually, she'd figure out why, and maybe she'd follow.

Yet this was for me more than anyone else, including Mr. McFarland. And sometimes, that was all that mattered.

"That's a great gesture, and I'm happy you did it. But I'm still confused."

Light flakes began falling like the motion of peace. Unfortunately, it was both breathtaking and intimidating as I knew the forecast. Beginnings were always the most exciting parts when everything was glazed with newness. Then it became an issue of momentum.

"I do have one more thing, but it's more action than words." I unzipped my jacket, then reached into my pocket. Grace drank some more water and yanked up her coat to cover her neck. The wind picked up even more, brushing across her face. She briefly closed her eyes.

"For every end, there's a new beginning." I spoke loudly, trying my best to overcome the deteriorating conditions. She watched me closely, her eyes blank and expressionless. She hadn't a clue what I was about to do.

My smile swayed to the rhythm of my heart.

I dropped to my knees.

"Grace, I fell for you in many ways." My left hand rested on my knee, my other grabbed hers. I steadied myself. Snow fell in large, heavy flakes, landing on both of us but melting quickly.

"You are the love of my life. I can't express how much you mean to me and how you've affected me in so many ways. You've forgiven me and accepted me for who I am, a blessing with no disguise. These last few months have been a whirlwind, and I was swept up in you."

Her right hand outstretched, the other covering her mouth. Her entire body shook.

"I want this moment to last forever. I want us to last forever," I snatched the small, white box and opened it. The hinges snapped. The padded box rested on my steady palm. "I know this sounds hasty, but it's really not. Grace… will you marry me?"

Grace wiped her eye. Everything was becoming damp — our hats and coats, the exposed skin on our hands and faces, some parts more than others.

What was she supposed to say? I wanted it to be quick 'yes,' to ease the suspense, to ensure I hadn't wasted my time and life on someone so valuable.

But that was selfish.

I also wanted to hear her fears and expectations, flowing from this eloquent speech, telling all of creation how she felt about me. How I was the perfect one for her.

But that too was selfish.

She tried to speak but couldn't. Her mouth frozen by the shock of it all. She had reservations. We were too young. It was rushed. Four months! What was I thinking? 'Let's wait until later. We have our whole lives to spend together.'

Luckily, my thoughts and reality never saw eye to eye. Only one was unexpected and strange and beautiful.

Her eyes danced around the world, around the lake, around us. "I would love to marry you, Shawn."

Chapter 37 – Shawn

December 12, 2003

The snow was sticking to the ground in ever-increasing piles, blanketing everything and dusting our coats faster than we could brush them off. Our boots sunk in and crunched beneath us, the depth almost reaching our ankles.

We scrambled down the boulders as fast as we could, trying hard to stay ahead of the storm. I hiked in front of Grace, so I could catch her if she slipped. The forest was not even visible below where I knew the trail continued. Twin Sisters had disappeared long ago.

We reached the bottom of the boulders, but we could only see about twenty feet in front of us. The trail headed to the right, tucked against a hill on one side and an infinite drop off on the other. A chilly sweat trickled down my face, hoping and praying to God my memory served me well.

I glanced back at Grace, barely feeling her hand with two thick gloves in between. She was smiling, even giggling. I stopped walking, waiting for everything to catch up. In that quick moment, she told me so much. And she was right. We were getting married, that we knew for certain. We'd share hopes and dreams, the future, the ups and downs of life, and kids!

I laughed. She had me.

Our steps lumbered forward as everything became heavy and dense. The intensity of the storm grew. Whistling. Howling. I was thrilled she was with me, but we didn't talk, muted by the growing whiteout.

The sky had a steely harshness, visible only because of its contrast to the army of white flakes that invaded the air. I smoothed my hand against a tree stump and found the blue flag pinned to it. We were still on the trail. A godsend. I'd never gotten lost on a hike before, and I wasn't about to now.

We rounded the drop off and reached the open field. Packed with smaller rocks, it became more an obstacle course than a trail. I let go of her hand, so we could swing out like tightrope walkers. The trail had a consistent downhill slope with switchbacks twisting around larger boulders and steep slopes.

While the snow provided a flat surface to hike on, it also hid the unevenness of the ground below. My ankle twisted as it landed between two rocks. I swore at myself for not noticing but shook it off. At least it was me and not her.

We finally reached the pine trees. At first, they were scattered, but soon became a worthy canopy of protection. A relief. They provided just enough cover, catching buckets of snow on their thick branches. I held Grace's hand as we pushed our boots hard into the snow, getting our best grip as we descended.

My other hand leaned against a large pine to steady myself. A stupid mistake. I ducked to get out of the way, letting go of Grace's hand. But I was too late. A showering of heavy, damp snow sneaked down the back of my jacket with chunks clumped near my neck. Grace's laughter almost kept me warm.

I was now shivering. And thirsty. We stopped below a grove of aspens; their champagne color so much more noticeable when surrounded by pure white. I removed my glove, placing it under my arm, then took a quick sip from my bottle. It was almost empty. I reached into my backpack, grabbed two Power Bars, and handed one to Grace.

"I'm sorry." I yelled so she'd hear me.

She smiled. "It's an adventure."

"I meant more than the storm."

She didn't hear me as she didn't react. Or maybe she did hear and simply accepted. Either way was okay. But as before, it was just as much for me as it was for her. And words were the easy part.

We ate then kept walking, gradually making progress toward the trailhead. The snow finally let up just enough for us to see where we were headed. Thank God.

We twisted around the final switchbacks then hit the flat stretch before the trailhead. I could see my Mustang off in the distance — the only car in the lot — albeit entirely covered in a blanket of powdery snow.

Grace hopped into my car, angled her legs toward the middle, and wrapped her coat tightly around herself. Her entire body was shaking. I glanced at the shiny solitaire, warmed by what it meant just as much as who wore it. I started the car, cranked up the heat, and brushed off the snow with the scraper.

The snow picked up again with flakes so thick, my wipers could barely keep up. Everything became a flat white. I turned my headlights on, but they didn't help at all. We headed down Highway 7 with its many steep and winding declines, my all-weather tires stretching the definition of *all*. I pumped my brakes at even the slightest downhill. I didn't trust my car, so I took over.

I turned the corner, the car hugging a rock cliff, when we both saw it straight ahead. The Chapel on the Rock was to our right, like a movie portrayal of a snow-covered, medieval castle. It was haunting yet beautiful.

Grace smiled. "My dream is to get married there. But let's wait till the weather improves." We both laughed. It was so easy to focus on simple things when the big things were out of the way.

A large vehicle was coming up the hill, going way too fast for the conditions. It plowed through the snow, creating a wake of slush. Alarmingly loud. It was a dirty white, so I would not have seen it without the up splash.

"That's the perfect place!" Everything about me smiled, both inside and out. "We have to. I almost forgot about it. Great place to tie the knot."

I briefly touched her hand, but quickly repositioned mine on the steering wheel. The oncoming vehicle was hurtling through the snow pack, swooshing with brashness. My hands firmly gripped the wheel.

It finally passed. I smiled at the overly confident thrill-seeker, his beard hanging low over his jacket.

Every so often, I stole a glance at Grace. She had this radiance to her. Her smile beamed. She looked and acted differently, somehow both calm and excited. I figured it was because of me, because of what I did.

My third selfish thought of the evening.

"Where are we headed?" She noticed I was looking at her. I could tell. She also knew I needed a distraction, my elbow twitching furiously.

"I found the perfect place for dinner. It's a place my parents loved, and my dad told me about." I stopped by Euclid Hall the other day to check it out. The untouched brick shouted its past, yet the place was eclectic and modern, with supposedly some of the best food in Denver. We had a ways to go, but luckily, I gave us ample time when I made the reservation. We had over two hours to get there.

We finally reached Lyons where the road leveled out. I slowed to a crawl as we reached downtown. We were out of the mountains, but the snow onslaught continued, my wipers still trying desperately to keep up.

"So much to look forward to." Grace finally unzipped her coat and shook it to remove the dampness. She glanced over at me with a huge smile. "We're gonna be parents, Shawn. Can you believe it?" Her hands landed on top of her head, elbows extended outward.

We reached the second stoplight in town. I pumped the brakes, my tires skidding to a stop.

I returned the smile and burst into a deep belly laugh. First time in forever. I instantly felt relief, as if I had searched and searched and finally found the last piece of a wickedly complex jigsaw puzzle. Scary and awe-inspiring, yet right.

"I love you, Grace." I turned to look at her, distracted by thoughts of her, of me, of the three of us. And in the telling of a truth, she had just radically changed it.

I never noticed the SUV barreling down the hill, skidding like a sled. The collision was instantaneous. The other driver slammed against his airbag. His front grill smashed against the top of my door, the metal panel bending inward against me, with the window breaking into a million pieces.

Grace banged her head on the windshield, a spider web of destruction. Her hands smashed the top of the dash. Her knees hit the bottom. Then her body ricocheted back like a slingshot.

My head hit the steering wheel. Blood smeared my eyes. An intense pain shot up my leg. I almost fainted.

It was a blinding instance of everything.

Noise and pain and memories.

I was a kid playing catch with my dad, leather glove dangling from my hand, the ball soaring through the air. He smiled and encouraged as only my father could.

I was at my father's funeral, walking up to the casket, saying goodbye to the man I admired and loved. Salty tears stained my cheeks, the place smelling of flowers and candles and grief. A sudden fire raged inside me — towards God, my father, everyone.

I sat on a rocky ledge overlooking a pristine lake. It was new and wonderful, but we didn't make anything that hadn't already existed. All we did was play the roles we were given.

But it was way more than that. Life stood still, life lurched forward, life plunged into space like a rocket ship. And it was different. We were different.

"I love you, Shawn." She was right next to me. I heard her whisper. It was real.

I thought of my boys at church — the annoying, squirmy, amazing boys who wondered and perceived and quite possibly, listened. Was it worth it? Did I have any impact? I'd never know their answers, but I definitely knew mine.

I saw my own family, laughing and playing in an immense open field. I reached out and held her soft, comforting hand as we watched our son bound across the tall, uncut sea of grass. With jet black hair and thoughtful eyes, he resembled me in many ways.

I smiled at Grace. She knew the peace I felt because she felt it, too. I squeezed her hand and told her, just not with words. A calm swept over us.

There was an importance with that. It wasn't my past, which was over but not forgotten. And it wasn't my future as I never knew it. Does anybody? It was here, and it was now.

A lightning bolt filled the vast sky around me. After the initial flash, I was surrounded by deep blue, soaring above the clouds. My journey had ended, but everything else that mattered was about to begin.

Chapter 38 – Aidan

<u>Case Number</u>: 58537228
<u>Date</u>: 12 December 2003
<u>Reporting Officer</u>: Deputy Bender
<u>Prepared By</u>: CPL Shamblin
<u>Incident Type</u>: Automobile Accident

<u>Address of Occurrence</u>:
Intersection of 4th Avenue and Broadway, Lyons, CO 80540
<u>Witnesses</u>:
Grace Liddell: passenger of first auto. Female, 19, White
Kevin Randall: driver of second auto. Male, 42, White
<u>Evidence</u>:
Skid marks from vehicle traveling southbound on 4th Avenue
Vehicle fragments and parts scattered across intersection

On December 12, 2003, at approximately 17:42, personnel from the Lyons police and fire departments responded to the report of an accident in the 400 block of Broadway in downtown Lyons. Thus far, the investigation has revealed that a Mr. Kevin Randall was traveling southbound in a Chevrolet Suburban. According to Mr. Randall, he had just left home a few blocks away and was unaware of the icy road conditions.

An analysis of traction marks was made on the scene, and it was determined the vehicle driven by Mr. Randall was traveling between 30 and 35 miles per hour at the time of collision. The speed limit at that location is 25 miles per hour. It was determined that Mr. Randall applied the brakes on his vehicle, but the Suburban skidded down the hill and through the intersection after the light had turned red.

After being struck by the Suburban, the other vehicle, driven by a Mr. Shawn Stevens, sustained numerous damages and slid to a stop near the light post on the southeast corner of the intersection. The left door and side panels of the vehicle were severely damaged by the collision, causing Mr. Stevens to be pinned between the door and the steering wheel. As Mr. Stevens was thrust against the steering wheel and front console of his vehicle, he sustained multiple injuries to his face and neck. The passenger, Ms. Grace Liddell, suffered only minor injuries to her face and hands.

Mr. Stevens was rushed to the hospital where he was treated for critical injuries sustained in the accident. He was later pronounced dead by a Dr. Martenson at Longmont United Hospital at 20:48. Ms. Liddell and Mr. Stevens' mother were on hand.

Pictures of the accident scene and this report were delivered to the District Attorney, Mr. Gonzales, upon completion. Until the District Attorney reviews the case, there will be no further release of information.

•   •   •

The police report fell from my fingers after I read the last line, sliding off my bed and landing on the floor. I wiped my eyes, hoping to clear any dust or debris. But there was none.

I scooted up on my knees on top of my bed then looked over at my mother sitting on a nearby chair. Our eyes were level, hers were damp. "Did he know about me before he died?"

She answered quickly. "Yes, he knew. I told him a few weeks beforehand."

"Where were you driving to?"

"You mean when we had the accident? We were returning from a hike to Chasm Lake. He asked me to marry him there."

"Why'd you hike all the way up there?"

She laughed. "Funny… I asked the same thing. I guess he wanted it to be in an unforgettable location. He was big on that. His memories were always tied to a place." She crossed her legs and placed her hand on the bed next to me. "He also made another announcement."

I squinted. "What was that?"

"He forgave the man who killed his father."

"Huh?" My head shook in total confusion. "What does that have to do with getting married?"

She made a deep, bouncy sound in her throat. "You know, I didn't get it either. But it makes sense now."

"And…"

"Well, sometimes, you have to finish one thing before you can start another." Her hand rested on my shoulder. "I know. It's confusing. But it'll make sense someday."

She didn't think I understood, but I did. Completely. His balancing act made sense to me only because I've had my own to perform. Sometimes, I dwell on the past, and sometimes I just let it go.

But there were hard to ignore coincidences in my father's story. I didn't want to talk about them, but now was my chance. "That's awful Dad and Grandpa both died young. And both from car accidents."

She sighed and rubbed her knee. I didn't think she wanted to talk about them either, which was why I asked.

"It was a difficult time for your grandma and me. I never met your grandpa, but losing your dad was tough enough. I'm not sure what we would have done without everyone at church."

My dad became a fatherless, directionless teenager lacking any support. No wonder he lashed out at everything around him. He was trapped without choices, and worse yet, no one was there to give him any.

"That's awful! For Dad, that is. And for you… and Grandma. Everyone!" My mouth turned dry, and my heart pounded like a drum. I latched onto my father's anger without exactly knowing why.

My mom stared at me, familiar with the whole detonation process. She finally answered. "It was awful, but I couldn't dwell there too long. I realized pretty fast I had to take care of you. It was my job… to save you."

My finger extended to scratch behind my ear. "Not sure I know what you mean?"

"Well, sometimes we save things from harm, and sometimes we save things so they last longer than us. This time it was both."

She brushed her hair back over her shoulder then slanted her head to focus on things that were close. I think that included me. When she stroked her chin, I knew. She was telling the truth.

For many years, I never understood my mother. She didn't want to talk about my dad, while at the same time I was desperate to know more. Now that she'd given me what I needed, I realized she was more than her words. And I, too, was way more than what I knew.

"Weren't you mad? At the people in the other car? At God? At anyone?"

"Yes and no." She reached out her hand and brushed my cheek. "It was a choice I had to make, to deal with the life I was given. I couldn't change it, even though I sure wanted to. So I moved on."

I guess I did have choices. But I still felt sorry for my father and all he went through. "It's still awful." I looked down at the textured rug spread across my bedroom floor. "Maybe other people helped. That makes sense."

Her body inclined forward. "That's right. Your father had his boys. They supported him, even though they were just kids."

I laughed. "Probably because they were."

She took a deep breath then smiled. "I think you're right. Harry, Peter, Sebastian…"

"And Zach."

"Yes, and Zach, too." She sat down next to me on my bed, balancing against her left hand and crossing her legs.

I cradled my knees with both my hands then swallowed hard. A bitter confusion lingered in my mouth. "Why'd they write letters? Couldn't they just tell me in person?"

"I wanted you to hear about everything. Your father meant so much to those boys, and they told me repeatedly how much they missed him. But the funny thing was they never told him. He never knew the impact he had. I didn't want you to miss out on that, too."

"So they wrote letters?" I loved them, I really did, reading them aloud to my mom, emphasizing what I thought was important. But who writes letters anymore?

She balanced against the headboard, curling up her legs and balancing her arms on top. "I could have told you, but I've struggled with that. I just don't like to dwell on things." She rubbed the underside of her nose. "I still love him. Very much, in fact. So I asked others to tell you."

The police reports had confused me much more than the letters. By themselves, they were awful to read. But I realized they were a necessary evil. "Thanks for keeping the letters... and the reports, I guess. Today was cool."

One more sheet of paper sat on the bed, wide-ruled and yanked out of a notebook with curly hairs dangling from one side. I picked it up and stared at it. 'Dear Son' was written at the top in smudgy, black ink. The messy handwriting looked like old schoolwork Grandma showed me years ago.

"What's this?" I asked.

She grabbed the paper, glanced at it, then shrugged her shoulders as if I just told her the sky was blue.

"It's a letter your grandma gave me a long time ago." She handed it back. "It's written by your father."

"Wait... what? When did he write it?"

She angled over the paper then looked up at me. "When he visited the prison, right after forgiving the man who killed his father. He wanted to write it — just for you."

"But... how'd he know?"

"Well, I told him we were expecting about a week before that." She massaged her neck. "He figured you'd be a boy. Runs in the family, I guess. And he already knew what he wanted to say." She rubbed her eyebrow. "It also inspired me to ask for the others."

I shuffled to my knees, clutching the paper in my hand. The sun peeked in through the curtains, making everything glow in its path.

I'd learn from my father. I never met him, but always wanted to be like him — thoughts, actions, reactions, whatever it was that made up him. The mystery drew me in, even more so because I was told not to.

But that was yesterday. I had searched and searched, unsure if I'd ever find him. Now that I did, I decided I wanted to be different. Not in a bad way. He'd teach, and I'd learn.

Tears rolled down my mom's cheeks. I didn't know what it meant, but in an odd way, it felt good.

"Don't cry, Mom. You'll smudge it." I stretched out my hand, holding the letter from my father. "I'd like to read this." I placed it on my bed and rolled my other hand over it. It had to be smooth. Unblemished.

She again balanced back against the headboard, curled up her legs around her arm then wiped her eyes. "Please do. I want you to know."

●　　●　　●

Dear Son,

It's odd writing this letter. We haven't met yet, but we will soon. My mind is racing with possibilities, but every time I see you, you're just like me: black hair, friendly yet ambitious, an honest smile (when you want to show it), and a big chip on your shoulder wishing life was better.

Let me give you a little background. I'm 18 and recently found out I'm going to be a dad. As I write this, I'm sitting outside admiring the snow-capped peaks, endless pine trees, and cloudless skies. But if I look behind me, I'm staring at a huge prison enclosed by an unscalable fence. It's such a metaphor for my life, I couldn't pass it up.

I also have to admit, I'm angry — at my parents, at my life, and at God who's shown me very few favors lately. My dad died four years ago, and I've been reluctant to forgive anybody for it. I loved him. He was a great man, and he shouldn't be gone. This has been my personal prison.

And that's why I'm writing you, to tell you things I wish I heard from him, things he would have told me if given the chance. I'm not good at any of these, but that's exactly the point. Experiences teach a lot, but they don't always have to be your own. So here it goes...

Don't blame others for your struggles and weaknesses. Own them, but don't let them define you.

Stand up for what you believe in. It's what makes you unique. The world needs more passionate people.

Be honest because lying sucks. It never works even if you think it might. It's a filled balloon just waiting to be popped.

Be someone people go to for advice. Only passionate people get asked for advice, and only honest people get asked twice.

Love your parents. You will find me and your mom (that's weird) annoying now and then, and trust me, I'm far from perfect. But you never know when you're going to need us or how much longer you'll be able to.

Trust God. There's a reason for everything, whether you agree with it or not. And be sure to tell yourself this over and over again. I do every day.

And last but certainly not least: learn to forgive but don't forget. My worst one. The past is important, but it can weigh you down if you're not careful. You'll make mistakes. Others will, too. Move on.

I struggle with wishing I had saved my father. Somehow, someway I could have. But I have also realized there is one person I can save. He's a hopeful dreamer who wants what's best for his son. It's me.

I can be there for others, and that keeps my world turning. But I'm the only one who can choose to save myself. And if I do it right, I'll last much longer than I'll ever know.

It'll take courage to do all that, but it'll be worth it.

I hope you find it, too.

I learned three things at the home. That's all. Honestly, they're the only redeeming qualities about the place, but they're well worth remembering.

I love you. I'm sorry. I forgive.

Love,

Dad

Acknowledgments

This novel was the culmination of so much work from so many people. Thanks to so many friends and family members who reviewed my manuscript and provided helpful feedback and encouragement, including Scott Jonas, Eric Lord, Linnea Tanner, and Anurag Dubey. Thanks also to Aviva Layton for her professional editing skills.

Thanks to my mother for her editing, support, and words of encouragement, and also to my father for putting up with my mother (just kidding). Thanks to Uncle Tom for his constructive feedback as he unleashed his English prowess on my poor, helpless book, only to make it ten times better in return. Thanks to Rick Archer for his helpful knowledge on juvenile crime and the confusing laws on public records. Thanks to Colin Sibert and Max Stevens for taking such awesome portraits. And thanks to Reagan Rothe for his valued expertise in the entire publishing process.

Special thanks to my amazing wife and children who put up with my stupid dad jokes and lend more than enough love and inspiration to convince me to pursue my passion for writing. For all of you, I am eternally grateful.

About the Author

Paul Schumacher lives in Colorado with his amazing wife, three wonderful kids, and two crazy cats. He pays the bills by day as an engineer and satisfies his passion for writing whenever he can. His award-winning first novel, *The Tattered Box*, was published in 2016.

Note from the Author

Word-of-mouth is crucial for any author to succeed. If you enjoyed *The Importance of Now*, please leave a review online—anywhere you are able. Even if it's just a sentence or two. It would make all the difference and would be very much appreciated.

Thanks!
Paul Schumacher

Thank you so much for reading one of our
Coming of Age Fiction novels.
If you enjoyed our book, please check out our recommendation
for your next great read!

What the Valley Knows by Heather Christie

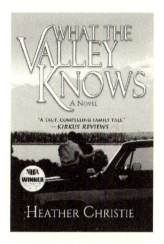

"A taut, compelling family tale."
–Kirkus Reviews

National Indie Excellence Awards- Young Adult Winner

Readers' Favorite Gold Medal Young Adult - Coming of Age

Maxy Awards Young Adult Winner

Made in the USA
Coppell, TX
29 May 2021

56517310R00132